VOICELESS

VOICELESS

E. G. WILSON

Atthis Arts, LLC

VOICELESS

Editorial services by Catherine Jones Payne, Quill Pen Editorial
Proofreading by Bob Michiels, Sarah Savage, and C.T. Templeton

Published by Atthis Arts, LLC
Centerville, Ohio
www.atthisarts.com

ISBN 978-1-945009-05-1

Library of Congress Control Number: 2017943954

For Ariana and Sarah,
who listened;

For Catherine,
who believed;

For David,
who supported.

CHAPTER ONE

<Adelaide Te Ngawai was thirteen when Maunga Richards stole her voice . . .>

The older girl sauntered into their classroom one crisp winter morning and announced that Kaiako Anita had told her to come across and make herself useful to the upper ninth.

"Tuck your shirt in," said Kaiako Katie, not turning around from where she was writing on the semi-transparent blue holoboard.

"Didn't you hear me?" Maunga demanded. "Kaiako Anita said—"

"Your shirt. Tuck it in."

Addy, sitting at the back with her best friend Challa, shifted in her chair for a better view. Beside them, Sofie and Nadia craned for a look, too.

Maunga wasn't Maunga's real name, but it was the one everyone knew her by. She was dark-skinned and solidly-built, with a thick braid of black hair falling over one shoulder and a mutinous expression on her square face. There was a lot more Maori than New Zealand European in her heritage, Addy guessed. Everyone had a bit of both.

Maunga huffed and crammed the tails of her white shirt into her school skirt. She made no move to straighten her tie. "Done."

"Now." Kaiako Katie turned around. "Anita didn't say anything to me about sending you across."

"You can message her if you don't believe me."

"I will. You may take a seat. Over there, by the wall."

Maunga slouched into the designated seat and smirked at the class.

"Back to work, girls," said Kaiako Katie.

Addy exchanged a look with Challa and bent over her holodesk. The metal leg of the horizontal frame felt cold where it touched her leg. Her left sock had crumpled around her ankle. She reached down and tugged it back up and then went on with her algebra.

"Sofie," Challa whispered a minute later.

Addy looked up. On Nadia's far side, Sofie stared out the window.

Addy rolled her eyes. Of course Sofie would be daydreaming when they had first-class entertainment here in the form of Maunga Richards. Challa tucked away a loose strand of chestnut brown hair that had escaped her braid and whispered again. "Sofie."

"Sofie," Addy hissed. "Do your work."

"Adelaide," Kaiako Katie said. "Challa. Nadia. Sofie. Less talking, more working."

Addy flushed, aware of Maunga Richards lounging at the front of the class. No doubt she was judging them. Anything she witnessed would be taken back to the lower twelfth and used as fodder for lunchtime taunting. The older girls could be merciless when they chose.

"Really," Maunga said, "when *I* was in the upper ninth, I never would have talked to my friends during lessons."

"That's because you never had any friends," piped a voice from the middle of the classroom.

Maunga jerked upright, scowling. "Who said that?"

Addy kept her head bent over her work and, from the corner of her eye, saw the rest of the class doing the same. Nobody looked at the third row, where a smile tugged at Kotukutuku Johnson's mouth. Tuku's older sisters were in Maunga's class, and Tuku delighted in sharing stories of the lower twelfth's antics with the rest of the upper ninth.

"Who said that?" Maunga's chair squeaked protest as she shifted her weight. "Own up, you little coward, or—"

"Miss Richards," said Kaiako Katie, "kindly stop disrupting my class." She swept a glance around the room, caught Addy's eye, and twitched an eyebrow in silent enquiry.

Ugh. Addy didn't want to spend the rest of the period with Maunga Richards, of all people, but she could see as well as anyone the way things were going. The longer the older girl stayed in the upper ninth, the more disruptive she'd become.

Addy shrugged and nodded. She just hoped Kaiako Katie wouldn't send her off alone with Maunga.

"Alright, Maunga. You can take a group to the study room downstairs for tutoring. You're to be back here with five minutes to spare—and they'll show me what they've been working on, so don't think you can shirk your duty. You were sent here to help, not to skive off."

"What do I tutor them in?"

Kaiako Katie turned to the class. "Adelaide. Challa. I'd rather not have you disrupting the class again. You may go with Maunga and work on your creative compositions for next week. No, Nadia, you and Sofie can stay right there. It won't kill you four to be separated for a while."

Addy wiped her screen and stood, hiding her relief. *Good.* She wouldn't be alone in the study room. And Kaiako Katie, the darling, had given them an excuse for going with Maunga. Bad enough to be exiting in disgrace—it would be worse if the other girls knew she'd volunteered. Her face warmed as she saw Aroha Waipori flash a malicious smile and mouth, *Sucks to be you.*

Addy dropped her gaze to the carpet. At least they hadn't seen her volunteer for the job. *Sucks to be you* was better than *suck-up, little teacher's pet.*

Not that there was anything wrong with earning high grades. She knew that. She'd been told often enough: by her parents, by Challa, by her brother Theo, older by four years and far past caring what his peers thought of him. She hid behind her fringe of dirty blonde hair and tried not to see the surprise in Tuku's eyes as she passed by. She'd never been sent out of class before. Being sent out meant you'd done something wrong.

Addy didn't do things wrong.

But now she'd been sent out anyway. The whispers and jeers seemed to follow her after the door closed. She pressed a hand to her cheek, sure that her face was flaming red.

They lagged behind Maunga as she strode down the hall.

"Alright?" Challa asked.

Addy nodded, looking down at her feet again. One of her shoelaces was coming undone.

"She didn't give us an official detention; it's only an hour in the study."

"I know." The lump in her throat made it difficult to speak.

"Is it Maunga? I know she's scary, but she wouldn't do anything really nasty." Challa sounded like she was trying to convince herself as much as Addy.

Addy cleared her throat and lifted her chin, making an effort to throw off the mood. "Of course not. But let's face it, she's not exactly head girl material, is she?"

They shared a giggle at that. Dark, tempestuous Maunga Richards would never deliver an impassioned end-of-year speech about the girls of Te Maru Girls' Grammar being the best and brightest. Just the thought of her scowling face repeating last year's infamously botched line set Addy laughing.

"What is it?" Challa asked.

"Can you imagine her giving last year's speech? Remember what Vickery Masters said after the choir sang their first song?"

"Do I ever! *Thank you for that performance, girls . . .*"

Addy joined her, and they chorused the last line, "*You never fail to disappoint.*"

They broke into giggles again and were still laughing when they reached the lift.

Maunga held the door open, looking bored. "Would you mind

keeping up? I know you can't help being *slow,* but some of us can't afford to stand around chinwagging all day."

The insult fell flat. They were among the best in the upper ninth, and they both knew it.

The study room seated eight. Addy and Challa sat together on one side of the table, and Maunga took a chair at the far corner. The older girl kicked her chair back on two legs, activated her wrist holo, and said without looking up, "Don't mind me. You've got forty minutes to work, and then you can read out what you've written, and I'll critique it. Talk or don't talk, I don't care."

They brought up their screens and set to work. As tempting as it was to skive off—which was clearly what Maunga was doing, despite Kaiako Katie's warning—the time would be better spent working. If nothing else, it was one less piece of homework to worry about.

They worked in silence for twenty minutes while Maunga's fingers flew across her holo. Addy wondered who she was messaging. She didn't have many friends in school that the upper ninth knew of. Maybe she had a boyfriend at the Boys' Grammar school?

The thought was so absurd that she let out an involuntary snort.

Challa twitched an eyebrow in silent question.

Addy shook her head and went back to work.

"Time's up," Maunga announced fifteen minutes later. "Let's hear what you've got."

Challa went first.

"Comments?" Maunga asked Addy when Challa finished.

"You changed tense once or twice," Addy said.

Challa nodded. "I'll watch out for that. Thanks."

"Too many adverbs," said Maunga. "And you used the wrong word in a few places. For example: 'I should warn you that it would be most unwise to under-stimulate me.' *Under-stimulate* should be *underestimate,* or at least I assume so, unless you're writing something not entirely appropriate for a school assignment."

Challa blushed red, and Addy felt her own cheeks warm.

"Read ahead more when you're presenting," Maunga added. "You might catch any words that don't look right, and you can correct them when you say them out loud instead of reading the wrong word. Just because it's written down doesn't mean you have to read it. Okay, you can go back up."

Challa looked as startled as Addy felt at the genuine advice; she stammered her thanks before fleeing the room.

Maunga turned to Addy. "Right. Make it quick, or you'll be late."

Addy glanced at the timestamp on her screen. *Ugh. Really?* They still had ten minutes to get back to class. Reading her composition would take four minutes, tops. But it wasn't worth protesting. Biting back her nervousness at being left alone with Maunga, she scrolled back to the top of her composition and started reading.

Maunga stopped her at the end of the first paragraph. "Not a sentence."

"Sorry?"

"That last bit was a fragment, not a full sentence."

Addy flicked back and read over it again. "It's supposed to be like that. Stylistically, I mean."

"Oh," Maunga said with heavy sarcasm. "*Stylistically.* That's fine—don't let me shatter your notion of having perfect written grammar at age twelve."

"I'm thirteen," Addy muttered. She marked the not-sentence for revision.

The next two interruptions she accepted without comment, marking them and moving on. At the fourth one, Maunga strode around the table to lean over her shoulder.

"Adverbs. There and there. I thought you'd have learned from the other three."

Addy flushed. It wasn't a case of *not learning*—she'd picked out the adverbs in Challa's composition, hadn't she? But fixing her own work when she was supposed to be listening to Challa would have been cheating.

Maunga stayed standing behind her. Addy wished she'd go back to her seat. It made her nervous, the older girl looming over her shoulder like that. Her voice shook a little, but she made it through the next full page with no comment from her critic. She finished the page and paused, wondering if she'd missed something so monumental that Maunga wasn't even going to bother pointing it out.

Maunga must have caught her uncertain glance because she shook her head. "Keep going."

Halfway down the next page, Addy felt a pricking in her arm, as if she'd jostled her elbow on something sharp. She rubbed at it, faltering in her reading. Where had that come from? Was there a wasp in the room?

Addy glanced at Maunga. Had she noticed? No, she was staring at her wrist holo again and chewing her lip. Nice to know she was paying attention.

Maunga looked up. "Keep reading. You're nearly done."

Addy shrugged mentally and drew in a breath to launch into her concluding paragraph. Her gaze fell on her fingers, and her breath stuttered to a halt. There was blood on her fingertips. She frowned and looked down at her arm. A tiny hole had appeared in her shirt. Mum would be annoyed about that; it was the only school shirt that fit properly since her last growth spurt. As she watched, another drop of blood welled up, red and wet against the crisp, white material.

She prodded the wound. What on earth had caused that?

"Are you going to finish?" asked Maunga. "Or are we going to sit here all night while you poke your arm because it's so fascinating?"

"Something stuck me."

Maunga followed her gaze and grunted. "You'll be alright. Now, can you hurry up and finish?"

Addy pressed her fingers against the wound and began reading again. She'd hardly made it to the end of the first sentence when her gut clenched and turned in a lazy circle. She took a deep breath to quell the sudden nausea, and a jagged flicker of a headache burst behind her eyes.

"I don't—I don't feel well."

She expected another disbelieving snort, but to her surprise, Maunga didn't say anything. Maybe she hadn't heard? Addy pushed her chair back, half-turning to face Maunga. Her tongue felt thick and clumsy. "I said," she repeated, hearing the words slurring as she spoke, "I don't feel well."

Maunga's eyes were on her, dark and still and strangely intent. "No, I don't imagine you do."

Addy frowned, trying to make sense of that. "Wha . . ." *What does that mean?* she wanted to ask. Her mouth didn't cooperate. Another swirl of nausea caught her; she gripped the arms of the chair with shaking hands and tried to stand, but a stabbing dizziness lanced through her head, and then Maunga laid a hand on her shoulder, pushing her back down into the seat.

"Sit down," she dimly heard the older girl say.

She stared at Maunga, not comprehending, fighting panic. *I'm sick. I need to go to the sick bay. Help me.* She tried to stand again, but her arms gave out, and she fell back into the chair.

Maunga stepped across the room for a minute, then came back and set a small bag on the table. She activated her holo and flicked a message away.

Addy tried to speak again, to ask for help, but only a strangled whimper came out. Her pulse thundered in her ears. She couldn't move.

"Shh," Maunga whispered, an odd lilt to her voice. She brushed her fingers across Addy's cheek. They came away wet. "Don't say a word."

She couldn't. The panic clawed and scrabbled at her insides. A scream built in her throat. She couldn't give voice to it. Addy tried to speak again. All that emerged was a rasping sound, breathless, pleading, more animal than human.

Darkness gathered on the edges of her vision. The jagged dizziness felt as if it would split her skull wide open. She took a breath. Her ribs tightened around her chest. Her lungs screamed in protest. The pain crescendoed, and in the last moment before the darkness swallowed her, she saw Maunga Richards opening the bag.

CHAPTER TWO

Addy woke to find the room empty. Her head ached. Every movement felt stiff and slow, like she was fighting her way through a black fog. Her hands wouldn't stop trembling.

Somehow she made it upstairs to retrieve her bag. The room was empty; she must be late. Her bag felt unbearably heavy, even though there was hardly anything in it.

She loosened the straps. It didn't help.

An incoming message sounded on her wrist holo as she stepped out the front doors onto the street.

Mum. <ARE YOU ALRIGHT? WHY AREN'T YOU HOME YET?>

She stared at it, mind blank. She didn't know. Didn't care. She turned off the screen without replying.

Around her, neon signs lit up, advertising teatime specials and happy hours. She ignored them, trudging north against the flow of the crowd, keeping her head down. Someone jostled her as they swept past, muttered a low apology, and disappeared into the crowd.

She'd been meaning to take the Gleniti train home, but instead she found herself sitting in a half-empty carriage on the Bay Line. The city sped past outside the windows, towering above her, overwhelming her. They used live feed holos along the tunnel walls to make it feel like the trains were still on the surface; usually she watched the view, but not tonight. She loved Te Maru, with the lights and sounds and the sense of millions of people inhabiting the city, but tonight she was just one more girl in the crowd. She didn't understand what had happened, and she didn't think she wanted to understand.

Her arm didn't hurt anymore. She tugged up her sleeve and saw that someone had stuck a smiley face band-aid over the pinprick. She hated it. The sleeve came down again.

She left the Bay Line at the top of the Piazza, bypassed the lifts, and took the stairs down to the fairground. A short walk across carefully maintained green grass brought her to the sandy dunes of the Bay itself. Another minute took her out along the boardwalk to the glass walls of the Shelter. She found a free bench and sat, watching the waves roll in, tugging her school jersey down over her knuckles and hunching her shoulders against the night breeze.

Something pulled at her mind. It was probably important.

Memory intruded, four words in a chilling whisper: *"Don't say a word."*

She shut the door in its face and left it hammering for attention.

Her holo chimed again.

Mum again. <ADDY, WHERE ARE YOU? ARE YOU OUT WITH YOUR FRIENDS? PLEASE LET ME KNOW.>

Addy sighed and selected *reply*. Her quivering fingers fumbled, turning the first word into a mess of meaningless letters. Something cold and slimy coiled in her gut as she stared at it.

She deleted the attempt and tried again. The same result.

It happened again. And again. And then again, by which time her hands were shaking so badly she couldn't make out any individual letters, just a shapeless blur of semi-transparent blue light.

She deactivated the holo and blamed her damp cheeks on the salt spray.

The waves ebbed and flowed with their own rhythm, wash and backwash, wash and backwash. The steady lap-lap, lap-lap slowed her racing pulse and quieted the hammering of the Very Important Something that wanted attention. It could wait. It could wait a long time. She closed her eyes and inhaled slow and deep, smelling the salt tang of the ocean and the subtle perfume of the heated wooden boards underfoot. Really, she wouldn't mind waiting forever.

Her holo chimed six times in the next hour. She ignored it. Ignored her hands trembling even as they gripped the bench, white-knuckled. Ignored the fact that she was growing colder despite the heated floor, that her whole body had started shivering. She watched the sea, letting her mind drift with the waves, seeing the city rise layer upon layer overhead and wondering what the stars would look like beyond them.

She didn't need to know what had happened. She didn't *want* to know.

But she had to go home sometime. Maybe she should try sending a message again. If it didn't work, she could ask someone nearby to send a message for her.

The sick, tight feeling in her gut intensified. She could ask someone nearby . . . unless she couldn't.

Addy pushed the thought away and activated the holo. Her first three attempts were failures, but each showed minimal improvement. The letters were a little closer to what she wanted. On the fourth attempt, she took her time, fingers tracing figure-eights in the air over a single letter before she could be certain they would land in the right place. When they shook too badly, she let them rest and forced herself to breathe deeply. By the time fifteen minutes had passed, she'd composed a three-word message.

<COMING HOME NOW.>

She sent it, switched off the holo, and stood, fighting giddy relief. She wasn't broken after all.

And then she started walking, not giving herself time to dwell on that last thought.

~

It had been late when Addy set off from school, and it was even later now. The trains were chock-full. She slipped into one of the lesser-packed carriages on the Gleniti Line, found a gap in the crowd, and planted her feet against the sway, holding the overhead rail for balance.

She was halfway home when the train took a bend too fast, sending her lurching into the man next to her.

He eyed her, his expression neutral.

She opened her mouth to offer an apology and then paused.

Don't try it, something deep in her mind murmured. *What if you're right, and you can't do it? The symptoms match. You're setting yourself up to fail.*

What if I'm wrong, and I can? she retorted but nodded anyway. Alright. Not here. She'd wait until she got home, where she had time and space and family around to catch her when—*if*—she fell apart.

So she closed her mouth, bit her lip, and gave the man an apologetic half-smile, half-grimace instead.

Clearly it wasn't good enough. He glared at her and turned his back.

Addy tried not to notice how her right hand clenched the rail or how her left hand trembled at her side. The black fog, driven away for a time by the sea breeze, came drifting back thicker than ever, rising up to choke her, dulling her senses, slowing her movements. She stared unseeing out the window for the rest of the journey.

~

No sooner had she closed the front door of the flat than she heard her mum call out from the lounge. "Addy? Is that you?"

The response was automatic—open mouth, inhale, exhale to push air past vocal chords to produce vibrations that could be formed into sounds and speech and words. This time, she let it happen. She tried, but even as she pushed the air out, her stomach writhed and sank like a deep-sea monster in its death throes.

She couldn't make a sound.

"Adelaide?"

Addy padded forward to stand in the doorway, unable to muster the energy for more than a half-hearted wave. Dad and Theo were nowhere to be seen. *Good.* At least she'd only have to tell Mum for a start.

A lump rose in her throat. She couldn't tell Mum, though, could she?

"Addy?" Mum swept across the room, frowning. "What's wrong?"

She couldn't tell Mum because . . . because—

The thought halted, stuttering, rocking back and forward in the antechamber of her mind. She couldn't think it. Thinking it would make it real. She'd made it this long without thinking it, hadn't she? Minutes, whole hours. She could make it another few hours, a day or two, a week . . .

The words echoed, hollow.

"Addy?"

She couldn't. She couldn't do it. She couldn't lie to herself; she couldn't lie to Mum and Dad, not even with her silence. She couldn't.

"*Adelaide.* Talk to me."

She fell forward into Mum's arms, tears running down her face, silent sobs ripping from her throat.

She couldn't talk.

She couldn't make a sound.

She couldn't *talk.*

Mum held her as she cried, rubbing her back, murmuring comforting nothings, empty platitudes. "There there, it's alright. You'll be alright. That's it—let it out. Have a good cry, and when you've calmed down, you can tell me what's wrong. We'll fix it, okay? You'll be alright."

But she couldn't tell her, not when she couldn't talk. So she cried. And cried. And cried.

Eventually Mum sat her on the sofa and went off to find some tissues for Addy's runny nose. When she came back, she not only carried tissues but a glass of water and a cold cloth.

"Now," she said, her tone brisk but kind, "sit up, have a drink, and tell me what happened. Did something go wrong at school? Is it that composition you're struggling with?"

Addy wanted to laugh. *If only.* It would be easy if it were something that simple. If it were an assignment or a problem with her friends, or if Aroha Waipori had said something mean about her light hair and yanked her braid again. She sniffed, reached for the tissue, and blew her nose.

Mum perched on the other end of the sofa.

Addy couldn't avoid it. She just hoped Mum would understand what she was trying to say.

She sat up, sipped the water, and gestured to her throat.

"Your throat's sore after crying?" Mum half-stood as if to retrieve something else from the kitchen.

Addy grabbed her arm and motioned for her to sit again, shaking her head. She gestured again at her throat, opened her mouth, gave a helpless little shrug, and closed her mouth again.

Mum didn't understand—Addy could see that.

"You're feeling ill," Mum said. "Your throat's sore. You've lost your voice."

Addy nodded and then shook her head again, grimacing in frustration. It was close but not close enough. How was she meant to make Mum understand when she couldn't *talk?* A germ of an idea came to her. She couldn't talk, okay, she knew that now. But she could still move her mouth. She could shape the words, even if she couldn't verbalise them.

I, she mouthed. *Can't. Talk.*

"Use your words, Adelaide."

Addy closed her eyes, despairing. *I can't,* she mouthed again. *Can't you understand? I. CAN'T. TALK.*

Mum leaned forward and activated the holo embedded in the

coffee table. "Well, if you won't talk, you can write, surely. You've always been a good writer."

I can't, Addy wanted to say. *I can't, I can't I CAN'T.* Her hands were shaking again. It was no use. Under Mum's expectant gaze, she lifted a hand and stabbed a string of letters.

What she tried to write was: <I CAN'T TALK.>

What emerged was: <O VSSNRT YTWAKLK.>

I can't talk, she mouthed again.

Mum sat back and blinked at her. That frown appeared again. *Good.* Maybe she was finally on the way to understanding.

"You're not just acting up, are you?" asked Mum. Her voice wavered on the last words.

Addy wanted to scream. *NO. I'm not acting up. She stole . . . she . . . she stole my voice.* Tears welled up again. She rubbed a trembling hand across her face, dashing them away. One more try. One more attempt; she'd try two words, two simple words to make it more real than anything she'd tried to say so far.

She waited until she was sure she had Mum's full attention and then mouthed, *Vox. Pox.*

The colour drained from Mum's face. "No."

Addy nodded. The tears came again, burning hot, streaming down her cheeks. She wiped them away, hiccupping on a silent sob, and wiped them away again. They kept coming.

"No. You can't. You can't have . . . Vox Pox . . ." Mum trailed off into a whisper.

But Addy did. She could. She nodded again, hating it, hating the flat look that crept into Mum's eyes at the confirmation. *Vox pox,* she repeated, hardly able to form the words amidst her tears.

Mum's mouth opened. Closed. Opened again. "I see." She moved closer, put an arm around Addy, and drew her into a hug. "I see."

Silence. Addy felt Mum shudder, but with her face buried in Mum's shoulder, she couldn't see her expression. Something wet dripped onto her shoulder. Mum sniffed and shuddered again.

Maybe it was easier this way. She didn't want to watch Mum cry.

The silence lingered, broken only by stifled sobs from Mum. Addy couldn't speak. It was obvious Mum didn't know what to say. She closed her eyes, burrowing deeper into the embrace, and tried to stop shaking.

The first cases had emerged just over a year ago. A few people across the city, not more than five or six, spontaneously lost the ability to produce sound. They couldn't talk, couldn't scream, couldn't even weep out loud. But it was more than that. They lost their creative abilities.

Two had been singers, one in a thrash band, one in a choir. No voice meant no singing—that was self-evident. But it wasn't only voice-related talents. A former concert pianist could only produce a tuneless mash of notes and chords. The man who painted in his spare time couldn't hold a brush steady. The girl who went to street dancing lessons after school lost all sense of coordination. And the news showed a teenager at a prestigious science academy gazing blankly at a physics formula of her own design.

Their voices had been stolen—and with their voices, somehow, vanished their whole creative identities.

Nobody knew how it happened. One man found a ring of bruises on his upper arm; another was unmarked but noticed that an old blister on his heel had reopened.

Experts were called upon, and they found no answers. Some people called it Vox Pox, others the Dumb Disease, still others the Silent Sickness. Despite its names, it was neither virus nor disease as far as any medico could tell. They confirmed it didn't appear to be a natural ailment. Artificial, they said, human-designed, human-made, and probably human-inflicted. They didn't know the cause. There was no cure.

Cases remained rare and, as far as Addy knew, contained to Te Maru. There might be two attacks in a week, then nothing for a month, then another solitary victim. There couldn't be more than thirty people who had it in the whole city.

Thirty-one now, Addy thought. She suddenly felt exhausted.

She stood, grabbed her schoolbag, and jerked a thumb upstairs. *I'm going to bed.*

"You're going to your room?" Mum asked, voice choked. "But you haven't eaten yet. You should eat something."

Addy was already halfway out of the room. She didn't look back, didn't want to see Mum's tearstained face. If she could still talk, she would have muttered *not hungry*. But she couldn't talk. There was no point in trying. She waved a hand in dismissal and took the stairs two at a time, fruitlessly trying to blink back tears. How could she still be crying? There were no tears left in her. There was nothing left in her.

She slipped into her room and shut the door. Her bag went on the hook; she slung her school jacket over the back of a chair. Then she stood, staring around at the familiar blue armchair, the thick duvet on the bed, the picture of Challa and herself stuck to the wall. Books covered her desk and clothes covered her floor. It was exactly as she'd left it this morning.

It should have changed. She had changed. She'd been changed so radically, so fundamentally that nothing was left in her. Her room, this space that was her own, should have changed, too.

She could change it.

Should change it.

But not now.

Addy kicked off her shoes. Took her uniform off. Hung it in her wardrobe. She found some old, flannel pyjama pants, the legs so long they fell over her feet, and a worn-in-worn-out shirt, thin and soft and comfortable. And then she curled into a ball under the duvet and let the clouds come down.

CHAPTER THREE

Dad took her to the clinic the next morning looking like he hadn't slept a wink. The senior medico, a man in his fifties with silvering hair, greeted them with a solid handshake.

"Call me Ian," he said. "And this is Junior Medico York."

"Harper, please," said the blonde young woman in medical blues. "How can we help?"

Dad lost no time getting to the point. "We think Adelaide has Vox Pox."

"Really?" Concern flashed across Ian's face. He pulled up a new file on his desk holo. "What symptoms is she showing? When did it happen?"

Addy tuned out as Dad filled them in. Beyond nodding in the right places, there wasn't much she could do.

Cream walls enveloped them on three sides. A misted window took up the fourth side, running from the deep blue ceiling to the polished concrete floor. The office was a study in industrial minimalism: metal desk, navy leather chairs, a stool on the side where Harper perched. Two certificates of medical practice hung on the wall beside a framed picture of a water drop.

Addy watched the droplet fall, hit the ground, and freeze solid. Once the image looped back to the start for the fourth time, she lost interest. The conversation went on. Ian took notes, Harper interjected questions, Dad carried the flow, and Addy . . . Addy just sat there, really.

After a while, Dad touched her shoulder to get her attention.

"I'm sorry," Addy said, focusing on Ian with an innocent smile.

"I was enthralled by the picture on the wall. Who's the artist, do you know?"

At least, that was what she was going to say. The words lined up in her mind, ready to come tripping off her tongue to charm them into forgetting her dreadful manners—

And then she opened her mouth and remembered she couldn't talk. The smile collapsed. She closed her mouth, blinked back tears, and nodded miserably when Dad asked if she was paying attention.

"Harper's going to take you for some tests," he said. "They could take two or three hours. I'll wait for you in the café downstairs, alright?"

She nodded. Again. At this rate, her head was going to fall off before her fourteenth birthday.

Harper took her into the next room and told her to hop up on the bed. Addy tuned out the explanation of the tests. They were a waste of time; surely it was obvious she had Vox Pox. She stared at the wall beside the bed and pretended she was down at the Shelter again, drifting with the tide. Instructions floated through the sea-fog. She obeyed them automatically.

"Turn onto your left side, please."

"And onto your back."

"You didn't take any medication this morning, is that correct?"

Nod. Drift.

"What about caffeine?"

Shake head. Drift.

"Shoes off and stand on the scale, please."

"Shirt off and take a few deep breaths."

The cold metal of the stethoscope pressed against her back, paused, and moved on. She'd been so embarrassed about this last time, having to stand half-naked while a stranger listened to her breathe. Now, she didn't care. Emotion at all hardly seemed worth the effort. Much easier to drift with the tide.

"You can put your shirt back on, thank you. A couple more tests, and we'll head down to the machines, okay?"

Nod, like a puppet on a string. Follow. Drift.

Downstairs, they gave her the option of the needle or the mask to make her sleep. She chose the needle. The sleep came as a welcome respite—Addy closed her eyes and drifted, felt the jab, and then the fog rolled over her and she knew no more.

The scans went well, they told her when she woke. Harper helped her dress and took her along to the café, keeping an arm at her elbow in case she fell. Addy didn't think she'd fall; she floated with the waves, pushing away the chemical smell of the corridors in favour of saltwater tang.

"She did wonderfully," Harper told Dad. "No problems at all. I'll trot down and get you when the results come through."

Dad thanked her, refilled his coffee cup, and poured Addy a glass of water.

"I messaged Mum," he said. "Told her what was happening. I'm pleased they could carry out the tests today."

She wanted to ask him about that. Surely most people weren't scheduled for hours of tests on the same day as their appointment? But she couldn't ask. Could she message him from her holo? No, she couldn't write a message that long. She could mouth the words, maybe, but it needed eye contact, and Dad wasn't looking at her.

The unanswered questions burned in her mind.

Harper appeared twenty minutes later and escorted them up to Ian's office.

"Henry. Adelaide. Sorry to be the bearer of bad news. The results confirm that Adelaide does have Vox Pox."

What a surprise. It wasn't like the symptoms matched perfectly or anything.

Dad's shoulders sagged. "I see. And there's nothing you can do . . . ?"

"I'm afraid not. There's no known cure. But if I may give you some advice?"

"Of course. Please."

"By all means give Adelaide a day or two off school to adjust.

But she should go back as soon as she feels ready. Isolation from one's support network after a major change does more damage than most people are aware of. Even if she's not actively participating in the lessons, she needs to be present."

Silence. Addy could feel them looking at her. She nodded acknowledgement without looking away from the water drop.

Dad sighed. "Alright. I suppose that makes sense. Thank you. If there's anything more we can do for her—"

"You could enrol her with a counsellor if you think she would benefit from that. It couldn't hurt."

"Has she lost anything other than her voice?" Harper asked.

"Yes," Dad said. "She wrote stories. Now she can't even write a full sentence. Lana, my wife, showed me the message Addy sent last night; it was only three words."

Ian leaned forward, sounding intrigued. "She still has some control of her motor skills? That's a good sign." He brought up a blank file on his holo. "Adelaide, please come here."

He's going to make me type a message, isn't he? She pressed her hands together, trying to stop the ceaseless trembling, and crossed to the desk.

"Write something," Ian said. "Anything."

She lifted a shaking hand and took a stab.

They looked at the result for a long moment, and then Ian said, "Thank you for trying."

He was giving up already? Addy held up one hand and used the other to delete the meaningless hash of letters. She took a breath, stretched her fingers out until they cracked, and began again. She could do this. She knew she could. She'd done it just last night.

Her finger wove figure-eights above the holo pad. *H.* She let her hand rest for a moment. *O.* Good. *M.* Their scrutiny bore into the back of her head, nervous tension spreading down her arm. She clenched her hands tight, demanding they hold still.

Figure-eight, figure-eight, *there.*

<HOME> proclaimed the holo.

She slumped back into her chair. Last night hadn't been a fluke. She wasn't broken. She *wasn't.* She could still write; slowly, yes, painfully, yes, but she could write, and by writing she could communicate.

Harper smiled. "Good on you, Adelaide. That's great. Fantastic."

"Excellent," Ian said. "Keep that up, and there's no reason you shouldn't be speeding through assignments again in no time. Henry, in light of this, I'm going to prescribe weekly physical therapy to go with the counselling sessions."

"I—yes, thank you," said Dad. "That would be helpful."

"If you take this note out to reception, they'll fix everything up for you."

Out on the street, Dad glanced at his holo and grimaced. "I have to get back to work. The Dusky Moose Café isn't far. Grab yourself some lunch, and I'll see you tonight."

~

Nobody knew what to do with her, Addy concluded glumly a week later.

Mum and Dad tried their best, but conversations flew over her head, or, when they tried to include her, fizzled and died. She couldn't type fast enough to keep up, miming was a waste of time, and mouthing words ended in a mess of mistranslation.

Theo was no help. He sat there in his calm seventeen-year-old superiority and tossed out complex phrases from his lessons like *catalytic cracking* and *dihydropyrometallurgy.* He wasn't *trying* to rub in the fact that he could still talk, she knew; it was just how he spoke. He was sympathetic, as were Mum and Dad, but they floundered when it came to effectual ways of helping.

Sympathetic but ineffectual described most people, really.

She'd gone to school the day after the medical tests with a

slip from Dad explaining what had happened. Challa hugged her tight and whispered that she was sorry and she couldn't imagine how Addy felt, and it would be okay, and she would field any questions from the class. Sofie proffered an open bag of Raspberry Crocodiles and said it wasn't so bad, they could still pass notes during class, couldn't they? And Nadia looked a bit lost before muttering *at least you won't have to do your oral defence of the peer critiques now.*

Kaiako Katie made the announcement first thing.

"I am very sorry," she said, her face grave, "to report that our own Adelaide Te Ngawai has lost her voice. She was tested at the medical clinic yesterday, and the results confirmed that she has Vox Pox." She waited for the murmurs to die down before continuing. "I would ask that you refrain from pestering her. She has elected to return to class in order to continue as much study as she can. Obviously this is a very difficult time for everyone involved, and for Adelaide most of all, but we will get through it together, and we will be stronger for it. Are we agreed, ladies?"

The upper ninth murmured assent. Addy kept her eyes fixed on the surface of her desk, not wanting to see the stares.

That first day passed in a dull haze of misery. She felt useless. She couldn't speak to join in the discussions. Her hands shook so much she couldn't type. She sat, hands clasped in her lap, sometimes listening to the lesson but more often staring out the window.

When class broke up for the weekend, Kaiako Katie asked her to stay behind.

"I'm sorry, Addy. I know you must be having an atrocious time with everything. But," she paused, looking uncomfortable, "if you're not going to participate in class, I'm afraid there's not much point in you continuing to attend."

Addy spread her hands helplessly. If she couldn't come to class, what would she do? Sit at home with shaking hands? At least here she had her friends and classroom chatter and familiar routines.

She'd lost her voice, her typing, and her stories. Was she going to lose everything else, too?

No. She refused to give up; she had as much right to be here as anyone else. Addy met frustrated tears with the heat of her anger, forcing them back. She would work. She would show them.

The emotion must have shown on her face because Kaiako Katie clasped her shoulder. "It's alright, I'm not going to kick you out today. I simply wanted to make you aware of the wider situation. We'll say a fortnight, shall we? And re-evaluate then."

Two weeks didn't sound like much, but Kaiako Katie appeared to think that even giving her that long was a grand gesture. Probably thought it was pointless. Alright. A fortnight. Addy had a fortnight to prove herself.

She could do this.

~

She spent the weekend in her bedroom with the door shut tight, hunched over her desk, practising. When she could type the alphabet in less than a minute, she moved on to simple words.

<RED. GREEN. ADELAIDE. TE MARU.>

Longer words made her hands shake worse. Resting her hands and stretching her fingers helped a little, and music helped more, she found. It let her concentrate on something other than the overwhelming pressure of the two-week deadline.

Mum knocked on her door late Sunday afternoon. "Addy? Are you there?"

Addy finished the last *s* of *linguistics* and went to open the door.

Theo skulked at the head of the stairs. Mum held her hands over her ears and shouted to make herself heard. "Can you turn the music down, please? It's rather *LOUD.*"

The last word echoed in the silence. Addy contrived to look as innocent as possible.

"Thank you. I'm not against music if it helps you with, er, everything, but do try to keep it to a civilised level."

Addy scratched her collarbone, thinking. It did help. At first, her music had screamed because she couldn't, but now it had become something almost therapeutic.

"Is that your assignment?" Mum peered over Addy's shoulder. "Have you been working on it?" Something terribly like hope lurked in her voice.

That's private, Addy wanted to say. *It's barely half a paragraph, and it's taken me the last hour to type. Please don't start thinking I'm going to regain my motor skills overnight.* She nodded begrudgingly, lifted her hands to cup them over her ears, and raised her eyebrows in silent question.

Mum frowned. "You want Eareos?"

Addy nodded again.

"Oh. Well. I suppose if it will help . . ."

It will, Addy mouthed. She repeated the ear cupping and made her hands into blinkers on either side of her face. *It helps me concentrate.*

"I see. No promises, but I'll have a talk with your father."

Addy smiled her thanks and retreated.

Monday wasn't much of an improvement on Friday. By Thursday, the rest of the upper ninth had stopped darting glances at her every five minutes, and the shaking in her hands had settled enough that she could make an attempt at keeping up in class. Friday would have been almost normal if not for two things.

She couldn't talk, and nobody knew how to act around her.

Addy was slowly getting used to not having a voice. The black fog lingered, but she was getting used to that, too. Music helped; Mum had knocked on her door on Tuesday and presented her with a gorgeous set of cutting-edge Eareos, all distressed black metal and gleaming blue leather and brass detailing.

"Consider them an early Christmas present," she'd said. They synced seamlessly with her holo and became a constant companion. If they weren't on her ears, they hung in easy reach around her neck.

She was adapting to it. Why couldn't everyone else?

The stares died down, but the awkwardness lay as thick as ever. Kaiako Katie never called on her in class anymore—not that Addy could have answered if she had. Aroha Waipori broke a six-month streak of mocking looks in favour of ignoring her. Nadia hadn't talked to her since Wednesday apart from saying, "Good morning."

Challa did her best to include Addy and persisted in sitting close enough to bump shoulders in silent support. Addy almost wished she wouldn't. It made it worse, somehow. She just wanted to slip away into her thoughts, into the fog, into the music, but the contact kept jolting her back to the here and now. She didn't want to be here and now. She wanted it to be Wednesday last week, where she could avoid eye contact with Kaiako Katie and not go off to that tutoring session with Maunga.

Kaiako Katie asked her to stay behind again on Friday.

"I won't hold you up for long," she said. "It's good to see you're doing better with everything."

Everything. It was the euphemism of choice for what had happened, Addy noticed. *How are you doing with, you know, everything? You seem to be coping well with . . . everything.* Sometimes she wanted them to call it what it was, and sometimes she thought that if they did, it would break her.

She smiled noncommittally.

"I'll check in with you again at the end of next week," Kaiako Katie went on, "but I wanted to say well done for your hard work on the assignments these last few days. If this week's progress is any indication, there won't be any trouble at all letting you stay on."

Letting you stay on. She said it like it was such a privilege. Addy's parents paid her school fees like everyone else's; they had no right to kick her out of class.

"Anyway. Keep your chin up, Addy. You've done well. Ka pai."

Addy took the compliment with a nod, shouldered her bag, and left.

~

The first time she saw Maunga Richards across the close-cut grass of the quad, the spike of nausea in her gut forced her to bolt for the bathroom. Maunga watched her go and said nothing.

The second time, her hands started shaking so badly she could hardly get a grip on her schoolbag. Maunga sidled up behind her and murmured, "Hey, dumbo. Don't try to tell anyone; they'd never believe you, and it'd be a shame if the same thing happened to your friends."

Addy's blood ran cold. Maunga had vanished by the time she turned around.

The third time, her hands still trembled, but it was manageable. She swallowed hard and jerked a nod at the older girl. Maunga was right. Who would believe her? Correlation wasn't causation; Maunga may have been in the room when Addy ran into trouble, but she had no proof. And if she did tell someone and Maunga found out . . . her gut clenched. Nadia, Sofie, *Challa*—they'd all be infected with the Pox, too.

No. She couldn't risk it.

She couldn't tell anyone.

~

Sick of people staring at her for being different, Addy dyed her hair a shade of brown so deep it looked black in low light. When she walked into class the next morning, Aroha Waipori sneered at her for the first time in weeks. Challa eyed her quizzically, then nodded and said, "Nice. It suits you."

The black fog became a constant companion. She stopped

fighting it. The hours passed, making a day; the days passed, making a week; and soon whole months were passing. She hardly noticed.

Nadia stopped talking to her entirely and then moved desks to sit beside Meghan Kim. Sofie lasted a little longer. Challa did her best to bridge the ever-widening gap; it wasn't enough, and she fell back on Sofie for conversation. Addy listened to them discuss plans for the weekend and told herself she didn't care.

She completed her assignments on time without fail. Kaiako Katie praised her ongoing recovery and never asked about the dark circles under her eyes. Mum and Dad didn't question the nights they went to bed late and saw her bedroom light still shining under her door. She bumped into Theo in the kitchen at two o'clock in the morning once. His brows twitched downward. He didn't say anything. All-nighters were traditionally his domain, but not anymore—now Addy was putting in six or eight hours a night just to finish her assignments on time.

The long hours became routine. Her typing slowly improved. Her grades for ninety percent of her work remained high—*technically proficient but lacking spark* was the invariable comment. The other ten percent was a different matter. Regardless of grade handicap or extra time granted, she failed every assessment that required the slightest degree of creativity.

She told herself she didn't care, and eventually she believed it.

CHAPTER FOUR

Someone knocked on her bedroom door late on the night of her fifteenth birthday, more than eighteen months after she'd lost her voice. Theo cracked the door open.

"Can I come in?"

Addy slipped her Eareos off and eyed him for a long moment. It wasn't like him to pop in for a visit. The late hour was nothing unusual—he often didn't get home from university until nine or ten—but the fact that he wanted to talk to her specifically . . . no, that wasn't normal.

She shrugged and nodded. He slipped inside, carrying a canvas sack in his arms, and nudged the door closed with his foot. She watched as he untied the knot and withdrew a large, gift-wrapped box.

"Here." He held it out to her. "Happy birthday. Careful—it's heavier than it looks."

It looked light. She took it from him cautiously. Hmm. He was right; it was heavier than she'd expected. She set it on her desk and took a minute to flash a message on her holo.

<THANKS.>

"You're welcome. Now hurry up and open it. I want to show you how it works."

Addy picked at the tape that held the wrapping secure. It came away easily, and she peeled away the gift-wrap to reveal . . . another layer of wrap.

She rolled her eyes at Theo. <REALLY?> He was so childish sometimes.

He grinned, unrepentant. "Keep going."

She thought he might have stopped at three layers. Or five. Or even ten. But no, he had to wrap the box in *fifteen* layers of wrapping, all different shades of blue. She hadn't realised he cared so much.

"One layer for each year," he said when the box itself was finally revealed. It wasn't anything flashy—just a plain brown box, no pictures, no labels or descriptions.

The lid came off. She lifted out a handful of tissue paper and detached the cushioning cone. The gift came next: a stiff keypad, light and slim, a perfect match for her Eareos in colour and materials: black metal, blue leather trim, brass details. It was a physical keypad, too, not the smooth, featureless sheet of a holo pad.

"I thought about making a normal keypad. But then I remembered back to when you learned electric guitar; you always had trouble with the holo frets. I figured you'd prefer a physical keypad."

He'd figured right. Addy smiled at him. Her confusion must have shown because he added, "That's only half of it. Look again," and nodded at the box.

She looked. More tissue papers, another cushioning cone. And the second half of her gift: a hollow metal shell, intricately carved, matching the keypad in appearance. It looked a bit like an elegant piece of shoulder armour from her Medieval History texts.

<THANKS,> she typed on her desk holo. <WHAT IS IT?>

Theo stepped closer and took the shell from her. "Here," he said, the amusement in his eyes giving way to the familiar light frown of concentration. He clapped it onto her left shoulder—she'd been right about the design, then—and waited.

After a moment, it warmed; Addy watched as it seemed to melt around the edges, the articulated plates stretching and contorting until it fit perfectly. She frowned at Theo, confused. Was it meant to be some sort of jewellery for her shoulder? She'd never dare wear it out of the house. It looked nice, sure; the colours made a statement against the drab grey of her jersey, but it was very odd.

Theo handed her the keypad. "Now." He took a deep breath. He sounded almost nervous. "Hold it upside down."

She flipped the pad so the keys faced the floor.

"No—sorry. Leave it facing out, but turn it so you can read the keys from your perspective."

Oh, *that* sort of upside down. She rotated the pad, wondering where this was heading.

"Okay. Hold it against your right leg, at about the right height for you to reach it without stretching. You want it to be comfortable . . . maybe a little higher. You'll need to reach the whole pad. Good. Feel down the edge, there's a little switch. Hit it."

It was like balancing a short and rather awkward plank against her thigh. She held the pad in place with one hand and flipped the switch with the other. *Aha.* The pad warmed and then, like the shoulder piece, melted a little and curved around to fit her leg before hardening again. Addy kept her hand in place for a moment, making sure it was secure before lifting her hand. It clung to her trouser leg and followed the lines of her thigh when she took a few experimental paces across the room.

Okay, she had a keypad attached to her. So what?

"Shrug," said Theo.

She looked at him incredulously.

"Shrug," he repeated, a grin tugging at his mouth. "Just your left shoulder."

The one with the shoulder piece on it. She lifted her shoulder, keeping her eyes fixed on Theo in case it was a joke, and lowered it again.

The shoulder guard felt much like the keypad: firm enough that she knew it was there, light and flexible enough to not be annoying. And then the spike that she'd thought was purely decorative lit up, projecting a pinpoint of light into the air above her shoulder that unfurled into a familiar blue holo screen.

Her mouth dropped.

Theo grunted. "Shouldn't have been that slow. Shrug again."

Addy did. The holo curled up and vanished into the spike. Shrug. Uncurl. Shrug. Disappear. The faster she shrugged, the faster it moved.

Theo nodded, looking satisfied. "That's alright then. Activate it, if you will."

She shrugged and watched the holo unfurl.

"Type something."

Type—? Oh, the keypad.

<SOMETHING,> she typed and watched the word appear letter-by-letter on her shoulder holo. <SOMETHING,> she typed again. <SOMETHING SOMETIGHN AYNTIHGN.>

Tears pricked at her eyes. Her wrist holo was fine for a few words or for simple, private messages, but it was small and clumsy, and it took too long when she had to stop and read what she was writing every five seconds. *This,* though—this was something entirely different. She could *talk* with this.

"It'll take practice," Theo cautioned. "It's a bigger pad than you're used to, and the curve will take a while to adapt to, especially when you're moving and talking at the same time. But the physical keypad should help with that. You won't even need to watch what you're saying." He smirked at the no-doubt-intended double meaning.

Addy choked back tears. <THANK YOU,> she typed. They were paltry words; she could say them a thousand times and not come close to conveying the depth of her gratitude. She borrowed a phrase from one of the classics, cutting it short in deference to her clumsy fingers. <I CAN NO OTHER ANSWER MAKE BUT THANKS.> He would understand the reference.

Theo nodded and stepped toward the door. "Oh." He turned back. "Almost forgot. It'll sync with any holo around, including your wrist holo—and, through that, your Eareos. You shouldn't need to activate the visuals, though. You can control your music from the keypad."

Even sending messages on her wrist holo would be a lot easier with the keypad. And schoolwork, too—she'd gotten used to the desk holo, but a physical keypad might help speed up her typing.

"I made it myself," he continued. "Started it last semester for a design assessment and carried it through to this semester for the practical. Figured it would make up for last year's present."

Last year he'd given her a scarf for her birthday. It had been lovely and warm, but—well. It was only a scarf.

Addy stared. He'd spent the last nine months working on this? She *really* hadn't known he cared so much. She darted forward and threw her arms around him.

Theo patted her back awkwardly. "You're, uh, you're welcome."

He disengaged himself from the embrace and opened the door. "Last thing, I promise. If you get desperate, you can attach the keypad and the shoulder piece to bare skin. And they're waterproof. In case you want to, I don't know, work on assignments while you're in the shower."

He shot her a fleeting grin and was gone.

~

Three months later, Addy stumbled across an old creative writing assignment in the records of her desk holo.

She'd been cleaning out the archives to make way for a new term of assignments. It was an old assignment; she hadn't labelled it properly the first time around, and the odd title caught her eye. She opened it to see what it was so she could re-label it and file it in the right place. It was a story.

She hadn't meant to start reading. But she did, and twenty minutes later she was huddled in a ball on her bed, crying.

How could she have forgotten? She dimly remembered what it was like to write something like that, searching for just the right words, the right emotions, the right ebb and flow of rhythm. But of course she'd forgotten. She never used those skills anymore. She couldn't.

Her voice had gone and with it her creativity. She couldn't write a story, couldn't play an instrument, couldn't sing a simple tune. She could write, yes; since Theo had gifted her with the shoulder holo, her writing had improved by leaps and bounds. But even at her most energised, she couldn't deny that the writing was dull. It didn't have any life to it. Oh, it was technically sound, she had no doubt of that, but no more than that. It wouldn't make her cry.

It wasn't *proper* writing, she thought with sudden clarity. Proper writing had vim and vigour and *spark;* all she'd been doing was stringing words together. Anyone could do that.

She wasn't *anyone.* Or was she? Her hands trembled at the thought. No, she wasn't. Anyone else could speak in class. So she might not be *anyone,* but it was for different reasons than it might have been two years ago. She had two years behind her of writing that was *technically proficient but lacking personality;* before that, she'd had four years of writing that was *well structured, emotive, vivid.*

Could she do it? Could she break through whatever was blocking her and write something worth remembering? Her heart quailed. Nobody else had been able to. She'd never heard stories of the ballroom dancer who started dancing again, or the physics girl who understood her own theorem. But she wouldn't know until she tried.

Her hands scrabbled for her headphones and slipped them into place. She moved to her desk, dropped into the chair, and did her best to quell the trembling in her hands. It took half a second to activate the holo; another half-second to bring up a blank file.

Her foot tapped out an anxious beat in double-time, tap-tap, tap-tap, tap-tap.

Just think of it as an essay. A creative essay, that's all it is.

Where to start, where to start. How about the most common definite article in the English language? *The.* The, the, the.

The what? Description, she needed some description. An adjective. A colour? *The brown.*

Okay, the brown something. The brown what? Animal, vegetable, or mineral? Animal. A common animal. *Dog.*

What about it? Was it male or female? Did something happen to the dog? Did the dog happen to something else? She needed a verb. *The brown dog ran.*

Where did it run? *Across the . . . road.*

Addy sat back, drained, hands shaking worse than they had in a long time.

<THE BROWN DOG RAN ACROSS THE ROAD.>

It was hardly a masterpiece of emotive writing. She could almost use it in an assignment, it was so dry. And her mind had gone blank. That was it. That was the entirety of two years' reserves of storytelling used up in a single sentence.

But she had written it.

And maybe she could write it again, even if it took another two years' reserves.

Bah. Wishful thinking, that's all it was. If there was anything this last two years had taught her, it was the value of sheer slog. Wishing for her voice to come back had never gotten her anywhere; sleep deprivation and hard work had.

And this wasn't the sort of thing she could dedicate six hours a night to practising.

She slapped the file shut and went back to cleaning.

~

Theo barged into her room one night without knocking.

The shrug to activate her shoulder holo was reflexive, as was the question she tapped into the keypad without looking. <WHAT ARE YOU DOING?>

"Check your holo," he said. "I sent you a link to a news article."

She pulled the article up, shot a curious glance at him, and started reading.

Science Lab Claims Psychotherapy Sim
Isabel Mabait, Channel 43 News

Could a virtual reality simulator solve more problems than a therapy session? Scientists at Breach Laboratories think so. In a statement released today, Weka Koltsov, Public Relations Officer for Breach, claimed that the laboratory and research institute has succeeded in building the first Virtual Psychoidentity Simulator in the modern world.

Addy glanced up at Theo. <VIRTUAL PSYCHOIDENTITY SIMULATOR?>

"That's what they're calling it."

<WHAT IS IT?>

"It's pretty much exactly that."

She furrowed her eyebrows.

He paused, thinking. "Let me put it this way. Imagine if you crossed one of those multiplayer RPGs with a psychotherapy session."

Addy blinked. <SOUNDS IMPRESSIVE. AND AMBITIOUS.>

"Yes to both. Nobody's ever seen it in action. The concept itself is ambitious, but so far as we can tell, it's only a concept. Sure, they're claiming they've built the simulator. Anyone could claim that. It's good PR. Until they prove that the simulator exists and, more importantly, that it works, it's all talk and no substance. Even if the prototype does work, Breach will have a long way to go before they can certify it fit for consumer use. But if it works, if it consistently does what they're claiming it can do, and if they can *prove* that it does . . ." He whistled. "If it works, it'll be very, *very* impressive."

<WHAT'S THE POINT OF IT?>

Theo leaned forward and lifted a finger. "They say half our problems come from our psyche. If we can get in and see, really *see*, what our individual identities look like and where they stem from and what causes them . . . we could fix those problems. Or, okay, maybe not fix them, per se. But we could certainly have a better understanding of them. I don't know, I'm not a psychologist, but that's the spin they're putting on it."

She quirked an eyebrow. <YOU DON'T KNOW? I THOUGHT YOU KNEW EVERYTHING.>

"Ha." He nodded to her desk. "Keep reading."

The next paragraph covered what Theo had just told her, albeit in twice as many words. The conclusion read:

> *Whether the claim is a hoax or not remains to be seen. Authenticity tests are underway by independent consultants. Until they are complete, all anyone can do is wait. Whatever the outcome, the laboratory is certain of increased interest in the coming weeks. This is groundbreaking science—if it can be proven.*
>
> *When contacted by Channel 43 News, Breach Laboratories declined to comment.*

Addy deactivated the holo. <SO IT COULD ALL BE A HOAX?>

"Could be. But I don't think it is. Breach isn't an unknown entity; they've been around for decades, and they're notoriously tight-lipped about new prototypes."

<YOU'LL LET ME KNOW IF YOU HEAR ANYTHING NEW ABOUT IT?>

"Yeah," he said. "Of course I will."

~

The Breach Laboratories claim wasn't a hoax. In six months it went from 'unsubstantiated wild rumour' to 'the newest fad for people with money.' Everyone wanted to try it: celebrities, politicians, experts in every field, the average person on the street. The media took full advantage of the uproar, with almost round-the-clock coverage.

One of the first interviews was with a student at Richard Pearse University who was a selective mute—or former selective mute, now. Addy watched and re-watched the video feed, examining it for any evidence of tampering, any sign that the young man's speaking was faked. It looked real enough. If the RPG programme could fix something like that . . . what else could it fix?

A fierce glow lit her insides. She banked the embers, not daring to hope.

She followed another instance closely: the case of one of the very first people to come down with Vox Pox, the middle-aged painter. He went into Breach escorted by his psychologist, looking calm and composed; the reporters caught him emerging a bare twenty minutes later, hair dishevelled, a murderous expression on his face. Addy noticed his hands shaking and filed the thought away.

"We're here outside Breach Laboratories," said Isabel, the designated Breach reporter, "where Frank Hadlow has just attempted—is that right, attempted?—to undergo the popular procedure known as RPG Therapy or TheraRPG. We understand the endeavour didn't quite go to plan. Can you tell us more, Frank?"

Hadlow glared at the holocam, made an obscene gesture, and kept walking.

"Ah," said Isabel, looking taken aback. "Well. That's unfortunate. Here's Frank's psychologist, Hika Claremont. Kia ora, Hika. How are you?"

A tall woman with dark red hair appeared on the screen. "Kia ora, Isabel. I'm well, thank you."

"Can you tell us anything about what's happened in the last thirty minutes?"

"Not much," Hika said. "I'm sure it wasn't a fault on the part of the Breach team, but the, ah, entry requirements for the procedure aren't calibrated to my client's needs. He was turned away during the initial preparation phase."

"Entry requirements?"

"I don't know how much I'm allowed to say." Hika glanced back over her shoulder at the Breach building.

Off camera, Isabel made an encouraging noise.

"Alright. I'll say this: the procedure assumes a basic level of reading comprehension and writing ability on the part of its participants. My client cannot write, and so he was ineligible for the programme."

"And how–"

"I'm sorry, that's all I have time for. Thank you for your questions. Good day."

Addy saved the feed to her archives for future reference.

~

Five months before Addy's sixteenth birthday, Maunga Richards walked into their classroom.

"Shouldn't you be at university?" asked Kaiako Clarissa.

"No." Maunga stuck her hands in her pockets and stared around at the class. Her gaze passed over Addy without pausing. "I don't have any lectures until three o'clock. This must be the old upper ninth?"

"We're the eleventh," Kotukutuku Johnson said.

Maunga shrugged. "You're still the upper ninth in my mind. There was that tutoring session, wasn't there? With, uh, Kaiako . . ." She trailed off, frowning.

"Kaiako Katie."

"Yeah, her. I need the paperwork signed off," she added, turning to Kaiako Clarissa.

"I'm sorry?"

"The paperwork for the tutoring session. I need you to sign it off, to say that I did volunteer tutoring as an extra-curricular activity. Please."

"It was one time," protested Nadia from two rows in front of Addy. "For, what, about an hour? And you only did it because Kaiako Katie made you. That shouldn't count."

"Shouldn't Kaiako Katie sign it off?" Kaiako Clarissa asked.

"The upper ninth room was empty. I don't know where they went."

"Did you try the library?"

Maunga shrugged and chewed her caf-cud.

Addy could see the moment Kaiako Clarissa decided it wasn't worth the trouble to argue. "Alright, Maunga. Do you have the file there, or shall I write you a note?"

"I have the file. You just need to fill in the spaces." Maunga checked her wrist holo. "Sending it through to you. There, it should have gone through now."

Kaiako Clarissa pulled the file up and started filling it in.

Maunga wandered over to the nearest occupied desk and looked down at Ruthie Scarborough, who had been runner-up for the position of Quietest in the Class for the last two years.

"Hi," said Maunga.

Ruthie's eyes widened. She swallowed hard and didn't reply.

"It's polite to answer when someone greets you, you know." Maunga stuffed her hands back in her pockets and somehow managed to look as intimidating as ever.

"Hi," whispered Ruthie.

"There we go. Well done." The sarcasm was evident.

"Hey," called Challa from the back of the class. "Leave Scar alone. What'd she ever do to you?"

Maunga's head came up; she picked Challa out of the crowd with unnerving accuracy. Her eyes narrowed. "Just making polite conversation. Nothing wrong with that, is there? Sorry, mate," she added, not sounding apologetic in the slightest, and patted Ruthie on the head. "I'll stop talking to you now since it scares you so much."

She sauntered down to the back of the class and slouched against the wall in the aisle between Challa and Aroha Waipori.

"Hello," she said to Aroha.

Aroha's mouth turned down in distaste. "Hi."

Maunga laughed; Addy expected the sound to be coarse and

ugly, but it emerged low and clear. "You're not scared of me, are you? Good."

"We're not scared of you," Challa said, looking bored. "We just don't like you."

"Don't like me all you like," said Maunga. "Or all you don't like, as the case may be. Do I look like I care?" She pulled a folded piece of paper from her pocket and held it up.

"What's that?" asked Aroha.

"This, Aroha Waipori, queen bee of the upper ninth—I'm sorry, eleventh—is a piece of paper."

Aroha rolled her eyes. "What's *on* the piece of paper?"

"Read it for yourself." Maunga unfolded the paper, smoothed the creases, and passed it to Aroha.

There was a long moment of silence as the whole class looked at Aroha.

"Out loud," Maunga said. "Otherwise it wouldn't be fair, would it?"

Aroha sighed and read the paper aloud. "This document is to confirm that the applicant—there's a black scribble where the first name should be—Te Whirikoka O Nga Rau Maunga Richards, preferred name 'Maunga,' has been accepted for a three-hour session in the—*keek*," she swore, looking startled, and then darted a guilty look toward the front of the class.

Kaiako Clarissa didn't react.

"Read on," said Maunga.

"In the TheraRPG programme at Breach Laboratories."

"What!" exclaimed Hannah James from the other side of the class.

"Eh," said Tuku. "It's not that great." Her dad held some high-up management position at Breach, and she'd done a session a few months ago for her birthday. By all reports, reactions varied wildly. Some people came out shaking with emotion and vowing they'd never go back, while others raved about how much they loved it. When the class quizzed her, Tuku had shrugged and said it had been fun enough, but it was nothing to rave about.

"Are you serious?" said Jessica Te Waiora from two rows in front.

"Shut up and let her read," Maunga snarled.

"In the TheraRPG programme at Breach Laboratories," Aroha repeated, "pending participation in, and proven competency during, the preparation phase. The aforesaid preparation phase is to be held on the day of your TheraRPG programme. Please arrive thirty minutes before your scheduled group session, and bring the attached participation swipe card to allow you access beyond reception. The card will be activated forty minutes before your session and deactivated ten minutes after the session ends. The time and date of your approved session is as follows: one-thirty p.m. on the afternoon of—" her brow furrowed "—the twenty-third of April. Please contact us when you receive this letter to confirm your attendance of the programme on the above-mentioned date. Yours sincerely, Caroline York, TheraRPG Overseer, Breach Laboratories."

"It's not until April?" Challa asked. "But we're only in October!"

"Yeah." Maunga plucked the paper from Aroha's fingers and tucked it away in her pocket again. "They're booking six months out at the moment, and I daresay it'll be seven months in another week or two. The whole city's mad keen to try it. I hear one guy amputated his own hand and tried to sell it on the black market to raise funds for a session." She snorted. "He was arrested two days later when his buyer turned out to be a cop, but it's the thought that counts, right?"

She grinned at their horrified faces and wandered back up to Kaiako Clarissa's desk, where the finished file was in the process of transmitting.

"There you are, Maunga," said Kaiako Clarissa. "Take it and go, please, before you traumatise my class beyond repair."

"Sure." Maunga turned toward the door. "Thanks. I might stop by the library on my way out—you said Kaiako Katie could be there? I wonder if the uni would accept two copies with different signatories . . ."

Addy watched her go with narrowed eyes. Her thoughts churned. There could be an opportunity here if she kept her cards close to her chest and played them just right. She deactivated her shoulder holo with a shrug and reached for her Eareos.

Sofie cast her a quizzical look but didn't comment. The class was used to her habits of concentration after two and a half years. With her shoulder holo down, they knew not to try to engage her in conversation unless it was important.

Kaiako Clarissa wouldn't notice her lack of attention. Addy slouched down in her chair and stared at her desk until the surface blurred.

She had a *lot* of thinking to do.

CHAPTER FIVE

Three dozen half-formed plans coalesced in a single, crystal-clear moment on the thirtieth of March, a week after her sixteenth birthday. It was Friday night; school had finished for the week, and Addy was looking forward to a weekend free of homework, courtesy of Kaiako Georgiana's view that it wasn't healthy to be slaving over one's books all the time and that teenagers should be able to go out and have fun on their weekends.

The knowledge that Maunga Richards would be going into a TheraRPG session on the twentieth of April had been lurking in the back of her mind. A quiet warning sounded every morning: *one less day to plan whatever you're planning on planning, if you're even planning on planning something. Are you?* And then on Friday the thirtieth of March, when there were three weeks to go until the deadline, the sirens reached a fever pitch, and she knew she didn't have a choice.

She was sitting down to tea with Mum and Dad when the front door opened and closed.

"That's early for Theo to be home," said Mum with a frown. "Maybe he's going to study at home tonight instead of at the university."

Maybe he is. It would be unusual, but she supposed he might prefer a bit of variety once in a while.

Theo appeared in the doorway, and the warning bells sounded in her head. His red-rimmed eyes glinted with a stony light; his hair was dishevelled far beyond its usual artfully tousled curls.

"Evening." Dad either didn't notice Theo's state or pretended not to notice it. "You're home early. Would you like some tea?"

Theo stared around the room. He shrugged out of his backpack and lowered it to the floor, the movements stiff and slow.

The warning bells grew louder.

"Theo." Mum half rose from her seat. "Are you hungry?"

"It's alright, you don't have to eat right now," said Dad, a thread of concern in his voice. "Come and sit down. Tell us about your day. Did you get your marks back on that project?"

A quiver ran across Theo's face. Amusement? Frustration? Anger? Addy couldn't tell. Then his expression hardened. He shook his head and jerked a thumb at his throat.

Addy's stomach dropped in a dizzying whirl of queasiness. She knew what he was going to say—or rather, *not* say. She reached for her keypad even as his mouth opened—

And he mouthed, *Vox Pox.*

<VOX POX,> her fingers echoed.

"Sorry, I didn't catch that," Dad said.

But Mum looked from Theo to Addy, and her face grew pale. "Henry," she whispered. "Henry. It's Vox Pox."

Dad followed Mum's gaze. His face dropped, and his eyes swung back to Theo as if pulled there by a magnet. "Vox Pox?"

Theo nodded, the movement short and sharp. His hands trembled at his sides.

The silence lingered. Mum and Dad sat frozen.

Addy didn't know what to say either, but someone had to say something. They couldn't sit in silence for the rest of their lives.

She shifted in her seat and waited for Theo to look at her.

<WELCOME TO THE CLUB?>

He bared his teeth in a maybe-smile that held equal parts rage and despair, turned on his heel, and left the room.

"Let him go," Dad murmured.

They heard footsteps on the stairs followed by the slam of a bedroom door.

Addy finished her meal and excused herself. Mum waved her

away. She scooped up Theo's pack on her way out of the room; it would give her an excuse to drop in and check on him.

She knocked on his bedroom door and waited.

Silence. No sound of movement.

She knocked again, a little louder. And waited. Another minute or two went by before the door cracked open. A sliver of Theo's face appeared and glared at her.

<Can I come in?> she asked.

He didn't move.

<Please? I brought your backpack up.>

He looked away, ran a hand over his face, and stepped back.

Theo was one of those naturally tidy people; his hair was always brushed, clothes neat, boots polished. The mess that greeted her was a shock. Clothes had been slung all over the floor, books lay in a heap in the corner, and his bed was a tangle of untucked sheets and rumpled blankets. It looked like he'd purposefully tried to make it as disordered as possible.

But that made sense. He was a mess, so the room was a mess. Addy had felt like that herself, the first night she came home with Vox Pox. She'd changed so swiftly, so dramatically, that she wanted—needed—to make her environment change too, in an echo of what she was feeling. But she had been too drained to do it that very night.

Theo clearly wasn't.

<Here's your bag.>

He snatched it from her and threw it behind him without looking. Now that she could see him fully, she was surprised to see a holo piece on his right shoulder. The pauldron shape was similar to her own shoulder piece, but the materials were different. Black metal and dark green leather formed the base. The matte-silver designs were more utilitarian than decorative. She ran a casual eye down him. Sure enough, a matching keypad clung to his left thigh.

Well. Perhaps it wasn't surprising that he'd built and stored his own shoulder holo, especially after seeing the leaps and bounds of progress that Addy had made upon being gifted hers. The number of reported cases had skyrocketed these last two years. He always had believed in being prepared for any eventuality.

He'd seen what it had done to Addy, that first eighteen months without an adequate means of communication. Of course he would want any slim advantage he could get right from the start.

Addy gestured to the shoulder piece. <ANY LUCK WITH THAT YET?> The way his hands wouldn't stop shaking, she doubted it.

He jerked his head in a sharp *no.*

<GIVE IT TIME. IT TOOK ME A MONTH BEFORE I COULD TYPE A RELIABLE SENTENCE.>

He rolled his eyes and nodded, and she could just hear his sarcastic comment in her head: *Yes, thank you for that incredibly helpful information.*

<I KNOW IT'S BEYOND FRUSTRATING,> she added.

Another nod.

<BUT IT DOES GET . . . NOT NECESSARILY BETTER, BUT MANAGEABLE.>

No response. He stared at the corner of the bed.

<I — >

They swung around at the same time. Addy didn't need Theo's upraised hand to tell her to stop communicating. Footsteps came up the stairs, and then they heard the sound of quiet voices.

"Just give it time, Henry," Mum was saying. "I know it's a huge shock. It is for all of us, but we'll get through it. We got through it with Addy, and we'll do the same with Theo."

"I know we will," said Dad, his voice choked.

Addy felt a stab of awkwardness. Parents weren't meant to cry. She darted a glance at Theo, but his head was turned away, and she couldn't see his expression.

"But," Dad went on, "it's both of them. *Both* of them, Lana. One was keeking bad enough. How are we going to cope with both our children having the Pox?"

"Others have it worse. Like Ettina Clarence, the poor woman. You think two kids is bad. Imagine trying to cope with a husband and *five* kids."

Addy saw a shadow move across the gap where the bedroom door hadn't quite closed.

"Six," Dad murmured.

Mum drew a sharp breath. "I thought that was only a rumour."

The shadow shook its head. "Her sister works down the hall from me. I've picked up bits and pieces of the story over time. Ettina and Micko had six kids. Ettina ducked out one morning to grab some groceries, and when she came back, Micko and the kids had the Silent Sickness." He paused. Ducked his head. "They did their best. That's all anyone can do. But one of the boys couldn't handle it. Held on a couple of months and then . . ."

Silence.

"I need a shower," said Mum. "No. A walk, I need a walk. A good—a good brisk walk."

"I'll get my jacket."

Addy sat, hardly daring to breathe as they went down the hall to their bedroom. She heard footsteps coming back to the stairs a minute later.

"We're going for a walk," Mum called without pausing. "Back later!"

Addy heard them go down the stairs. The front door slammed, and they were gone.

She blew out a breath and snuck a look at Theo.

His trembling hands were clenched white-knuckled on his thighs; his eyes were hard and cold as he stared at the far wall. Without looking at her, he pointed to the door.

Addy swallowed, feeling sick. There was nothing she could say. Even if she tried, he'd never hear it.

She left.

~

Friday the twentieth of April dawned clear and cool. Addy woke early, her thoughts whirling, her gut churning. The smell of ocean spray lay heavy in her memory. She'd spent hours upon hours at the Shelter these last three weeks, thinking, plotting, letting the sea breeze drive the lingering black fog away. Even on wet days, she threw on a jacket and went down to stare at the blurred horizon where high sea washed against low cloud.

Today was the day.

She made herself wait until her usual waking time to send a message to Mum.

<I DON'T FEEL WELL. GOING BACK TO SLEEP. CAN YOU MESSAGE SCHOOL AND TELL THEM I WON'T MAKE IT PLEASE?>

Five minutes later, Mum cracked the door open and slipped inside.

"How bad is it?" she asked. "Do you need the medico?"

Addy shook her head. <NO MEDICO. THROBBING HEADACHE. JUST WANT TO SLEEP.>

"If you're sure. I have to go to work, but message me if you need me, okay? I can slip home at lunchtime."

The door closed. When she was sure Mum was really gone, Addy sat up and waved the lights on.

Let's do this.

She grabbed her daypack from its hook and shoved supplies in. A hooded jacket. Water bottle, wrapped sandwich, apple, chocolate bar. Three pieces of ID. A book. A miniature medical kit. Clothes came next. Accounts of what the TheraRPG programme consisted of varied, so she'd gone with practical choices. Charcoal-grey cargo pants. Blue shirt. A black jersey, soft and warm. Thick socks. Chunky black boots. And over the top, the ever-present shoulder piece and keypad, black and blue and bronze, and her Eareos.

Mum and Dad left for work together at quarter to eight. She waited until eight o'clock to be safe and then shouldered her pack and slipped downstairs. Breakfast crossed her mind. It could wait. She was heading for the front door when she remembered she hadn't left a note.

If she was late back, Mum and Dad would wonder where she'd gone.

She dashed back upstairs and scribbled a quick note on her desk holo: <NEEDED SOME FRESH AIR. BACK SOON.> That should stop them worrying. If they needed her urgently, they could always message her wrist holo.

On the Bay Line, the live feed holos along the tunnel walls flashed with frenetic energy, a stark contrast to the sweeping strings of her electric orchestral music. An advertisement for the *Southern Alps* restaurant chain dissolved into a view of the city, which gave way to a slow-motion panorama of scenic country inland, all jagged mountains and flowing streams. She drank it in; she'd love to get out of the city someday, take a train west to the mountains. It would be gorgeous.

Addy took the steps down to the fairground on a route that she could almost walk in her sleep. Across the grass and out over the boardwalk, she found the Shelter empty except for one or two people on the bottom level.

She took her usual seat on the top level and stared out through the glass walls at the crashing waves below. It was a familiar sight; the smell of sea salt and the lapping sound of the ocean were just as familiar.

It wasn't too late to change her mind. She could still turn back if she wanted. Nobody would know. Mum and Dad thought she was in bed sick. Theo was at university. Her friends wouldn't know. Breach wouldn't know. Most importantly, Maunga Richards wouldn't know. There was nothing keeping her on this path.

But there was. She'd been on this path for the last three years, even if she'd only realised it in the last six months. Everything had been leading to this moment—Maunga stealing her voice, the visits to the medical clinic, her remnant of an ability to write, the lifesaving gift of the shoulder holo and keypad, the Breach developments . . . and now the catalyst. Theo.

She had to do this, if only for him. She had no doubt that he could learn to live with it, like she'd learned to, like the other hundreds of people who had Vox Pox had learned to. But he shouldn't have to. With the four-year age gap, they'd never been all that close, but sarcastic Theo with his clever hands and whacking great intellect should never have to live without his voice. He *needed* his voice.

It was alright for her, Addy knew. It had felt like the end of the world when she first lost her voice and her writing along with it, but she had learned to cope. She'd withdrawn into herself for a long time. There had been days when the black fog had been a welcome companion. There had been weeks when she felt utterly disconnected from reality. There had been months with only the fog and her thoughts, or a frightening lack of thought, and she had nothing but her music to keep her sane.

It was okay. She'd dealt with it in her own way. She had fought it with her music and the sea.

But Theo was different. He always had been, even when they were at primary school together. Where she was quiet out of natural reserve, he was quiet out of casual superiority. Some kids wouldn't respond to a question because they didn't know the answer; he wouldn't respond because, to him, the answer was self-evident and therefore not worth wasting breath on. Before the Pox, she'd turned her talents inward, using her hands to pour out words in a riot of emotion and introspection; he turned his outward, using them to make things out of metal and wood and electronics. And after the Pox, where she had withdrawn, turned soft without her voice, he was doing the opposite. She'd seen it that first night he came home and in the three weeks since—his expressions and his body language had hardened with brittle anger. Perhaps it was his way of coping.

Or perhaps it was a sign of his inability to cope.

She only knew that she was afraid for him—afraid of what might happen to him if this was left unchecked. If he grew too brittle, would he shatter?

He might. The sea breeze swirled around Addy, and she shivered.

She was one of the few with this disease who had maintained some writing ability beyond the barely functional. She knew that Breach could help her if she could get into one of the TheraRPG programmes; they'd helped that boy with the stammer last year, hadn't they? And she knew that Maunga would be at the session this afternoon. Maunga had admitted to stealing her voice. And so, three years later, Maunga was her best bet at getting it back again.

They said your headspace affected your session; if she was in the same session as Maunga, if she focused with every shred of her being on getting answers, she might have a chance of finding out more about Vox Pox.

Rumour said a single session in the virtual psychoreality simulator could cure everything from bad fashion sense to the common cold. Fact said that bad fashion sense and common colds alike remained rampant among those who finished a session. But it couldn't be denied that a uni student had gone into Breach selectively mute and emerged talking.

Could a session cure Vox Pox?

Addy didn't know. But she had to try.

Find Maunga. Find her voice.

It wasn't worth taking the City Line into town from here; she walked, making it to the Dusky Moose in thirty minutes. If this went wrong, she'd probably be grounded for the rest of her life. With an air of one going to one's last meal, she ordered a breakfast roll: bacon, egg, cheese, tomato, and mushrooms, woven into a scroll of cheesy garlic bread and baked until toasty.

"And what will you have to drink?" asked the server.

Well, if she was going to be grounded for the rest of her life, she may as well go out with a bang.

<TRIPLE-SHOT FLAT WHITE, PLEASE.>

Her breakfast was fantastic.

At ten o'clock, a familiar form stepped through the doors. Addy ignored Kotukutuku Johnson as she made her way to the pigeon holes at the side of the shop, checked her box, and left again.

Good. That was the worst of it over. Addy hated waiting. She hated relying on other people to do things that she was capable of doing herself, too, but this was a special case. She might be capable of draining every cent from her bank account and applying for the TheraRPG programme, but she couldn't get herself into the session this afternoon, not with a nine-months-and-growing waiting list.

So she'd gone to Tuku for help. Tuku had thought for a minute, then shrugged and said she'd do her best.

And now she'd come through.

Addy waited ten minutes, picking a time when four other people were at the boxes to slip the spare keycard from her pocket and join the crowd. The papers and ID card were exactly as Tuku had described. There was a short note attached:

> *Hey Addy,*
>
> *My dad wouldn't agree to do it—he's too high up the ladder if anything went wrong. But I've got a few friends lower down on staff at Breach. Doug was more than happy to help you out. If you see him around, say hi from me, would you?*
>
> *Tuku*

Addy breathed a sigh of relief. Now all she had to do was show up on time with the papers completed, flash her card at reception, and try not to vomit from the nerves.

No worries.

~

Addy stepped through the door from reception and tried not to show her relief too overtly. She'd made it. Her hands shook from the adrenaline. She stilled them. Time enough for that later.

"Welcome," said a woman with short black hair waiting on the far side of the room. "Once everybody is here, we'll head on through."

There were three thirtysomethings already waiting. As the escort spoke, an older man with long hair stepped through the door from reception. In five minutes, twelve participants had gathered, with ages ranging from Addy's sixteen years to a short, spry woman with grey hair who must have been sixty-odd. Maunga raised her eyebrows when she saw Addy but otherwise showed no reaction.

"That's all of us," the escort said, breaking into the quiet chatter. "Welcome, everybody. You must be here for the afternoon TheraRPG session; if you're not, you're in the wrong place. You can either leave now or be incinerated later."

A ripple of nervous laughter spread through the group. Nobody moved.

"Excellent. My name is Caroline York. I'm the Overseer for the TheraRPG programme. If you'll please come with me?"

They followed her down a wide hallway and into a lift. To Addy's surprise, the carriage started to fall. Somehow she'd expected it to move up, not down. Her first instinct was to activate her shoulder holo and ask the escort about it; but no, better to wait and see. Maybe one of the others would say something.

One of them did.

"I thought the sessions were run on one of the upper levels?" a soft-spoken woman asked.

"They used to be," said Caroline. "We updated a few months ago. Now we have a fully equipped set of chambers downstairs." She grinned. "Or downshaft, you might say."

They completed the rest of the short trip in silence, save for the three thirtysomethings who were obviously travelling together.

They continued to talk at the rear of the lift. The room at the testing level proved to be similar to the reception foyer, but on a far larger scale. The floor was warm timber, the walls clad in metal panelling. The arched ceiling high overhead had been painted a cool off-white.

Caroline led them to a wide table at one end of the room.

"Okay, you've all read the information pack you were given, I'm sure, so I won't waste time going back over that. Open a booklet each, read it, and fill in the blanks. Once you've done that, take a number"—she crossed to a small box attached to the wall and lifted a piece of thick card from it in demonstration—"and go through the red door at the end, where you'll find the corresponding individual session chamber.

"If you find anything in the booklet you don't agree with or cannot fulfil, just tell me: you'll be free to leave directly or to wait at the couches until the session time is up. The same applies to ending your session early for whatever reason. Complimentary tea, coffee, and snacks are available at the station near the couches. Bathrooms are through that door there; I suggest you make use of them before you start your session. If you have any questions, please ask. I'm here to help you."

Addy was relieved to see that the booklet was an electronic file embedded in the tabletop. Her keypad synced to it without a hitch, and she started reading, keeping half an eye on the time. They had to be inside their individual chamber by twenty-eight past one; it was three minutes past already.

> *Health and Safety Briefing for the TheraRPG programme, public session 550, taking place between 1330 and 1630 on the afternoon of Friday, April 20. Read the following information and sign in the marked space.*

It was standard stuff, albeit somewhat quirky. Whoever wrote it had a sense of humour. She read it, signed, and moved on to the next section.

Entailment Briefing, or: What The Session Entails, And How We Entail Your Belongings, Your Money, or Your Body If Anything Happens.

Read and sign. She'd covered most of it in her research or in the information pack she'd borrowed from Tuku. The in-depth explanation of what the three hours consisted of was helpful, though.

Your session technically begins two minutes before the half hour. A warning bell will sound at twenty-eight minutes past the hour. When it does, the door to your individual testing chamber (3m x 3m x 3m, all surfaces set to default colour off-white, all surfaces holo-interface capable) will lock to prevent outside interference. You may begin writing at this bell. You then have two minutes to begin inserting yourself into the programme. This is done by writing a brief description of yourself and your background (minimum word count 100, maximum ∞, arbitrarily calculated average 127) to start the personal psychological trace. Once you reach 100 words or two minutes is up, whichever comes second, the trace will activate the Virtual Psychoidentity Simulator. At this point, your body in the chamber may or may not continue writing; this varies according to the individual, and as you will have no control over it, there is no need to let it concern you.

Once submerged in the session, you may or may not remember that it is a simulation. The session is real, and the session is in your mind; the two concepts are not mutually exclusive. The main thing you need to know is that the TheraRPG programme is neither a fully psychological mindtrip nor an accurate representation of the real world. Psychologists did not design the system, nor did cartographers.

The session world is not a parallel universe populated by real people, nor is it a metaphorical or literal journey into the individual's mind. It is something of both. Think of it as another country populated by the people in your session group and influenced, but not controlled, by those same minds. There may also be a few ghosts in the system from previous sessions. We like to keep things interesting.

Your VPS guide for this session will be Caroline York, Overseer of the TheraRPG programme. Her assistant, Jenkins Le Cren, will supervise the physical testing chambers and will be available at all times if you require help. Ninety-five percent of the time he can be found at the coffee machine; the other five percent, in the men's bathroom.

Addy read through the rest of the booklet, filling in her name, address, and other details as she went until she came to the final warning.

The VPS has the potential to change you. The change will not necessarily be physical. If you are killed in the programme, you will find yourself back in your testing chamber, unharmed. Mental and psychological changes in past participants have been documented, which is hardly surprising—it is called the Virtual Psychoidentity Simulator, after all. If you have read this warning and wish to continue, sign below. If you have read this warning and do not wish to continue, advise an overseer and walk away.

She signed. Change was what she'd come for.

Booklet completed and filed away, Addy took a moment to look around. Maunga and four others had gone through the red door already; one person lounged on the couches at the far end of the chamber, chatting with a man who must be Le Cren; and the last five, including the three thirtysomethings, were still reading their booklets.

It was twenty-four minutes past one.

She crossed to the wall and took a card. Five. The red door slid open as she approached; she stepped through and found herself in a short, squat hallway with six numbered doors on either side. Number five was second from the far end on her left.

She took a moment to breathe, then opened the door and stepped inside.

The interior proved to be exactly as the booklet had described it. Three by three floor, three high. Clean, white surfaces with that particular sheen that only came from holo-capability embedded into solid surfaces. No furniture.

She supposed it didn't matter whether she stood or sat, or how she sat, for that matter. As long as she got her hundred words down, she could hang upside down and scratch her armpits for all Breach cared.

She settled cross-legged in the middle of the floor, facing the one wall that wasn't an unbroken, smooth surface. There were seams where the door was located, small but not invisible to the naked eye. To her surprise, the floor felt warm. They kept it heated? Neat.

One minute to go.

She activated her keypad and made sure it could sync to the chamber. It connected seamlessly. Good.

Thirty seconds.

The nerves built. What if this didn't work?

Twenty. She shoved the questions aside. Mind on the programme, Adelaide.

Ten. A warning light flashed on the walls.

Her fingers hovered over her keypad, trembling. Five. Her mind was blank.

Three. Two. One.

The starting chime blared, the door locked with a hiss of firing pistons, and her fingers hit the keypad in the same nanosecond. There were no rules to this sort of writing, no time for hesitation or nerves or even conscious thought.

<Adelaide Te Ngawai was thirteen when Maunga Richards stole her voice . . . >

She poured out words in a flood and hit fifty as the first minute ticked over; the second fifty took longer, the word count rolling over at two minutes and eight seconds. But she didn't stop. She couldn't stop. She felt an intense itching behind her eyes; her head pounded; her fingers, abnormally hot, kept typing of their own accord. She was no longer in control.

The itching and the aching intensified. She screwed up her face against the sensation. When she thought she could bear it no longer, it grew even greater, and then greater again. All she knew was the pain and the mindless need to scratch, agonising beyond belief, but her body wouldn't move.

The world flared white, and the chamber vanished.

INTERLUDE

WE ARE THE VOICELESS.
HEAR US.

CHAPTER SIX

Addy didn't know what she'd been expecting. A bullhorn blaring for attention would have been a bit much, she supposed. But she thought there might have been . . . well . . . something. Anything.

She found herself on a long, gentle slope. Underfoot lay soil and a scattering of rocks and an overgrown carpet of dry tussock grasses. They were mostly the indeterminate sandy-brown of the common species, although she could see a few with the red or blue tinge of rarer species. The sky was overcast, but the clouds didn't look heavy enough for rain—at least she didn't think so. It was hard to judge distance without the constant backdrop of city buildings. She'd never seen so much sky in all her life.

The light came from everywhere and nowhere, whiter and clearer even in its diffused state than she was used to in the city. A faint breeze blew across the hill. She turned her nose into it, smelling clean dirt and open air and vast space.

Beautiful. And eerie.

Where was she? More importantly, where was Maunga? Addy turned on the spot, looking up the hill and then down. There were no tracks, no buildings, nothing but the sea of grass. The place was deserted, but all the same she had the sensation of being watched.

She started downhill, winding her way through the clumps of tall grass and keeping an eye out for jutting rocks. After a time, the ground levelled out and then, to her left, rose again in fits and starts. A shallow depression ran down to her right, winding its way along the base of the hills. She struck right, following the gully as it snaked downhill.

Her neck itched. She threw a glance over her shoulder. The slope behind her was as bare as the track in front. She was alone . . . for now. The feeling persisted.

How long had she been walking? It felt like at least an hour. She went to check the time on her wrist holo, but it wasn't there. The shrug to activate her shoulder piece was automatic. Her hand went to her thigh—and stopped.

She touched her leg again. Patted it. Yes, the flash of gut-wrenching panic had been right; that was linen and her leg beneath it, not a keypad.

For the first time since the simulation had begun, it occurred to her that she might not be wearing the clothes she'd so carefully chosen that morning. Addy looked down.

Crisp white shirt. Heavy grey skirt, complete with outdated pleats. Skinny blue tie knotted loosely around her neck, looser than she'd ever have gotten away with in class. Scratchy, knee-high socks, also blue.

She was wearing her school uniform.

At least she'd kept her own black boots.

Addy lifted a hand to feel the familiar outline of her Eareos sitting around her neck. Good. She still had those. Never mind that she couldn't use them without her holo; it was the thought that counted, right? But her sleeve felt far too smooth to be the usual wool of her school jersey. She looked again and grimaced.

Her outer layer was a hoodie, dark green and far too big for her. The cuffs had been rolled to her wrists, and the left sleeve bore a triple ring of contrasting black leather around the bicep. She knew that design. She slipped the hoodie off and held it up. All the signs were there—the minimalist logo on the left breast, three horizontal lines bisected by a black circle, the faded initials *TTN* on the inside of the collar, the distressed crest on the back featuring a historically inaccurate triplane and the Richard Pearse University banner.

This was Theo's hoodie.

Addy shrugged it back on. Why had the programme decided to gift her that, of all things? It was warm, which she was grateful for down here in the hollow between the hills, and it was comfortable, sure, but she'd much rather have her own jersey.

But she didn't have the jersey. Or her backpack. Or any method of communication, even supposing she met anyone else out here. The hills rising to either side blocked much of the light; she shivered, the isolation weighing on her mind. She could spend days wandering these shadowed hills and not meet another soul.

Addy started off again down the gulch. At least the hoodie gave her pockets. And from the feel of it, the sim had also gifted her school gym shorts, so it wasn't too breezy under her skirt.

Things could be worse.

She kept walking, trying to ignore the nagging at the back of her mind. The day turned muggy under the grey sky as she lost altitude. Mouth dry and lips chapped, she tied the hoodie around her waist and rolled up her sleeves. She was grateful she hadn't been given her old thin-soled school shoes to wear; they would have been murder on her feet in this terrain. The boots made everything hot and sweaty, but they gave her solid soles and stiff ankle support, not to mention protection against the prickly strands of tussock. Between her skirt and socks, only her knees remained uncovered, and the grass rarely came that high.

Time wore on. The hills to either side drew back and diminished until she was walking across a level plain. Grass stretched as far as the eye could see.

There was nothing to do but keep walking. She hoped she was going the right way. Was there a right way? She hoped there wasn't a *wrong* way.

Was that a line on the horizon? Addy squinted ahead. It was too far away to tell for sure, but she thought she could see a change in the unbroken sea of grasses. Keeping one foot pointing straight on, she turned and looked behind her. The hills were already a fair distance away. She tried to fix their location and height in her mind to get a feel for what they might look like after she'd walked another hour. She didn't know how well it worked. The scale of this country was massive. Everything looked so different from what she was used to.

She faced forward again and started off. The faint depression she was following grew darker and widened a little, and before long she was following a proper track of compacted dirt. It was barely wide enough for one person, but it was something. A sign that people had come this way before, perhaps. It was certainly better than the directionless field of tussocks, where there'd been nothing she could do but keep the hills at her back and hope she'd end up somewhere of significance.

Ahead of her, the grassland seemed to come to a stop. She quickened her pace, forgetting the heat. What would it be? An easy, downhill slope to a village? A road where she could hitch a lift with another traveller? A city where she could find Maunga Richards?

Eager feet took her to the edge of the grass and jerked her back half a pace without conscious thought.

It was downhill, alright. A vertical downhill.

She stared, dizzy, at the gaping chasm that opened at her feet, plunging down into infinite space. No wonder the grass had stopped. The ground itself had stopped.

Addy swallowed and lifted her gaze to the other side. *Much too far to jump. Left?* The fissure stretched in an unending line to the horizon. *Right?* The same. Her head spun. Anticipation fled, leaving hollow panic in its wake. Where was she meant to go now? The trail came this far, but she couldn't follow it over the edge of the cliff. That would be madness.

She sat on a lump of tussock and waited for her head to settle. How long had it been since she'd had something to eat? Or drink? She didn't know.

The track had come this far. . . She scratched her collarbone. She hadn't seen any other trails. This track was her ticket out of here. She couldn't go back—the track ran out less than halfway to the hills. Nor could she spend hours wandering the edge of the chasm in hopes of discovering another trail or a bridge. The simulation would finish long before she found anything.

She stood and saw a matching trail on the far side of the yawning gulf. That couldn't be a coincidence. She kicked at a clod of soil and watched the shattered pieces fall into blackness.

There was only one thing to do.

She wavered at the edge and then found her courage. She couldn't leap the gap. She knew that and saw no point wasting energy. In one swift movement, she lifted a foot and stepped out.

It came down on solid ground.

Addy opened her eyes. When had she closed them? Never mind that. What happened?

She looked back. Her left foot was on the track she'd come down, a vast distance away. She looked ahead. Her right foot was safely on the track at the farther side of the divide, also a vast distance away. She looked down and saw her legs straddling a crack in the earth that was no more than a single pace across.

Her head reeled. For a terrifying moment, she thought she would fall. *Move!* She tore her left foot from the ground, swung it with a huge effort to the far side, got her feet tangled, and sprawled headlong in the dirt.

She lay there, panting. It was okay. She'd made it. She was on the other side.

She picked herself up and dared a quick look back. The gulf was as wide as ever; beyond it, the hills rose, brown and tan, to meet the grey sky. This really was the far side.

The track ran straight ahead, took a wide bend through the grass, and disappeared. The back of her neck prickled. A glance around showed nothing but grass and the gaping chasm.

She started along the path at a trot. To her surprise, the tussocks ended in a sharp line after perhaps five hundred metres. Before her, the track ran down through a green gully to a stream, cool and clear. A line of stepping-stones crossed to the far bank before the track rose again up a steep slope.

Down in the dip, the sensation of being watched faded. Addy took a few minutes to rest. It was a relief to pull off her boots and socks and bathe her tired feet. She splashed her face and neck, wincing a little at the cold, and washed the worst of the sweat off. The raging thirst, never far from her mind, reared its head again. She cupped her hands and drank her fill, and then drank some more. Who knew when she'd find clean water again?

She gave herself a couple more minutes and then waded across to the far bank. The breeze dried most of the moisture from her legs. She wiped away the last drops with the sleeves of Theo's hoodie. The grass sprang back upright as she passed, and she suppressed a pang as she pulled her scratchy school socks back on. Her black boots felt hotter than ever as she retied the laces.

The green slope loomed before her. The track zig-zagged to the top; she eyed it and tried to summon a spark of enthusiasm. It felt like she'd been here for days already without any food or sleep.

Sleep. She pushed the thought away. She wasn't here to sleep. She was here to find Maunga. Find Maunga; find her voice.

The path steepened with each switchbacking turn. Her steps slowed. Two turns from the top, she could see over the top of the rise to where the topmost peaks of a long, iron-grey roofline jutted into the overcast sky. Her heart leapt. A building! She plodded onward and came to the next turn. Now she could see an oversized roof, gabled windows, and the dark lines of eaves. It looked like a large house. Was Maunga here? Another turn, one final push, and she stood at the top of the hill, panting, thighs burning, looking out across manicured lawns.

Strike that. It wasn't a house. It was a mansion.

Dark stone rose, layer upon layer, into the grey sky. A flight of shallow steps led up to a veranda where huge doors stood shut fast. Two great wings splayed out from the central section like open arms. In front of her, the trail turned from packed dirt to paving stones, widened to a preposterous degree, and swept down the centre of the lawn to end in a courtyard at the bottom of the steps.

The house called to her, tugging at her thoughts. *Come here,* it seemed to say, while the double doors grinned mockingly. *Maunga's waiting for you.*

She gulped and set off. The walk seemed to take forever. Ranks of sightless windows stared down at her. The silence pressed on her like a physical weight. No birds sang; she hadn't heard birdsong once since she'd found herself in the hills.

The mansion drew closer. The windows grew larger. She tried to tread as quietly as she could, but her boots weren't made for catlike tiptoeing. Every step echoed. Now she was within the outstretched wings of the house. She found herself holding her breath, waiting for those vast arms to close upon her. Her heart pounded. Her pulse sounded as loud as her footsteps to her ears.

Addy paused at the foot of the stairs. She licked her dry lips. How long had it been since she'd had that drink at the stream? A hundred years, at least.

She tightened Theo's hoodie around her waist and started up the stone steps.

Clomp. Clomp. Clomp. It took an age to reach the top. Clomp. Clomp. A dreadful thought occurred to her. *What if the doors are locked? What if I can't get in?* Maunga was waiting; she had to go in. Clomp. Clomp. At last, she stood on the terrace.

She approached the doors, laid a hand on the tarnished metal handle, and hesitated. One last glance around revealed manicured green lawns glowing under the leaden sky. In the shelter of the house, the heat proved stifling. She shuddered under the glare of ranks of windows and blank stone walls, opened the door, and slipped inside.

CHAPTER SEVEN

The sound of the door shutting behind her echoed in the vast space. Addy stared. The entrance foyer was far larger than it had any right to be—larger even than it had seemed from the outside. Polished concrete floors stretched forever. Blue-black panelled walls towered at the edges of her vision, pockmarked with empty alcoves and mirrored glass doors. In the middle distance, chunky staircases of bare black metal rose on either side to the upper floors.

It wasn't the most welcoming place in the world.

She took a hesitant step forward, fighting an impulse to wipe her dirty boots on the nonexistent doormat. Another step, and another. Her footsteps echoed on the hard floor, reverberating off the walls and bouncing back to her ears. Far too loud. What if someone heard? She brushed sweaty hair off her forehead and tried to step lightly.

Ten paces, and the distance to the staircases hadn't shortened. She looked back. A line of muddy footprints marked a straight path from the front door, fifty metres away.

Wait, what? Her strides weren't five metres in length.

She took a step. Glanced behind her. Took another step. Nine more paces brought no change. The distance behind her didn't seem to grow anymore, but the tenth step brought her abruptly to the bottom of the staircases. Heart hammering in her chest, she chose the left-hand one and started up it.

It was one thing knowing that distance could be deceiving; it was another thing experiencing it. One tread on the staircase was so wide she had to take three paces to reach the next rise, the next so narrow she could hardly fit her toes on it. Some were so shallow she took them three at a time. Then came one so high it was almost twice her height. She jumped, caught the edge with her fingers, and wormed her way up.

And then she realised Theo's hoodie had come loose from around her waist. It lay in a puddle at the bottom of the step. She swung herself down, shrugged into the hoodie so she wouldn't lose it again, and heaved herself up once more.

Frustration welled inside her. What was the point of this? For all Breach's reassurances that the programme wasn't designed to be a mindtrip, it sure felt like one. What else was she meant to call a chasm hundreds of metres wide that she could straddle in one step? Or a staircase where no two steps were the same height or width? Or—she looked down at her boots and then back along the stairs—clean-ish boots that left perfectly formed muddy footprints across an expanse the size of the Town Hall? The footprints had even followed her up the stairs!

That wasn't normal. None of it was normal.

Addy shoved down the burgeoning panic and scrubbed a hand across her face. *Keep going.* If she could just find Maunga and get out of here . . .

In another minute, she stood on the first floor landing. The stairs looked quite normal from up here. The foyer looked like an ordinary foyer. She took a step toward the railing and leaned over, curious—and the floor of the foyer dropped away abruptly, sickeningly, until it lay a hundred metres or more below her.

She retreated, biting back an involuntary surge of bile. Her heart raced. Black spots crowded her vision; she blinked them away.

What if it had done that while she'd been walking across it? The manual had said that nothing could kill her here; if she died, she'd just wake up back in the testing chamber. But they hadn't mentioned her mind. Could she go mad? Would physical injury translate to mental injury? The floor could drop out from under her. What would happen when she hit the bottom?

What would happen if she *never* hit the bottom?

She shuddered, shoulders heaving, and reflexively shrugged again to deactivate her holo. Except she didn't have her shoulder piece. Right. She remembered that.

Where to go next? Staircases rose in spirals and switchbacks to upper landings, some five metres above her, others more like fifty metres. The house called to her again. She turned away and slipped through the doorway behind her, emerging into a wide corridor. *Left or right? Left.*

The walls here were the same blue-black panelling as those in the foyer, with mirrored glass doors at oddly spaced intervals. The floor and ceiling were done in white. She crept along, trying to look behind and ahead at the same time in case any surfaces shifted, hating the feeling of being watched whenever she passed a door. Her muddy footprints followed her with uncanny regularity. Even when she shortened her strides or hopped on one foot, the footprints remained the same distance apart, and they were always whole footprints, left, right, left, right, never heavier on one side than the other, never missing the shape of the little toe or the heel.

Her internal compass pointed her to the next door, and she stepped through. The room beyond lay dark. Before she could retreat, the door slammed. She tried the handle without much hope. Locked. *It's that sort of place,* she thought, irritated. Shifting walls, weird architecture, doors locking behind you—and all for no purpose beyond the amusement of the architects.

She was sick of it already.

Dim light filtered down from skylights. Her eyes gradually adjusted. Black marble seemed to be the order of the day in this long, low room. The floor, walls, and ceiling were all carved from it. An aisle ran down the centre. To either side squatted neat rows of uniform protrusions. She stepped closer and ran her hand along the curved white top of one.

A gravestone.

Creepy. Whoever said this place wasn't some sort of journey into the psyche really had been lying. Except . . . she looked again, counting. If the headstones represented those lost to the Vox Pox, there weren't enough of them. She'd expected more than four hundred, but the room only held eighty or so.

She stepped around the nearest stone and peered at it. *Picture,* it read. *Tests,* said the next one. *Water,* said a third. Baffled, she retreated to the aisle. Maybe they were meaningless after all.

The door she'd come through was still locked. She strode forward, down the aisle, touching the nearest gravestones with a light finger as she went. She couldn't have said why. They were smooth, and slim, and silent. If they were the dead, they rested in peace.

The door at the far end of the room was unlocked. She opened it and took a careful look. White stairs in a white room led downward. After the foyer, she didn't trust stairs, but she had no choice. She marched through.

Predictably, the door slammed behind her. She halted on the top step, hand groping at her back for the handle. Locked. Of course.

Addy rolled her eyes and then paused. *Hang on.* Skylights lined the ceiling. How did that work? She was still on the first floor; there should be at least two more floors above her, but the ceiling, a bare ten metres above her head, poured grey light into this white room. Shouldn't the ceiling of this room be the floor of the level above it?

Bah. Probably ordinary things like physics were too plebeian for a house like this.

Heart in her throat, she felt her way down the steps, testing each fall with her foot before she committed. Expecting another cliff-like drop, or at the very least a few steps of abnormal height or width, she was surprised to reach the bottom having found no irregularities. Perhaps the lack of surprises was the surprise.

The door at the bottom of the stairs led to a short antechamber, where two more doors waited on the far wall.

Oh. Choices. Great.

Her house-sense lay silent. She cracked the left-hand door open. Half a metre in front, the ceiling sloped down until it was maybe a metre clear of the floor. It wasn't a corridor; it was a crawl space. She opened the right-hand door. The same view presented itself.

A choice without being any choice at all, then. The two options were identical.

She took the left route and was soon crawling on her hands and knees down the tunnel. Ambient light panels let her see where she was going. The shaft took a right-hand bend before climbing, rounding another bend, and levelling off. Another few minutes of sore palms and banging knees brought her to the end of the tunnel.

The shaft ended just below the glass ceiling of a massive room. White light filtered through, showing everything clearly—dark walls plunged into oblivion, smooth and seamless, free of any handholds that she might have used to get down. She couldn't see the floor. Pungent black fog filled the lower part of the room. The odour tickled her nose, sharp and peppery, and she sneezed.

Down? Not an option. Sideways? Useless. Up? The siren sense chimed. *Yes.*

If the ceiling had consisted of a single sheet of glass, she would have dismissed the idea, but it was made of dozens of rectangular panes. The black frames of the glass panels jutted down into the room in a strange way. At first, she thought it was merely a quirk of the architecture, but closer inspection proved them to be sleek metal handles, like an elegant set of monkey bars.

Addy traced the line of them across the ceiling to an opening on the far wall and nodded. *Right.* It was the chasm all over again.

Now, what was the best way to do this . . .

She wriggled onto her back and scooted up as far as she dared until her head and the tops of her shoulders hung over empty space. One hand gripped the third bar out from the wall. The other hand reached to the next bar along. Grateful the frames were close together, she lifted a foot and hooked it into the bar closest to the wall. Gulped. Taking all her weight on her hands, she lifted the other foot and jammed it into the second bar out.

There. She was on the bars, safe above the ominous fog. Now it was just a case of lift a hand, stretch, place it on the next bar along. Repeat with a foot. Now the other hand. Good. Now the other foot. She could do this.

Thirty rungs out, she made the mistake of looking past her feet to see how much progress she'd made. Her heart sank. Fewer than five bars separated her back foot from the wall. She darted a look ahead at the opening. Too many bars to count. She'd hardly made any progress at all.

Back to it. Hand. Foot. Hand. Foot. She counted off another thirty and risked a second look.

What . . . ?

She was still only five bars out from the wall. *The TheraRPG programme is not a fully psychological mindtrip.* Yeah, right. What sort of drugs had they been tripping on when they wrote that?

Another thirty bars went by with no change. And then sixty. And ninety.

At two hundred rungs with no change, she stopped, wedged herself more firmly into her chosen bars, and reevaluated. At this rate she could keep going forever without getting anywhere. The distance in front never grew any less. And now she'd been going forward so long that she was afraid of going back.

She didn't know if she had that much energy left. Her arms and legs were tiring. Working her way backward would take more effort than moving this far forward had done.

She made her second mistake. She looked down.

Keek. She redoubled her grip. The black fog had risen. It loitered perhaps five metres below her hanging body. Her mind conjured a vivid picture of what would happen if the ceiling chose this moment to drop. Her stomach churned.

But now she knew what this place was. Where she hadn't

made a connection in the graveyard, she did here. She'd been here before, clinging to a lifeline, unable to move forward or back as the fog rose higher.

Mind you, it wasn't usually so literal.

What had she done then? She'd fought it. But it had been different. For one thing, she'd had her music, and for another, she hadn't literally been hanging over a room of rising black fog. A glance down showed the fog lingering maybe three metres below. It would continue to rise, she was sure. And once it was level with her . . .

She remembered the days of blank mindlessness, everything inside her at once screaming and numb, the vast disconnect with reality.

Well. She wouldn't have a choice once the fog came that high, would she? Which meant she had to choose now. There was no going forward. Going back would take more effort than she could muster. She had a feeling that there would always be five rungs between her and the wall.

Only one option left—never mind that combining the words 'one' and 'option' was something of an oxymoron.

She closed her eyes, released her hold on the bars, and fell through the black.

~

Addy landed hard. She staggered forward, caught herself on her hands before she could face-plant, and lay sprawled on the ground, panting. It had been a longer fall than she'd thought possible, even for a house of this size.

Nothing felt broken. She tested each of her limbs in turn. Nothing screamed in agony. Her hips twinged a little from the landing, but that was all. Could be worse. Maybe the fog had slowed her descent. Or maybe it was one more side effect of the wonky physics.

Who knew?

The ground felt scratchy under her cheek, like a million tiny blades of grass were reaching up with sharp fingers and tickling her. She dug her fingers into it, curious. It didn't feel like grass, it felt like . . . sand?

She sat up and looked around. Yes, she was surrounded by sand. It was real, smooth, golden-white sand like they had at the Bay. A faint sound came to her ears, foreign in this strange place. She almost laughed. Waves! Waves lapping at the shore. This was a beach, and somewhere—she turned, straining her eyes—somewhere there was an ocean. She sniffed and smelled the familiar tang of salt. There. Far away, over the sand, a glint of strong light reflecting off water. The sound of the sea grew louder as she hurried toward it.

Soon she was jogging down a slope, tugging off sand-clogged boots and socks and splashing up to her shins in saltwater. It was cold and wet and glorious. She didn't need the parallel to the last three years explained: only by going through the fog had she ever gotten beyond it, and she'd always found the sea waiting on the far side.

Before her the sea stretched, endless, into infinity. Behind her, the sand did the same. She looked up and saw the black fog floating far above, nothing more than a dark cloud scudding across a vast, grey-white sky. The house called to her again, and she nodded. Maunga was waiting.

She waded out of the water and started walking along the shoreline. Sand clung to her heels and the balls of her feet and rubbed coarsely between her toes. Her feet were still too wet to put her boots back on. She shoved her socks down into the toes, tied the shoelaces together, and carried them.

The shoreline curved to her right. She followed it, keeping to the edge of the dry sand, out of the wash of the waves. Something shimmered in the distance ahead of her. As she came closer, she saw it was a door of mirrored glass. But there was no wall attached to it.

Her reflection looked back at her, brows crooked.

She poked her image in the cheek. The door was solid. It felt real. An experimental prod in the air to the side of the frame proved that it was indeed air, not an invisible wall. She walked around to the far side. The door was identical from this side.

Her reflection appeared no less puzzled.

Opening the door revealed a white staircase ascending through a white room. She closed the door, moved around it, and opened it from the other side. The view was the same. Did it make a difference if she pushed instead of pulling? No. She couldn't push the door open. It only pulled open. From both sides.

Another false choice. She stepped through and let the door slam behind her. The white floor felt cool and smooth underfoot. The sand stuck to her toes would grow uncomfortable soon enough. She sat on the first step and, with a silent apology to Theo, used the sleeves of his hoodie to wipe the worst of it off before pulling on her socks and boots.

The steps on this staircase were infuriatingly shallow. She stomped up them two at a time and then three; even then, the vertical rise was only *almost* equal to one step on a normal staircase. The stairs reached a landing, turned one hundred and eighty degrees, and leaped upward again. She followed.

Several dozen turns later, she reached yet another landing. This one was different. A door stood in the far wall.

Interesting. To continue up the stairs, or to go through the door? She vacillated, looking from one to the other, considering. The house remained silent. She opened the door.

A white room with white stairs.

What a novel sight.

In the mirrored door, her reflection shrugged. *Why not?* She walked through the open doorway and onto an identical set of stairs.

Up another dozen turns of the second staircase lay an identical landing. Her thighs ached. She continued upward.

Another twelve turns. Another door. She took the stairs again. And again. And again.

The fourth time, lungs burning, she chose the door. And then the stairs. Door. Throbbing legs. Stairs. Stairs. Door. She stopped for a rest and then limped on. Door. Door. Door. Door. Would this ever end? Maybe it was like the monkey bars; maybe she'd gone so far into an infinite loop that there was no way of going back.

She hoped not. One of those was quite enough for one day.

Just when she despaired of ever reaching the end of it, she reached a dead-end landing. The door opened into a room that didn't contain more stairs. She knew how deceiving mere sight could be by now; hardly daring to trust her eyes, she slipped through the door and let it close behind her.

This room was small by comparison to any of the others she'd been in. Two couches faced each other over a low coffee table—the only furnishings. She padded across the cream carpet, eyeing them. They looked comfortable: wide, rolled arms and padded backs in gleaming brown leather, a little worn. The coffee table was a marvel of timber and glass.

Did she dare sit on one of the couches? She paused in front of the nearest one. It would only take a second. She perched on the edge of the seat. *Oh, that's nice.* Her body sank into it, the leather cushioning her without sagging too much. Very nice. She wanted one of these when she got home.

Addy sat for a moment longer and then stood. She had to find Maunga.

An open archway took her to the next room. She found another pair of sofas framing a coffee table. These couches were square and low, clad in deep red linen; the coffee table was a hard-angled monstrosity gleaming in chrome and blackened steel. She tested the couches and wrinkled her nose. A concrete slab would be more comfortable.

The third room featured yet another pair of couches, dark green this time, and a coffee table that looked like the mutant offspring of a footstool and a bookshelf. She moved on, wondering if there was a point to these rooms. This place had been strange enough to start with and was becoming increasingly illogical.

The next room proved to be a kitchen, warm and cosy. A tray of steaming brownies lay on the bench. Her stomach growled. If she could sit on the couches, surely she could eat a piece? She stepped closer, saliva pooling in her mouth at the sight. Double-chocolate, from the look of it. And the smell–*mmm*—yes, they were brownies alright.

Half a metre from the bench, she hit an invisible wall. She set her teeth and traced a hand along it. No luck. The barrier merged seamlessly with the floor, encapsulating the whole bench in an impenetrable bubble.

She could have cried. A hard slap against the wall sent dull pain shooting through her hand. She turned her back and made for the next room, hoping it would hold something kinder to her ravenous stomach.

It didn't. The second kitchen mimicked the second lounge: silver and black, all harsh lines and strong angles. A clear carafe of black coffee sat on the concrete bench, but like in the last room, she couldn't come closer than half a metre to it.

The third kitchen boasted an oven dish filled with carrots, kumara, pumpkin, and a whole roasted chicken. The smell was overwhelming, the invisible wall unbreakable.

If the kitchens had proved just how hungry she was, the bedrooms that came next showed her exhaustion. She kept moving. Bathrooms followed, and then libraries, thick with the scent of ink. The third library gave way to a plain hallway. A single, mirrored door greeted her at the far end.

More stairs. The house called her onward, whispering. *Maunga is here; Maunga is here.* She stepped through, and the door slammed.

~

An irresistible force yanked her sideways, off her feet, to press against the wall beside the door.

She shook her head to clear it and stood—with her feet on the wall and her body parallel to the floor.

Her head swam. *Gravity shift.* Her breathing came loud and fast to her ears, echoing in the silence. Surely even a house as creative with its physics as this one couldn't do that?

But it appeared it could.

She edged forward and peered down at the mirrored door in the floor. Her own face stared back at her, wide-eyed. Cautiously, she prodded it. She wasn't sure what she was hoping would happen. Even if the door opened, she wasn't going to jump down through it. The gravity on the far side could spin and send her rocketing back through to this side, and with the momentum she could be stuck in an infinite free-fall.

In any case, it was a moot point. The door remained shut fast.

Addy swallowed and looked around the room. It was predictably white. Stairs protruded this way and that, covering each of the three dimensions with ease. Her heart pounded. She couldn't rely on the gravity to remain stable.

A door glinted on the far side of the room. *There,* the house whispered. What she needed was to plot a route that somehow kept a surface on two or even three sides as she moved. If gravity shifted, she had to be able to grab an edge or land on a wall without losing her way.

She mapped a mental route. And then another. And a third, just in case. And then she moved.

A short sprint to the corner. She leaped, grabbed the rim of the hanging staircase, and hauled herself up onto it. The room spun. She threw herself flat, clinging to the edge of the step until the spinning stopped. Her heart felt like it would burst from her chest. But it was only a ninety-degree change. She was safe. She hurried down the stairs, legs shaking.

Down to the landing, hop across a gap to a matching landing, and up another staircase. The room tilted. She sprawled across the wall to her left.

Look around. Re-evaluate. Keep moving.

The staircase she'd been on was now a zig-zagging, waist-high wall. Addy vaulted onto the lip and ran along it, heart in her mouth. She was far too exposed here to be safe. She reached the corner as the room spun and spun again, and when she picked herself up, the door was tantalisingly close. Up a staircase, slide across the landing to a set of steps heading the other way, take them two at a time to another landing, which became a wall as soon as she stepped onto it.

The door was less than a metre away now. She no longer knew which surface had originally been *down*. This door was the right one, though—she knew it like she knew her own name. It tugged at her, drawing her closer.

Another tilt, sharp and jolting. She slid along the wall, scrabbled for a foothold, and realised with a start that she was in danger of falling into empty space. There were no stairs here. Panicked, she threw out a hand and gripped the nearest object: the rim of the mirrored door.

Empty space opened beneath her. Feet flailing, she struggled to yank the door open while the room turned. Her shoulders screamed protest. She kicked out, trying to find purchase, and winced as she slammed her shin on something hard and unforgiving. The door flew open; she tumbled through; it slammed shut.

Where was she now? Another hallway. She hauled herself upright, leg throbbing. The school socks hadn't been much protection. A few drops of blood oozed from the shallow scrape. No doubt she'd have a mean bruise there in a few hours. She tugged her sock back up and crouched, hesitant to move in case the shifting gravity wasn't confined to that room.

The hallway looked familiar. Blue-black panelled walls. Blinding white floor and ceiling. Mirrored doors at uneven intervals. She'd been here before. Or maybe it was identical in the same way that all those unmoving white stairs had been identical. It might look like the same hall, but it didn't mean it *was* the same.

Maunga, the house whispered. *Here. Along the hall. She's close.*

The hallway went on. And on. There was a short flight of stairs, and then it went on some more. A sharp corner, another flight of stairs, and on. And on.

She was well sick of this place. It had mucked her around for far too long. Was Maunga even here? Had Maunga ever been here? Or was it lying to her?

The walls widened. The ceiling rose. Pillars sprang up on either side. She walked through a space the height and breadth of a cathedral and halted at the door at the far end. Her reflection met her gaze with red-rimmed, exhausted eyes. *Maunga is here. Maunga is not here.* The thoughts crashed against each other.

Addy pulled the door open and went through.

The room beyond reminded her of nothing so much as a very exclusive art gallery. The floor was lightened timber, smooth and pale; the walls a matte cream two shades down from true white. The ceiling matched the floor. And the ratio of width to length, she thought, was so impossibly pleasing to the eye that it had to involve the *proportio aureum.*

Art pieces hung at regular intervals along the walls. A white canvas lay nearest, black-framed, sporting a simple quote in cursive black ink.

> *"When writing the story of your life, don't let anyone else hold the pen." - Unknown.*

The next piece was identical—black frame, white canvas—except for the offset, blocky type.

> *"It's not just about creativity. It is about the person you're becoming while you're creating." - Charlie Peacock.*

The third: a black and white picture featuring a mouth sewn up with needle and thread.

And then more spartan pieces of typography.

> *"You can make anything by writing." - C.S. Lewis.*

> *"Creativity takes courage." - Henri Matisse.*

> *"That black scrawl marked in rebellion held a thousand meanings. For me, it meant: I am here. I exist. I am known." - Leia Velluna Hartsfield.*

Her hands shook.

Addy moved down the gallery, reading each canvas in turn, dimly wondering how simple black ink on white canvas could impact her so much. It felt like someone was scooping out everything she'd thought, or refused to think, over the last three years and splattering it on the page for anyone to see.

Most of the quotes she'd never heard before—never even heard of the person who'd said them.

> *"From the shore, the ocean is forever. It's a beautiful, dangerous place. Music is tied to the sea, born from the struggle, looking for hope. Because hope belongs in the dark places." - Jon Foreman.*

She thought of the black fog, of her music, of the sea breeze and how the ocean always waited just over the horizon, and nodded.

> *"There's really no such thing as the 'voiceless'. There are only the deliberately silenced, or the preferably unheard." - Arundhati Roy.*

Again, it hit home. It wasn't just her. It wasn't just those with Vox Pox. She thought of the dark, deliberate look in Maunga's eyes on that day three years ago. With a pang, she thought of Nadia, who would often be talked over the top of in class, and Ruthie Scarborough, who had all but given up speaking after weeks of constant teasing about her deep voice. It was a plague, silent and cruel.

It had to stop.

Tears ran down her face by the time she came to the final canvas. It hung on the end wall, larger by far than any of the previous pieces. She steeled herself and lifted her eyes to read it.

Anger rose, swift and hot. That was *private.* Confidential. They had no right—!

The canvas held two simple lines of dialogue from a counselling session. It had been one of the early sessions, she thought, when she still ached from the loss, struggled to wrap her head around it. The aesthetic, stark black ink on white canvas, echoed the sentiment. There was no dancing around the issue here. She gulped back furious tears and read the words again.

The counsellor had spoken first: *"You fear being voiceless, don't you? You fear not having a voice, not being listened to."*

<YES. IT'S WHY I WROTE. BECAUSE PEOPLE LISTEN WHEN I WRITE.>

She stepped back, reeling. *No,* she thought. *And yes. And no. I don't know. Get out of my head.*

Get. Out. Of. My. Head.

Not a mindtrip, they'd said. *Yeah, right.* Endless stairs and untouchable gingerbread were fair enough in their own way.

But Maunga wasn't here. Maunga had never been here.

And now they'd gone a step too far.

She turned on her heel and strode back up the gallery, following the ruler-straight line of disastrously muddy footprints. No mess was that perfect. She took a raging delight in trampling over the prints, smearing them into oblivion as she went. She traced them back out through the door, down the pillared hall, into the absurd black and white and mirrors of the hallway.

Smoke and mirrors. It was all smoke and mirrors—all show and no substance. What had she learned here? What had she found that would help her? Nothing. Smoke and mirrors and spitting into the wind, that's all it had been.

A waste of time.

She stormed down the hall, past dozens of seething reflections, through one corner, two corners, down flights of stairs. The corridor continued, but the trail of footprints veered left, through an open doorway.

She could have sworn she'd come from the right-hand side of the hall. She followed the footprints left anyway and found herself on a landing at the top of the entrance foyer.

Oh, good. More stairs. She'd been starting to miss them.

It was a long, long way from this high landing to the ground floor, she knew. She sped down the stairs, boots clattering, and found herself at the bottom almost before she knew it. Through the haze of rage, something tugged at her. It should have taken her more than double that amount of time to reach the bottom.

Bah. The house was playing Creative Physics again and having a good laugh at her expense. She flung an obscenity at it in the privacy of her mind and marched toward the double doors. The sooner she was out of here, the better. She'd be well shot of the place.

The double doors swung open, and she strode out of the house—and into a bar.

CHAPTER EIGHT

Addy almost thought she'd gone blind at first. Expecting the clear grey light of the outdoors, she'd instead walked into a darkened room filled with people and pulsing with music and neon lights. The teeming crowd pressed against her, buffeting her this way and that, suffocating her. She retreated to the nearest wall and found an unoccupied space where she could pause and get her bearings.

Her initial feeling was that the room was claustrophobically small. A few deep breaths and further observation proved that to be false. It wasn't a huge room by any stretch of the imagination, but it was a more-than-adequate size for the number of people it held and its seeming purpose as a nightclub dance floor. It only felt small in comparison to the ludicrous vastness of the spaces she'd encountered in the house.

The music reverberated through her head. In the multicoloured lights, a swarm of sweaty bodies heaved and bobbed on the floor. On the stage at the far end, a trio of dancers wearing far too little clothing performed for the entertainment of anyone who cared to look. A few people sat on barstools on the other side of the room, drinking and talking and watching the stage.

She shuddered and drew her hoodie tighter around her, acutely aware of her school uniform under it. What a place. She could hardly hear herself think, everything was so loud.

"Alright there?" said a friendly voice at her side.

She started and turned to face the intruder. Male, early twenties, straight black hair. Wide smile with very white teeth. Low-slung black trousers. No jacket—or shirt, for that matter. She tried not to stare at his bare chest and found herself looking instead at the tribal tattoo wrapping around his shoulder and down his right arm.

Ngai Tahu. They were the dominant southern tribe. Well, that and Ngati Pakeha, for those who identified with the pseudo-tribe of European descent.

"Hello?" the stranger asked. "Anyone at home? You alright, love?"

Love. Who called anyone *love* these days? The colloquialism had been popular three or four years back, but the traditional *mate* had long since surpassed it again.

"Oi. Say something. You're starting to scare me, looking all spaced-out like that."

"I can't talk," said Addy.

There was a long pause.

"That right?" he said, winking.

"Sorry?"

"I think you'll find you *can* talk. Just did, in fact."

She frowned. "No, I—" She stopped.

He was right. Noise had just emerged from her mouth. Sound. Speech. From her mouth. Talking. From her mouth. Actual sounds, out loud, making verbal communication things. Doodads. Words. Words! She was making words! With her mouth! And they made noises! She could talk!

She could *talk.*

"Steady on," said the stranger. "I know, it's a head rush at first. Just breathe. You'll get used to it soon enough."

Addy felt for the wall at her back and dug her fingers into the rough brick, grounding herself in the here and now. She could *talk.* "I can talk?"

"Reckon so," said the stranger.

"I—I can talk."

"Yep."

"I can talk! Talk talk talk. Words. Speech. Talk. Sentence. I can make sentences! With my mouth! Out loud!"

"Technically that was just word vomit, not sentences, but yeah. Words. Good job. Well done you."

She gathered herself. "Hi. Um. Sorry."

"Quite alright," he said, grinning. "Happens to the best of them. I'm Seth, by the way."

"Adelaide. Addy." What did he mean, the best of *them?*

"Nice name."

"Thank you," she retorted. An Aussie name wasn't the magnet for taunts it had once been. She'd long since learned to deal with teasing.

"Come here often?"

She looked at him sharply, but the question seemed genuine. "It's my first time."

"Oh, well, in that case, I'll give you the tour."

Addy considered him. He seemed decent enough; his voice held no greasy over-familiarity, just honest amiability. His eyes crinkled with good humour as he returned her regard. She liked him, she decided. She didn't know that she trusted him, mind you, but she did like him.

"A tour would be nice," she said. "Thanks."

"This, as you may have guessed, is the dance floor. Bathrooms are through there." Seth pointed to a discreet door near the bar. "And through here," he said, leading her through a wide archway to another room on the far side of the wraparound bar, "is the restaurant. I know, it's an odd mix of spaces. Don't blame me, I didn't design it. We call it the pub. Are you hungry?"

The archway must have contained a sound dampener; the noise level fell to a background murmur, and her stomach chose that moment to rumble. "Starved. But I should warn you—the last time I tried to eat anything I couldn't get closer than half a metre to it."

"Is that so?" He cast her an intrigued look. "Hold that thought. Grab us a seat, and I'll be right with you."

Addy perched on a barstool down the far end where it was

quieter and hooked another seat closer with her foot. This was better. Her shoulders relaxed from their instinctive hunch. She felt far more comfortable here; it was like any family-friendly pub on a fish-and-chip night.

"Taieri!"

"Seth," the ponytailed woman behind the bar said. "You're off for the night?"

"Yeah, I've done my sets. Can I get a bowl of hot chips for my new friend here?"

"Sure," Taieri said. "Did you want to pay up now, or—"

"Nah, put it on my tab. Thanks, love."

"Welcome."

Seth wandered down the bar and slid onto the stool Addy had saved him.

"Now," he said. "What were you saying about not being able to eat anything the last time you tried?"

She told him about the kitchens in the house, the fresh food on the benches, and the invisible walls stopping her from touching them.

"Interesting," he murmured. "Infuriating for you, of course. But interesting nonetheless."

"Have you ever been there?"

"That house? No, I can't say I have."

Addy blinked. "But it's just through that door—the one right there by the dance floor, the one I came through. You've been here—how long?—and you've never gone through that door?"

"I don't know how long I've been here. Three, maybe four years?" Seth shrugged. "Time here doesn't flow the same as time out there."

"I'd gathered that. It feels like I've been here more than a day already, but it can't have been—the session's only three hours."

He grinned. "Time is not time which alters when it alteration finds, or bends with the remover to remove."

"That was a terrible misquotation."

"Thank you."

"I'm impressed that you know Shakespeare well enough to misquote him, though."

"Again, thank you."

"But really," Addy said, choking back a laugh, "you haven't been through that door once in all your time here?"

"Oh no, I've been through the door alright, too many times to count. But I've never been to the house you were in."

It clicked. "The crazy physics aren't just confined to that place, then?" But of course they weren't. She'd had that bottomless chasm to cross before she even got to the house, hadn't she? Her heart sank. So much for hoping she wouldn't have to deal with any more shifting doorways or rotating gravity fields.

"No-o-o," he said slowly. "They're not, but they're usually far more stable than whatever madness you experienced. From what I've observed, that door only changes once or twice for every group of outsiders."

"That's a relief. I don't think I could handle another hour of that chaos, let alone another three days."

Seth's eyes narrowed. "I doubt it would feel like three days if you ended up there a second time. Actually, I doubt if you'd get put there again. It sounds like you've seen whatever you were meant to see."

"That was my impression, too," Addy said. She didn't mention the gallery.

Taieri appeared and set a massive bowl of steaming fries in front of Addy. "There you go. Did you want anything to drink?"

"Er. I'm underage. I'm only sixteen."

"We have sans-alcs. On the house—or on Seth's tab, rather."

"Do you have Paeroa beer?" The drink bore a passing resemblance to ginger beer but featured more of a citrus tang.

Taieri retrieved a bottle, uncapped it, and passed it across. "Seth? Anything for you?"

"Thanks." Seth shook his head and waved a hand in polite refusal.

Taieri vanished down the far end, leaving them to their conversation.

"You're not thirsty?" Addy sipped her drink, set the bottle down, and blinked as the lemony aftertaste kicked her in the throat.

"I don't drink, love," said Seth.

"There are sans-alcs—"

"I don't drink," he said again, laying a slight emphasis on the words.

Addy thought about that for a minute. "You don't drink," she said, "or you don't *drink?*"

He leaned across to snatch a chip from her bowl. "I don't drink alcohol. I can drink liquids when I want, but generally I don't feel the need."

A mental warning bell chimed. His line earlier about *happens to the best of them* flashed through her mind. *Them,* not *Us.* She probed a little deeper. "You're not part of the session group?"

Only one group went into the system at a time, she knew that. She didn't think she'd seen him at Breach, but she hadn't been looking closely at anyone besides Maunga. It was possible . . .

His mouth twisted. "No."

Happens to the best of them. He didn't feel the need to drink. And he wasn't part of the session, which meant . . .

The pieces fell into place, cemented by the bittersweet grin on his face. "You're a ghost in the system." She'd read about the concept in the material Tuku had given her and then again in the briefing instructions. They weren't actual ghosts, of course. That was just the label Breach had given them. They were copies of real people—a shadow or an echo left behind from previous sessions.

She'd imagined they just floated aimlessly through the sim. If they made any sound, she would have imagined vague ghost noises, moanings and such. She hadn't thought about carrying on a conversation with one, hadn't thought a ghost could be as real as any flesh-and-blood person.

She'd been wrong.

Seth tipped his head in acknowledgement. "Yes."

"They told you?"

"Of course they did. Who knows what sort of havoc I could wreak if I didn't know I wasn't sentient?" There was rather more bitter than sweet in his tone, that time.

"But . . ." Addy stared at him, thoughts churning. "You're conscious. You're talking. You *are* sentient, aren't you?"

"In a rather limited sense of the word. I'm self-aware. I share the memories of the person who planted me in the system. I have autonomy within a set area. That's about it."

"So you're, what, a virtual clone? You're a copy of someone out there in the real world?"

His gaze slid away. "Yes and no." He didn't elaborate, and Addy realised it wouldn't be polite to push the topic any further.

"What about them?" She nodded through the open arch to the seething mass of humanity—or not-humanity—on the dance floor and the spectators at the bar.

"Restricted A.I.s," Seth said. "NPCs, you might say. They each have a face and a name and maybe even something passing for a personality. You could have a conversation with them, but it would be short, and you'd find it looping back to where it started without much effort on your part. They can't leave their designated area. Even if they could leave, they'd never seriously think about it, let alone do it."

"And Taieri?"

"She's a ghost like me."

Addy bit a chip in half and ate it. "Why are there so many people here—hang on, are they people?"

"You can call them people, yeah. I call them loopers, myself."

"Why are there so many here when I didn't see a single person out on the wasteland or anywhere in the house? And that house was *huge*. It could fit the entire population of Te Maru inside without breaking a sweat."

He shrugged. "Who knows? Maybe Breach wanted to test you? Or your mind influenced your environment to give you that level of isolation? It could be any number of factors. I've never even heard of that house before; it's possible it was a construct formed for you and nobody else can even get to it."

"There were no ghosts, either. No one. Just . . . me." Addy idly drew a line through a puddle of spilled beer on the bar top. She added another line below it, and a third, and finished it with a small dot in the centre to make the stylised triplane of the Richard Pearse University logo. It soaked into the worn oak in moments, leaving a stain atop what looked like centuries of other stains.

"Breach tends to only have a few ghosts in play at any one time," Seth said. "Two or three for every person in the session. And we're concentrated in spots where pilgrims tend to congregate, like here or the bank."

"The bank?"

"Yeah. Amazing how many people buy their way into a session in hopes of striking it rich."

"Do they have much luck?"

He laughed. "Absolutely none. But they try."

"And—did you say pilgrims?"

"That's what we call session participants."

"Why?"

"Let me take it back a bit. You've got your loopers—not much personality, not much conversation. They're content to go where the programme tells them and be part of the background scene, so to speak. I have my doubts as to whether they're even self-aware."

Addy nodded.

"Then," Seth continued, "you've got your ghosts, like me. I'm essentially a copy of a real-life person—or a copy of who the person was at the time they left their session. We live in the system. We're able to move around within a set area, and we're put to sleep every so often so that Breach can change the environment and introduce new ghosts without disturbing us too much. We tend to hang around the areas that Breach constructs, like the pub, although we can go to areas constructed by session participants if the conditions are right."

"Okay."

"And then we have people like you. Pilgrims. We call them that because they're always looking for something, even if they don't know it themselves, and they treat the programme like a sort of sacred experience. They might want something emotional like closure from trauma or something mental like a deeper look inside their own mind or something material like money. I've encountered a few who wanted a spiritual experience. Once a woman spent her whole time sitting in non-space. She didn't even do anything. Didn't make any effort to change her environment. I don't think she wanted to change it. She just sat there, breathing. Said afterward that it was the most peaceful experience of her entire life."

He cleared his throat. "Whatever they're looking for, they all come here. Sometimes they find it; sometimes they don't. They're the real-world people who visit for three hours and then vanish, and for the most part, we never see them again. Really, it would be more accurate from our point of view to call *you* the ghosts."

Addy leaned forward. "You mean some of them come back?"

"Oh, yeah. If they've got the money and the time. A fair few come back a second time if they feel they've got unfinished business here. Some come back a third or fourth time. I think the record was a woman who made twelve separate visits over eight months."

"And then they wouldn't let her in again?" She reckoned even a company wanting to maximise their profit margins might balk at that many repeat visits. Who knew what the woman had been up to?

"No," Seth said. "They'd done all the regular vetting tests and updated her file after each visit, and they would have let her in again; she wasn't a danger to herself or to anyone else. She stopped coming of her own free will. She'd finished whatever her business was here." He gazed into the middle distance. "I remember she spent a lot of time at the hospital. And the cemetery."

He didn't volunteer any more information, and Addy didn't ask.

She made an effort to change the subject. "Have you seen anyone else from my group?"

"I have." He reached across to steal another chip, dripping tomato sauce onto the counter. "There was a long-haired chap in here earlier, but he left. A woman arrived half an hour or so ago. She's sitting down the back with an espresso martini—her fourth, unless I've miscounted. Second table from the end wall."

Addy cast a casual look over her shoulder, spotted the woman down the far end of the restaurant chatting with a neighbour, and turned back to her chips. "Anyone else?" Maybe Maunga had wandered through here. "Someone around my age?"

"Looking for someone in particular?"

"Maybe."

He eyed her speculatively. "Why do you want to know?"

How much to tell him? She couldn't tell him the whole story, but he wasn't going to bite without knowing something of what had happened. She sipped her Paeroa beer. "She took something of mine a while ago. I'd quite like to get it back."

"She stole something?"

"Yes."

"How long ago?"

"Three years."

"And for some reason you had to wait until now, years later, when you're both in a virtual reality programme, to get it back?"

Addy bit her lip. It sounded ridiculous when he put it like that. "Yes. It's—it's quite important. To me."

Seth grimaced and looked away, and then he started and his gaze swung back. "You said you couldn't talk. She stole your voice?"

"Yes . . . ?" She'd thought he knew that already.

"*She* stole your voice."

Oh. He was fixated on the person who had done the stealing, not on the act of theft itself. But how did he know? "Who—?"

"Maunga Richards. That's who you're talking about, isn't it?"

She blinked. "It is, yes. How did you know?"

"Process of elimination," he said after a pause. "She's the only female around your age from your session group." He ran a hand across his face. A bleak look flashed in his eyes, disappearing so quickly she half-thought she'd imagined it. "Maunga Richards stole your voice."

"That's what I've been saying, yes."

"You're certain?"

Addy fought an urge to slap a hand on the table. "I was there. I'm certain. We were in a tutoring room at school, just her and me, and she injected me with something, and I felt woozy and passed out. When I woke up, my voice was gone and so was my creativity. And my writing ability. And a dozen more minor things, like any chance of passing oral presentations for the rest of my life. Not to mention," she added, anger pushing the words out, "adding insult to injury by sticking a band-aid over the injection site. It had a smiley face on it. A keeking smiley face. On a bright keeking yellow band-aid. After she keeking stole my keeking voice."

"I can't—" Seth heaved a shuddering breath and then gathered himself. He cleared his throat and straightened his shoulders. "Sorry. I didn't mean to imply that I don't believe you; I do believe you. And I didn't mean to pester you. I, um, I can't believe she'd do that. She just—she didn't seem like that sort of person when I . . . uh . . . talked to her."

"So you have talked to her?"

He gave a low laugh. "Oh, yes."

She waited.

"Maybe half an hour ago. She asked me what the best route to the mountain was. I told her that accurate times depend on your mindset, but if she meant the prettiest, the scenic route would probably take two days. Then she asked for the quickest. That's much more doable in her timeframe."

"Are you having me on?"

He frowned. "No. Why would I?"

"Maunga's going to the mountain?"

"Yes."

"Maunga," Addy repeated slowly and clearly, "is going to the mountain."

He held her gaze, looking perplexed.

"You're not joking." *He really doesn't know?*

Seth shook his head. "I have no idea what you're talking about."

"Maunga—"

"Is going to the mountain, yes, I know, but *what does it mean?*"

She'd thought it was obvious. "Maunga. Mountain."

"What?" He barked a disbelieving laugh. "Really? *That's* what you meant?"

Clearly, she'd misinterpreted. "That's—er, yes. I thought—well, it's obvious, isn't it? Maunga means mountain. Thought you were having a nice joke at my expense."

"I'm sorry, love," he said, still grinning, "but you've got your wires crossed on that one."

"You weren't joking, then."

"No."

"And she really did—"

"She really did ask me for the quickest route to the mountain, yes."

"Oh," Addy said lamely. "Sorry."

"Quite alright. Don't worry about it."

"So can you tell me how to get to the mountain? Please?"

"You want to find Maunga. Why? So you can get your voice back somehow?"

She nodded. "That's the idea. I don't know how—"

"No, I imagine you don't," he muttered, not quite under his breath.

"But I want to corner her and get as much information as possible."

"And how are you going to do that?"

"I—what?"

"How are you going to corner her? How are you going to get all that information? I assume you have a plan for when you reach her and she laughs in your face and walks away without answering a single question?"

Addy swallowed. She didn't. She hadn't gotten that far; she'd thought she could wing it as she went.

"And bargaining chips?" Seth continued. "I doubt she's going to answer your questions out of the goodness of her heart. She'll want compensation of one kind or another. I hope you're rich or have a large stash of Whittaker's dark chocolate—and by a large stash, I mean several dozen crates at the very least. Alternatively, she might accept you completing all her assignments for the duration of her university life or maybe the indentured servitude of your first child." He clapped her on the shoulder and grinned. "Tough luck, love."

Addy didn't return the smile. "So what you're saying is that it's hopeless and I might as well give up and go home now, is that it?"

And once more he surprised her. "Not at all."

"No? Then what?"

"I'm suggesting," he said, sitting up straighter and rescuing the last now-cold chip from its lonely fate at the bottom of the bowl, "that I come with you."

She nearly dropped her beer. "You what?"

"I should come with you. You don't know the way to the mountain. I do. I can get us there faster. Plus I have some small idea of what makes Maunga tick, which is, if you'll excuse me being blunt—"

"Go for your life."

"Rather more than you have."

Addy wrinkled her nose but conceded the point with a tip of her head.

"And I'm curious, to be honest," he continued. "If a cure for Vox Pox is possible or if Maunga knows more than she's letting on, I'd like to be there when you find out."

"You're a complete stranger. Why should I trust you?"

There was no time for beating around the bush; if she was going to embark on a severely time-limited cross-country trip with a stranger, she wanted to know a bit more about him.

He shrugged. "Would you take my word for it? I can't provide hard evidence one way or the other; I don't keep a portfolio of Reasons Why I'm Trustworthy. You can only believe me—or not. If you do believe me, I won't be able to convince you not to, and if you don't believe me, well, the reverse holds true. I'm curious. I think what she did was absolutely horrific, and I quite like you, young Adelaide."

"I'm sixteen," she muttered.

He had a point, though. If he'd launched into a monologue about why she should trust someone she'd only known for half an hour, she would have found it reason enough to *not* trust him, but by being honest and giving a couple of very human reasons for why he wanted to play a part in this, she was inclined to, yes, trust him. Or at least to accept his offer of an escort.

"Ah," he said with overly-dramatic nostalgia. "Sixteen. I remember being sixteen. Or at least I remember my original being sixteen. It was a horrible time. He hated it."

"He?"

"Seth," said Seth with a wink. "He's named after me."

"I see." Addy bit back a grin. "I don't mind being sixteen. There are worse ages to be."

"Oh?"

"Thirteen, for instance."

"That was when Maunga stole your voice?"

"Yeah." She drank the last mouthful of her Paeroa beer and set the empty bottle on the counter with a vehement *clink.*

Seth slid his stool out from the bar and made as if to stand. "Shall we go?"

"We're not getting anywhere by sitting around talking, are we?"

"Taieri!" Seth called.

Taieri poked her head around the corner of the wraparound bar, saw Seth, and came toward them, wiping her hands on a cloth. "Seth. You're finished?"

"We are, thank you." He pushed the bottle and the empty bowl across the bar. "Would you tell Jezza I won't be in tomorrow? I'm taking a day's, ah, annual leave."

"Sure, I'll tell him. Where are you off to?"

"Adelaide and I have some questing to do."

Taieri raised an eyebrow. "Do you just?"

"We do."

"You might want to put a shirt on first, then."

He glanced down at himself. "Ah. Yes. I will. Thanks."

"Welcome." Taieri picked up their empty dishes. "I'll let Jezza know first chance I get. The sooner I can tell him, the less likely he'll be to blow his top."

"Tell him to put me down for a few extra sets the day after tomorrow. That should appease him."

She nodded. "I'll do that. Good luck on your quest."

"Thanks, T." Seth squeezed her shoulder before motioning to Addy. "Right. Come on . . ."

Addy lifted a hand to cover the tail end of her yawn and smiled sheepishly. "Sorry. I told you it felt like I'd been here ages already, and I haven't slept at all."

"Oh, that's not good. Let me see if we can't do something about that. Taieri?"

"A Sparkling Fizzbee, do you think?" Taieri was already turning away to the fridges behind the counter.

"No, no, no, we want something rather more potent. What about a Spitting Mad Maui?"

They named a drink after Maui the Trickster? That sounded dangerous. "I've had my fill of fizz for the night, I think," Addy said. "Have you got anything without bubbles in it?"

Seth exchanged a glance with Taieri. "We can do that," he said. "A Flat Mad Maui, then? Sans alcohol, of course."

"A Flat Mad Maui it is." Taieri plucked six different bottles from the fridges and retrieved a double shot glass from under the counter. She kept her back to them as she made the drink.

Addy leaned sideways to try to get a look without being too obvious, but she still couldn't see. "What's in it?"

"Twelve ingredients," said Seth, "nine of which are secret, rare, borderline illegal, or a combination of the above. The other three are Bundaberg bitters, Watties tomato sauce, and concentrated artificial caffeine."

Ew. "That sounds disgusting."

"It's not too bad."

"And I tell you what," said Taieri, placing the full glass in front of Addy, "it does the trick. You won't want to sleep for a week after you've had that shot."

Addy eyed it suspiciously. The liquid was a light caramel-brown colour and viscous, with a thin layer of creamy foam on top. She tapped the glass. The drink wobbled and settled back with a deep *gloop.*

"Stop thinking and just drink it," Seth advised. "Plug your nose if it'll help. Come on. We need to go."

She held her nose and threw the shot back. *Ugh.* It sat at the back of her mouth for a long moment, and then, with a mammoth effort, she swallowed. It slid down easier than she'd expected, leaving a lingering aftertaste of liquorice. She let go of her nose.

"Not as bad as I'd expected," she said. "Thanks."

"Right. This way." Seth led the way toward a door she hadn't noticed, set in the wall beside the bar. "Bye, Taieri. I'll be back tomorrow or early the day after. You'll be okay holding the fort while I'm gone?"

Taieri rolled her eyes. "No, I'm going to collapse in hysterics as soon as you walk out of the room."

"You can't wait until I get back? I'd pay good money to see that." He grinned and slipped out the door, Addy sticking to his heels.

To Addy's surprise, they turned left down the hallway and started up an impressive polished oak staircase. She ran her hand over the banister, admiring its smoothness and the subtle twists in the uprights.

"Just up here." Seth indicated the next flight.

She followed him up to the next landing and then along a short corridor. He stopped outside a solid oak door that had been retrofitted with a card scanner.

"Sorry about the mess," he said, scanning a card to unlock the door. "I wasn't expecting company."

The bedroom was small and sparsely furnished—a bed against one wall, desk hard up against the window, wardrobe and drawers built into the wall. An uncomfortable-looking armchair with yellow and grey stripes squatted at the end of the bed, covered in clothes. A full-length mirror hung on the wardrobe door.

Somehow the room managed to look messy and abandoned at the same time.

Seth yanked open a drawer and rifled through it. "Won't be a minute. I just need to find a clean shirt and some shoes. Can't go questing in bare feet."

Questing. It was such an odd word choice. But she supposed, if they called outsiders pilgrims, quest could well be the right word for it.

He pulled out a white t-shirt and tugged it on, found some socks, and slid his feet into a pair of boots before knotting the laces. "There we are," he said, slinging a red jacket around his shoulders. "All ready to go."

"You don't want to take a pack?" Addy asked. "A water bottle? Food?"

He shook his head. "Not from here. The fewer things we have to cart and the less distance we have to cart them, the better. We can pick up supplies on our way out of the city."

"Okay." He was more familiar than she was with their environment. She assumed he knew what he was talking about.

"You've got everything you came with?"

Addy checked herself. Boots, the treads still a little clogged with sand. School uniform, her socks and the hem of her skirt stained with salt in places. Theo's green hoodie, looking rather worse for wear after she'd used it to dry herself off twice, sand-spotted and now with greasy finger-marks on the cuffs where she'd wiped them after the chips. And, of course, her Eareos, useless without a holo, hanging around her neck. "Yes. This is everything."

Seth nodded and stepped past her to the door.

Addy followed him from the room.

INTERLUDE

We are the voiceless.
Hear us.
Our silence is not consent
nor rejection
nor ignorance
nor knowledge.
Our silence is the imposition
of nothing
instead of something.
Our silence has been
forced upon us
by you,
the noisome masses.

CHAPTER NINE

Outside, Addy was surprised to find the city basking in bright sunshine. It couldn't have been much past noon, or whatever passed for noon in this seemingly timeless place.

"I thought it was night," she said to Seth.

"Why, because the pub was open?" He veered around a group of hagglers at the roadside stall. "The pub's always open. And I told you, time doesn't flow right here. It plays havoc with our circadian rhythms, but most pilgrims aren't here long enough to notice."

"You're kidding?"

"No."

"Our session's only three hours. I swear I've been here two days already, and you're saying that most people don't notice the discrepancy?"

He nodded. "Seems like Breach might've played with your perceptions a bit, or else your mind is influencing your environment to a ridiculous degree. Most people only experience the three hours as three hours. Obviously, there have been exceptions. I did hear a rumour of one guy who lived a month in the system in the space of a three-hour session."

"A *month?*"

"Yeah. He was a right mess when they pulled him out. He'd managed snatches of sleep here and there, but it wasn't nearly enough to function on. The rest of his group had in-system times of anywhere between an hour and four hours, and then he produced his record of twenty-nine days. Breach went ballistic. The rest of the group wasn't too happy about it, either."

The smile playing about Seth's mouth didn't quite distract her from the intent look in his eyes. He was frowning a bit, too. What was he thinking about? Maunga? The fastest way to reach her? Or something else? For the first time, it occurred to Addy that this cross-country trip might not be entirely safe.

She shook her head. What had Seth been saying? Oh, right. "I can understand Breach being unhappy, but it wasn't any business of the rest of the group, was it? They weren't the ones stuck in the sim for a month."

"Exactly," Seth said. "They *weren't* in there for a month."

She frowned. "I don't get it."

"They'd spent the time and money to get into a VPR session, the same as this other guy. Most of them would have been quite happy with their average three hours; the person with four hours was elated, while the poor sod who only had one hour was, as you might expect, disappointed. But one to four hours is still in a reasonable range. Throw in this one guy who's spent twenty-nine days—not hours, but *days*—in the system, and you've got a big problem.

"Bad enough that Mr. Four Hours had four times as long in the session as Miss One Hour; now you're dropping Mr. Twenty-Nine Days into the mix." Seth waved a hand and squinted skyward, clearly doing some mental arithmetic. "That's, what, five, six, seven hundred . . . seven hundred and nineteen hours? Say seven-twenty, then."

She was beginning to understand why the rest of that group mightn't have been too happy. Keek. Seventy-two hours was bad enough. She couldn't imagine being here for ten times that long.

"So," Seth continued, "Miss One Hour is already disappointed because Mister Four Hours got four times the experience that she got, and then Mister Seven Hundred And Twenty Hours comes swanning along and has the gall to *complain* about his session. The whole group kicks up a stink, demanding free sessions and a full refund and whatever else. Mister Seven Hundred And Twenty is traumatised from being forced to live a month in one world when it only translated to three hours in the other world . . . and you can see why Breach had a little bit of a problem on their hands."

"Keek, yeah. I hadn't thought about that side of it. Hang on, how did you know all this if you've been stuck here?"

"Oh, Caro—that's the Overseer—keeps a ghost of herself in the system. She claims it's for easier maintenance and A.I. wellbeing, but we all know she's a total workaholic. Two of her, see? She can get twice as much work done. Anyway, she told the ghost, and the ghost spread the word around to us to find out what had happened from our side."

Seth sped up as they turned a corner. Addy matched his pace at a brisk trot. She noticed his eyes darting from side to side ahead of them, sweeping from one building to an alley and onto the next building. Were they being watched? Would the system try to stop them from leaving the city? She opened her mouth to ask what he was looking for and then closed it again. If he wanted to tell her, he would. In his own time.

"So what did happen?" she asked.

"We don't know. Even *they* don't know. Breach called it a temporary system glitch, apologised, issued refunds, and took full liability for any psychiatric costs incurred. The contracts had confidentiality clauses, of course, so the clients couldn't go public with the story."

"And they fixed the system?"

"Yes and no. They put a research team on the job to figure out how the guy had managed to bend the timeframe that much. The team took six months to compile their report, and in the end found practically nothing of any use. So they labelled it an isolated incident, tightened the in-system timers to a strict range of between two and four hours, and left it at that."

"Let me guess, there were more isolated incidents?"

"Yeah, but not half as many as there used to be. The ratio's down to about one in nine hundred."

"That's about one a year?"

"A bit over a year. And there's never been a month-long session again. The longest incident since then was forty-eight hours. Left here," he added, turning down a wide avenue.

Addy chewed that over as they walked. The city was starting to bear more than a passing resemblance to Te Maru; or rather, it was something like what Te Maru could have been if the city had wider streets, far more green space, and a perpetually sunny sky, and if it was then overlaid with a saturation filter to make everything impossibly rich in colour.

"Have I been here forty-eight hours?"

"Eighty-one," said Seth, "and a half."

Good grief. She hadn't thought it would be *that* long. But how could he tell? She shot him an enquiring look.

"It's a knack. Don't worry about looking for your timer. You'd never find it."

They turned down a private lane and emerged in a grassy courtyard. Seth led her to one side where a row of what looked like unfurnished bathroom cubicles stood. Doorless, they contained nothing more than a shallow gutter around the edges of each square. He walked into one and stood with his back to her.

Addy turned away hurriedly. Surely he wasn't . . .

"Are you coming in?"

"Uh, let me think about that . . . *no.* Why didn't you go to the bathroom before we left?"

He huffed a laugh. "I'm not peeing. It's a lift platform. We need to get down to the station, and this is the closest drop point."

Oh. She stared at her feet, feeling a dull flush climb her cheeks. The grass was particularly fascinating. "You could have said something earlier."

"I'm sorry. I forgot the boxes can look a little dodgy. Now, would you come in, please?"

She turned and joined him in the cramped space.

"It really does look like a loo cubicle," she muttered.

"It does a bit. I suppose I'm just used to it. I'll do my best to warn you next time."

"Thank you."

"Now." He stamped twice on the floor. "Down!"

With a quiet whirring, the square lowered. Concrete walls rose around them; Addy looked up and watched the patch of cloudless sky grow smaller and smaller. She had time to feel the first stirrings of unease at descending into the darkness—what if they never stopped?—when the air grew brighter again. A slice of golden light fell across their feet and spread upward, and they emerged into an underground cavern lit with lamps that shed a soft yellow light.

She stepped off the lift onto solid ground and felt more than saw Seth move to stand beside her.

"Welcome," he said, "to Lysaght Station."

She blinked and blinked again. Her eyes adjusted to the light. A vast roof arched high overhead, supported by carved beams and cross-braces; before her lay a wide platform and a short drop down to a series of train tracks, with another platform on the far side. To her right, a flight of stairs led up to a graceful, glass-floored walkway that spanned the gap. The space was empty.

"It's a station for what, trains?"

"Ghost trains, in fact."

She cast a slantwise look at him. "Ghost. Trains."

"Trains for ghosts, I mean. Not—the trains themselves aren't ghosts. That wouldn't make any sense."

"Oh, trains for ghosts. I see."

A rumbling came up the tracks, and in another minute a train pulled up in front of them, sleek and almost silent. The doors opened with a hiss. Addy was about to hop into the nearest carriage when Seth halted her with a hand on her shoulder.

"Do me a favour?" he asked.

"What sort of favour?"

"Touch the carriage. Don't get into it yet. Just touch it with a finger."

She eyed him curiously but nodded. "Alright."

"Now," he prompted. "You've got about eight seconds before the train leaves."

She prodded the side of the carriage.

The whole train flickered, wavering. Seth pulled her back from the tracks as the side of the carriage rippled, metal bulging with a whine and settling again, and then the train dissolved into nothingness.

Addy stared at the empty space where the carriage had been.

Seth blew out a gusting breath. "I was afraid of that."

"What was that?"

"Ghost trains. Trains for ghosts." He frowned at the empty tracks in front of their section of the platform. "Not for pilgrims," he added, almost to himself.

"So we can't use them to get . . . wherever we're going?"

He made a thoughtful noise. "Not sure. Let me think about it for a bit." He loped over to the stairs, climbed six or seven steps, and sat with his back to the railing and his legs bent. When it became obvious that 'a bit' was going to be more like twenty minutes, Addy joined him.

After a few minutes, she thought of something. It was wonderful being able to ask questions whenever she felt like it, without the fear of being ignored if the other person wasn't looking directly at her. "Maunga couldn't use the train, right? She's not a ghost. So how did she get out of the city?"

"It sounded like she'd been in the sim before. I'd guess she's learned the knack of planting headspace suggestions to make her trip easier. Or maybe she took a bus."

"There are buses here?" He couldn't have mentioned that before?

"Pilgrim buses, yeah. Buses—"

"For pilgrims," Addy said. "Not for ghosts. Right. We can't split up and meet up across the city?"

"It'd take too long."

Ugh. She was starting to think Breach hadn't designed their transport systems all that well. She glanced around the empty terminal. "Why are there no people here?"

"It's a ghost station."

"I know. So why are there no ghosts?"

"How many people are there in your session?"

"Twelve."

Seth picked at the knee of his trouser leg. "There are three ghosts per pilgrim. We tend to be concentrated around where the pilgrims are—like the pub—or assigned to float around pilgrim-specific territory in case anyone wants directions or intelligent conversation. Only ghosts can use the trains, and this is only one station out of dozens across the city. It's not surprising it's empty, really."

Oh. That made sense.

Another question occurred to her. "Can we trick the sensors somehow? How do they know I'm a pilgrim?"

"It's a tad obvious," he said, not unkindly.

"But how does the train know? It's not sentient; it's a machine. Is there a fingerprint scanner, or a blood tester, or some sort of DNA collection laser? How does it know for sure?"

"That's a bit like asking how anyone knows you're human. It's so self-evident that there's no way to explain it."

"But surely you can *try*—"

"I can't," he said, cutting her off. "I'm sorry, but I can't. There isn't a way for me to explain it in any language you speak, or if there is, I don't have the capacity or the ability. There are more things in heaven and earth, Adelaide, than are contained within your vocabulary. Alright?"

"Shakespeare."

"Yes. Hamlet."

She tried not to sound too grudging. "Alright. Sorry."

Seth dropped his feet to the step below and stood. "I'm going to take a walk down the platform while I think. Don't go too far, okay?"

"Don't worry. I'll stick around here."

He sauntered down the steps to the platform. She watched him go, suppressing an impatient sigh. Shouldn't they be doing something instead of just sitting here? He didn't seem to be coming up with any grand ideas, and, much as she hated to admit it, she didn't know enough about this parallel Te Maru to contribute anything useful. If the trains were a no-go, the time would be better spent moving on. Couldn't they walk?

And where were they going? Seth hadn't even told her that yet.

She settled her chin into her cupped hand. *Hmph.* It was so nice to be trusted.

Seth reached some arbitrary mark down the far end of the platform, turned, and wandered back. Her foot bounced up and down on the step. *Hurry up.* Who knew how long Maunga would stay on the mountain? She might be getting ready to move off right now.

Seth halted at the bottom of the steps and let out a rumbling chuckle. "Don't be so impatient, love. We'll be out of here soon enough."

Addy trotted down the stairs to join him. "Do you have a plan?"

"I do." Seth shrugged off his red jacket and held it out. "Put this on."

She reached for it and then hesitated.

"Please," he said.

She took the jacket and slipped it on over Theo's hoodie. One layer of oversized clothing over another layer of oversized clothing. She felt like a kid playing dress-up. "Okay. Now what?"

"Give it a few minutes while we wait for the next train to pull in."

"Give what a few minutes?"

"The jacket," he said patiently. "If we're lucky, it will have absorbed enough of my ghostliness, for lack of a better word, that it will hide your pilgrimity."

Addy choked on a laugh. "Pilgrimity?"

"Or whatever you want to call it."

"So your jacket should mask my . . . pilgrimity . . . from the train sensors?"

"If we're lucky."

"And if we're *not* lucky?"

"Then the carriage does what it did last time, and we fall down onto the tracks and die." He held a straight face for a few seconds before cracking a grin. "Sorry. No, I'll get you to touch the side of the carriage like you did last time. It seems to be a pretty good test."

"Your confidence is overwhelming."

"Isn't it just?" His gaze swung down the tracks as the low rumbling began. "Here it comes. Ready?"

"Ready."

They moved forward as the train drew up to the platform. Addy lifted a hand to touch the carriage; the too-long sleeve of the jacket fell over her hand, and she poked the smooth metal through the material of the jacket. No flickering this time. She glanced at Seth. He nodded. She stepped across the gap and put a foot on the carriage floor.

"No—!"

Seth yanked her back by the waist as the train flickered; they overbalanced, falling backward to sprawl painfully on the platform. Addy watched aghast as the metal bulged and rippled, and a split-second later, the train vanished. Breathing fast and light, she stumbled to her feet, unable to tear her gaze from the empty tracks.

Dimly she thought that she should say something, but she couldn't think of anything to say. At the pub, riding the high of being able to speak out loud for the first time in more than three years, it had been easy to blurt out words with no regard for whether they were necessary. But now, that freedom felt like sacrilege. She remembered those three years: the slow, shaking effort of trying to type out words on her holo, how much time and energy it had taken to communicate the simplest and most important of things.

Words were a gift. She would treasure them.

Addy turned and offered a hand to Seth, who was still lying on the ground. He accepted it with a murmur of thanks, and she hauled him to his feet. *Ooof.* He was heavy. Came with all that muscle, she supposed.

"It's alright," Seth said after he'd taken a thoughtful walk down the platform and back. "I know where we went wrong."

"Can we fix it? That was too close for comfort."

"We can fix it. You touched the side of the carriage through my jacket sleeve, yeah?"

"Yes."

"But those boots are pilgrimatic."

"They're mine, if that's what you mean by—did you say *pilgrimatic?* It sounds like a disease. Or a clothing brand."

He grinned. "Pilgrimatic boots, now with ten percent more tread! Yes, I meant that they belong to you."

"They do," Addy said. "They're the only thing from the outfit I was wearing in the real world that transferred over. I don't know where the rest came from; I wasn't wearing my uniform, and the hoodie is my brother's."

"I see." Seth looked thoughtful, but he didn't elaborate.

She was grateful; three weeks wasn't nearly long enough to take away the sting she felt at the reminder of Theo with Vox Pox. Even the thought of it brought a lump to her throat. It wasn't *fair.*

No, it wasn't fair, but what in life was?

"So," Seth said, "you touched the train through my jacket and it was fine, but as soon as you touched it through something of yours, it went on the blink. The solution looks easy enough. We just have to make sure you don't touch the train with bare skin or anything belonging to you."

Easy. Sure. "I can't even stand up without my boots touching the ground. I may have seen some crazy physics in the last eighty hours—"

"Eighty-two hours and twenty minutes."

"But I haven't come across any *that* crazy. My feet still have to touch the ground for me to move—and your boots would fall off my feet as soon as I tried to walk in them, so don't even think about trying that."

"You'll have to climb on my back."

She blinked. "I'm sorry?"

"Climb on my back," he said, turning away and bending his arms at his back. "I'll carry you. That way you won't touch the ground."

There were so many ways that could go wrong. She jumped on his back anyway, gripping with her knees and trying not to choke him with the arm around his shoulders.

He took a few cautious steps. "That's fine. Put the hood on, please. I might bump into a wall, and I'd rather you didn't hit your head."

Meaning, of course, that he would rather her head didn't touch the wall because that would scupper their plan. Addy tightened her grip with one hand and used the other to twitch the jacket hood up and over her head. "Okay. It's on."

"Thank you."

In another couple of minutes, the train pulled up, doors sliding open. Seth moved forward with every sign of confidence and stepped into the carriage. He gripped an overhead rail with one hand, rapped on the carriage wall with the other—Addy redoubled her grip with her knees—and the doors slid closed.

They'd made it. The train started off.

"Try not to talk," Seth said. "The sensors might pick up your vibrations."

She nodded against the side of his head so that he could feel her acknowledgement. The train moved fast, faster than she'd expected. In fifteen minutes they had flown through six stations and were halfway across the city. Soon Seth knocked on the carriage wall again.

"It'll drop us at the next station." He shifted to the side, stretching out first one leg and then the other.

Something brushed against her calf. Addy looked down and froze. Her boot had followed Seth's motion when he moved. It grazed the side of a row of seats. She squeezed his shoulder hard, following the movement with a frantic double tap on his upper arm.

He turned his head.

The train flickered.

Her heart leapt.

Seth spat a profanity under his breath. Quicker than thought, quicker than the train could dissolve, his hand whipped out toward a sharp knot that jutted from the rim of the nearest seat. The first ripple came through the walls as he gouged a long line down his forearm, opening a wound that bled freely. He grunted in pain. The rippling wave spread. His arm came back to his side, slid against Addy's skirt, down her calf, across her boots.

The ripples wavered and then faded away into the straight walls of the carriage. The flickering stopped.

Addy closed her eyes and tried not to feel the blood trickling down her leg.

"Alright?" Seth muttered.

She lowered her cheek to his head and jerked a nod. She was sure he could feel her shaky breaths. Her hand trembled where it gripped his shirt.

The train drew into the next station and stopped. The doors slid open.

"Mind the gap," crackled an unseen voice overhead.

Seth leaped out onto the platform. Behind them, the train moved away and vanished down the line.

His arms loosened about her legs. Addy slipped off his back and onto her own two feet, relishing the feel of solid ground and, more importantly, ground that wouldn't dematerialise as soon as she touched it.

"That was, uh, good," she said. Her tongue felt clumsy in the aftermath of the adrenaline. "Good—good thinking. Quick thinking, I mean."

Seth had stripped off his t-shirt and was wrapping it tightly around his bleeding arm. He gave a shuddering laugh. "I'm just glad it worked. I'm sorry," he added, frowning. "I shouldn't have moved that much."

"And I should have looked where my foot was going," she retorted. "Don't be daft. It wasn't your fault."

"It wasn't yours, either. Forget it."

Addy straightened and looked around. This station looked smaller than the other one and dingy, like it hadn't had any decent maintenance in a good long while. She shrugged off his jacket and handed it to him. "Here."

"Thanks." Seth pulled it on over his bare chest. "This way." He led the way to a bank of lift platforms and stepped onto one.

They shot upward, emerging in a grassy courtyard that looked identical to the one they'd visited earlier. Addy was about to ask if they'd been here before, but remembering the change in stations, she held her tongue.

"Down here," said Seth.

They cut left down a narrow alley that bordered one side of the courtyard. It ran straight for a short way, sandwiched in a sliver of shadow between tall buildings, and then dropped down a flight of steep stairs. Seth opened a door at the bottom of the steps and waved her inside.

"After you, love."

Addy entered the . . . shop? It was dim and musty and, yes, definitely a shop. Neat stacks of clothing towered above her; to one side, shelving offered antique hardback books sorted by colour. Thick carpet swallowed the sound of her steps. She touched a finger to a brass statue. It came away sheathed in dust.

Seth closed the door behind them. Somewhere in the interior, a bell chimed.

Shuffling footsteps echoed in the silence. A wizened figure, bent nearly double beneath flowing white hair, appeared in the far doorway. "Hello there," it croaked. "Welcome to Old Ebenezer's Antique Emporium. How may I be of service to you on this fine day?"

"It's me, Dave," Seth said.

The effect was immediate. The figure straightened and cast off its white locks—a wig, Addy saw—to reveal shaggy chestnut hair. He came forward with the jaunty step of youth. "Seth! Welcome! Haven't seen you in a while. How've you been?"

"Oh, not bad. Same old, same old. You know how it is."

"I do know," Dave said. He cast a quick look over them, eyes lingering on the blood-soaked, makeshift bandage poking from beneath the arm of Seth's jacket, and frowned. "You're hurt. Head on upstairs; you know the way. I'll close up down here and be right with you."

Seth stepped around Addy and led the way down the aisle to the rear of the shop, where a narrow, twisting staircase was visible through the open doorway. Once up the stairs, he veered left into a living room.

The room startled her in its modernity. Gleaming slate tiles lined the floor. Subtle red and maroon patterned the walls. Leather couches on old-fashioned-turned-new-fashioned-again carved legs framed three sides of a coffee table, and to one end, an elbow-height bench and a wide hatchway set with steel shutters provided a view into the kitchen.

"Have a seat," Seth said. "I'll be back in a minute."

He vanished back out the door.

Addy looked after him for a moment before transferring her gaze to the room. Which sofa should she sit on? It didn't matter. With three couches to choose from, she doubted Dave would complain about her taking his favourite spot. She padded to the farthest seat and perched on the edge of the cushion, eyes fixed on the empty doorway.

Where had Seth gone? Maybe he was helping Dave close the shop. Why did Dave need to close the shop? Why did he even have a shop here? A pub was understandable, but an antique shop? There weren't enough pilgrims—or ghosts, for that matter—to make it worth his while.

Her knee itched. She scratched at it. That felt odd. *Ugh.* She eyed her blood-flaked fingers in disgust. *Yuck.* It wasn't even *her* blood. Maybe Seth had gone to get medical supplies. Did ghosts feel pain the same way that humans did? It had looked like it; Seth hadn't exactly been bouncing around like normal. His arm had to be hurting him.

She heard footsteps on the stairs and then a brief exchange in the hall. Dave and Seth came through the door together. Seth set a sizeable medkit on the table and stripped off his jacket.

"It'll need stitches," he said.

Dave pulled on gloves, unwrapped the bandage, and whistled. "You did the job properly, didn't you? Any other wounds? Are you hurt, pilgrim?" he added, keen eyes turning to Addy.

Of course he'd spotted her leg. She shook her head. "No. Thank you. It's—it's Seth's blood."

"Just the arm," said Seth. "Self-inflicted."

Dave started speaking, but Seth continued, talking over the top of him. "I smuggled her onto the train. We weren't quite at your station yet, and the sensors needed a little convincing."

"Hmm," said Dave after a pause. "What did you use? A knife?"

"A sharp nut along the top of the seat row."

Dave sighed. "Iodine," he muttered under his breath. He reached for a pressure sponge and pressed it to the wound. "Hold that. I'll get the gear sorted out."

Amidst the preparations, Dave retrieved a small packet of antiseptic wipes and handed them to Addy. "Here. Bathroom's down the hall. Why don't you go and get cleaned up? Take your time," he added with grim humour. "We might be here a while."

"Thanks."

"Dave, have you got any morphine?" Seth's unharmed hand clenched on his trouser leg.

"Not for you, mate," Dave said as Addy slipped out the door. "But tell you what, you can have some Panadol . . ."

Their voices faded as she padded down the hall. A metal plaque identified the bathroom door. She slipped inside. More black slate tiles met her eyes, their harshness relieved by terracotta walls and warm white downlights. It was deliciously quiet. Her heart lightened, relieved to have some space to herself.

But she didn't have long. As soon as Dave had patched Seth up, they'd be off again. No time for daydreaming; she'd best freshen up while she had the chance.

Perching on the closed toilet lid, she peeled off her boots and socks, wriggling her toes and relishing the feel of the smooth floor under her bare feet, and then she cleaned the worst of the blood off with warm tap water and the antiseptic wipes. The stains on her skirt were the heaviest; that was where Seth had wiped the initial spurt of blood. Under her determined scrubbing they faded from dark red-black to a lighter reddish-grey, but despite her best efforts they refused to disappear.

She glared at the streaks on the damp material.

The stains didn't budge.

The wipes lifted the blood off her knee. Warm water washed away any faint residue. Her socks were more difficult; she filled the sink with water and a drop of strong soap and left them to soak. The boots were easiest. The blood came off the black leather without a murmur.

She took the opportunity to relieve herself, washing her hands and face before splashing hot soapy water up her arms to the elbows and up her legs to the knee. Who knew when she'd get another chance for a wash? It wasn't a good soak in the bath by any stretch of the imagination, but it would do.

The water in the slate sink had turned a dingy grey-brown. She pulled the plug and rescued her sopping socks, wringing them out with a section of the towel. They weren't dry enough to put back on yet, but time was pressing. She'd better go and see how Dave and Seth were getting on.

Addy picked up her boots in one hand and her socks in the other and slipped out into the hall. No screams of agony echoed from the living room. She made sure to cough before stepping through the open doorway.

Seth lay back on a couch with his eyes closed. The lines of pain around his eyes had eased, and he was breathing easier than he had been when she'd left. Dave must've given him something to help.

Dave was wrapping a clean bandage around the injured arm. He nodded at Addy as she came in, fixed the bandage in place, and sat back with a stretch and a small groan.

"All done," he said. "That was a deep scratch he gave himself, but it's stitched up now. It'll be fine."

Addy perched on the nearest seat. "I've been meaning to ask about that."

Dave waved for her to continue as he started cleaning up the supplies.

"It sounded like he used his blood to convince the train sensors that I was a ghost. How does that work?"

Seth answered from the couch without opening his eyes. "Blood covers a multitude of sins."

Another misquote. She wondered if he was capable of quoting anything accurately. "I still don't understand how blood tricked the sensors."

"Blood's the strongest conveyer of individual identity that we know of," said Dave. "By smearing his fresh blood onto you, he convinced the train sensors that you were part of him, in a sense. It was quick thinking—the sensors picked up on the freshness, the scent, and the ghost markings and came to a single, inaccurate conclusion."

"For which we are grateful," muttered Seth.

"Ghost markings?" asked Addy at the same time.

"The signs of him being a ghost," said Dave. "I can't explain it. They're just *there.* It's as obvious as you being a pilgrim."

Seth grunted, opened his eyes, and hauled himself upright. "We should be going. Thanks for your help, Dave."

"Already? You've only just got here."

"Sorry, mate. We're questing on a tight time frame."

Dave raised his eyebrows. "Ah. And so you came here, of course."

"I'll pop in for a visit when we get back. No strings attached. But for now . . ."

"You need supplies."

"Please."

"Alright." Dave snapped the medkit shut and stood. "You two rest here. I'll get your gear. What do you need?"

"One pack," said Seth. "Keep it small and light. Blankets, food, water. The basics. We're only planning to be gone a day. Two nights at the most."

"And you're headed—where?"

"The mountain."

Dave nodded. "Right. Back soon."

Seth sank back on the cushions and closed his eyes. Addy draped her damp socks over the arm of the sofa and curled into her corner, content to rest and keep an eye on Seth. He might be bandaged up now, but the pain had drained him, that much was clear.

Dave returned in ten minutes, carrying a clean shirt for Seth and a daypack made from dark, shiny material. "Waterproof and wind resistant," he said, placing it on the floor beside Seth. "All your supplies are in there. You should eat something before you leave. How does hot chicken and buttered bread rolls sound?"

"Lovely," Addy said. "Thank you."

They didn't linger over their food and were ready to leave within twenty minutes. Addy pulled on her dry socks and boots, Seth shouldered the pack without even a hint of discomfort from his injured arm, and they followed Dave downstairs to the shop door.

"You know where you're heading to leave the city?"

Seth nodded. "Left from here. We'll take the back alleys to the western gate."

"Thank you for the food," said Addy, "and the supplies."

"Good luck, pilgrim," Dave said as they stepped out into the dusk. "And Seth—be safe, yeah?"

"I will."

Already ten paces down the alley, Addy heard Dave snort before the shop door snapped shut. Seth ran a few steps to come abreast of her, and together they set a steady pace. Addy could keep up a ground-eating walk for hours. She assumed Seth could, too; his legs were longer than hers, after all.

Half an hour of winding through narrow lanes brought them to a door set in a stone wall that looked at least fifteen metres high. Seth unlatched the door and pulled it open; Addy slipped through, he followed, and the door closed behind them. A cramped passageway, well lit by ceiling squares, greeted them. The wall must have been nearly as thick as it was tall.

They reached the other end without any trouble. Seth pushed the far door open, stepped through, held it while Addy joined him, and then let it go.

The outer door closed with an emphatic *clang*. They were out of the city.

CHAPTER TEN

Before them the ground sloped away westward, covered in a dense carpet of short, hunter-green grass. A line of shadowed trees showed on the horizon. Was it the near side of a forest? Or it could be a sign of a river. A dusky sunset painted the sky in darkening shades of navy blue and pink; a boiling mass of low clouds was shot through with bright gold. The distance and the failing light were too great for her to see anything more.

Seth started off down the hill at a long-legged lope.

"Come on," he said over his shoulder. "We should reach the trees before we rest for the night."

She trotted to catch up with him. "We're resting tonight, then?"

"Of course we are."

"I thought we were on a tight schedule?"

"No use forcing ourselves on until we drop dead from exhaustion. Besides—" and here his voice turned so dry she couldn't tell if he was joking or not "—time doesn't pass if you don't perceive it passing, right?"

He looked at her and added, "We've got time enough to sleep tonight, love. Don't worry."

Hmph. "Maunga might be gone by the time we get there."

He gazed away for a moment and then shook his head, light glinting off his short hair. "She'll be there. She had business that'll occupy her for a long while yet."

The tight knot of worry in her gut eased at that scrap of news. "I thought that shot of stuff Taieri made was meant to keep me awake for a week."

"Exaggeration. It might do you two days in a pinch, but you wouldn't like the feeling when it caught up with you." He adjusted one strap of the pack. "Happy? You're running on eighty-five hours without proper sleep, and I've been awake since four o'clock this morning. We both need to rest."

So ghosts *did* need sleep, then. She'd wondered. Seth might be something other than human, but he still appeared to have human needs, for the most part. He ate normally, even if he only drank a little, and he certainly bled and felt pain as much as any human out there in the real world. He'd had a bed in his room, she remembered. Maybe it hadn't only been for show.

The air grew cooler as the light faded. Addy zipped Theo's green hoodie up and tugged the cuffs down over her knuckles. That was better. Seth seemed content to walk in near silence, and she was happy to store up her questions for later.

Night fell. Something twinkled far overhead, and she stopped, craning her head back to see it. Had she been mistaken? No—there. A glimmer of light in the deep velvet of the sky. A star, so small and remote that she had to squint to see it. Her breath caught in her throat. It was beautiful. Was this what the sky looked like every night above the city lights?

Another star appeared, brighter than the first, and then another, and another. Some were larger and some smaller, some pure white and some glinting with colour, some far away and some so close together they looked to be joined. They shone in their clusters and constellations, each with its own splendour and fire. Magnificent.

"We should keep moving, love," Seth murmured, coming back to stand beside her. "If you're done stargazing."

Addy swallowed, feeling an inexplicable urge to cry. "It's so beautiful."

"Stunning, I know. But we need to move. It's a fair way to the tree line, and we're too exposed out here."

Exposed to what? she wondered, but she didn't ask. She didn't think she wanted to know. There would be worse things out here than bottomless chasms and endless flights of stairs.

"I can take the pack for a bit if you want."

Seth shook his head. "It's okay. I'm fine. You can take it when we hit the trees. We've come too far south," he added, scanning the stars. "This way."

They set off once more, angling to the right, away from their previous trajectory. The moon, nearly a full circle, shone brightly. It was a stroke of luck—they could see the dips and bumps of the land clearly, and between the stars and the looming tree line, Seth was able to guide them straight without pause. But looking at their shadows streaming away across the grass, Addy thought she understood what he meant about being exposed. The world was washed in soundless silver-white, and she and Seth were the only things moving on the plain. She shivered.

The feeling grew. It wasn't so much a feeling that they were being watched, although that was part of it. Rather, it was a terrible certainty that something would happen at any moment now—something sudden, unforeseen, and inexplicable. It started like a barely-heard whisper of movement in another room and grew at the back of her mind until she could hear the slow tread of heavy footsteps in the hall, coming closer . . . closer . . .

She tried walking behind Seth so she could steal looks back over her shoulder at the increasing distance to the city wall, but her pace lagged, and she had to jog-trot to catch up with him.

She tried walking in front, scanning side to side, but she still found herself checking behind her.

The next time Seth saw her looking, he sighed, beckoned her closer, and held out a long strap from the unused waist belt of the pack. "No, I haven't vanished," he said. "Hold this while you walk, if you want. Maybe then you'll be able to stop making sure I'm still here every ten seconds."

She took the end of the strap without a word, and they fell

back to walking side by side a few paces apart. The contact helped; she gripped the belt hard, able to feel with a slight tug that Seth was still there and still moving.

The feeling of dreadful anticipation remained. It was like being poised on the edge of a cliff top, knees bent, muscles tensed, head tucked, one hand reaching for a parachute cord and not being able to move. Constantly on the verge, constantly expecting the drop—and constantly waiting.

It was unbearable.

An hour's hard walking brought them under the shadow of the trees. Addy was sure Seth breathed easier once they stepped out of the moonlight. She knew she did.

He shrugged out of the pack and held it out to her with a murmur of thanks. She took it, tightened the straps to better fit her small frame, slipped it on, and tightened the straps some more. *There. All set.*

"Are we resting here?" she asked quietly. "Or do you want to keep moving?"

Seth cast a long look through the outer trees to the silvered plain. "Are you tired?"

"Starting to feel it. But I could carry on for a while yet."

"I'd rather get as far as we can in the first push. We've a long way to go yet before we find the mountain trail. We'd be safe enough here, I think, but we'll be safer still if we can get further in and find a good tree to climb."

"Harder to navigate in here. Light's worse, and we can't see the stars."

"Easier to get lost." He turned away from the plain and frowned at the dark under the trees, and then nodded. "We won't go far. Just far enough to be safe."

It was easy going at first. The trees near the border were slender and set far apart, leaving wide patches of light-dappled ground for Addy and Seth to pick their way through, but soon the trees drew close as if to guard against unwanted intruders. They changed in texture, growing coarse and thick, and their foliage increased, blocking all but the merest sliver of light.

The dimness made it easy to trip on wayward roots or walk straight into a fallen log. Addy's exposed knees seemed to be a magnet for the clusters of thin, springy shoots that poked out of knotholes here and there, and more than once she had to stop and free the pack from the snare of a sharp twig. Seth narrowly avoided having an eye gouged out by an overhanging branch at head-height.

"Alright?" Addy asked, hearing the muttered profanity and seeing his shadow pause in front of her.

"It's bleeding a bit." He pressed a hand to his right eye and cheek. "My eyelid caught part of it. Nasty scratch down the cheekbone, from the feel of it."

"We can't do anything to treat it in this murk. When do you want to stop for the night?"

"Soon." His shadow dropped its hand and prepared to move again. "As soon as I find a good tree."

A short way along, he halted under the thickest tree they'd seen yet.

"I should warn you," Addy said through a yawn, "I've never climbed a tree in my life, so I'll be rubbish at it."

"I'll give you a leg up. Find something to hold with your hands, grip with your knees, and work your way up. I'll take the pack."

She passed the pack to him and noted the muscles moving under his borrowed shirt as he slipped his arms into the straps, the contained power when he crouched. He looked strong. She stepped into his cupped hands. He lifted her in a single smooth movement as if it were the easiest thing in the world to heft a sixteen-year-old wearing heavy boots into the air; but he was a dancer. Of course he'd have the muscles to lift a partner.

Her grasping hands found a wide branch and gripped tight. She got her shoulders over the edge, and then the support disappeared from under her foot. Her stomach dropped. She kicked air once, twice, found some momentum, and flung a leg over to sit astride the branch. Heart racing, she clung to the bough with knees and hands and arms, feeling as if she were going to slide off any second.

"That's it," said an encouraging voice from the next bough over. "Good job."

She kept her eyes clenched tight, turned her head, and snarled an obscenity—or at least she'd meant to snarl. It emerged as a whimper.

Seth laughed. "You're doing fine. We need to get a bit higher, though. Can't hang around down here all night."

She wasn't planning to *hang around* at all. She was just fine right here, thanks.

"Come on," said Seth. "Just a little higher and then we can sleep."

Ugh. Why did he have to make so much sense? She groaned and opened her eyes. Okay. She could do this.

It felt like it took forever. Seth kept up a flow of quiet encouragement supplemented with a helping hand in the worst spots. By the time she hauled herself onto the chosen bough, her arms felt as weak as a puddle of gloop. She didn't know how on earth she was going to get down. Fly, maybe. Or fall.

Yeah. Probably fall.

Beside her, Seth whistled. "Nice bed for the night."

From the bottom, it had looked like any other bough, albeit very wide, but the top was a different matter. Some force of nature had flattened it to a smooth pulp, forming a level surface two metres wide and perhaps three long. The side furthest from the trunk tapered to a point, merging seamlessly into a natural curve for the remainder of the branch—or as much of it as Addy could see in the darkness, which wasn't much.

"It's not natural, I don't think," he added.

She felt a stab of unease. "You think someone made it?"

"No. I think your mind is affecting your environment. It's not uncommon in these circumstances."

Oh. She settled with her back to the broad trunk and tried not to look over the side at the drop.

Seth opened the pack. "Hungry?"

"Tired. Let me see your face, and then we can sleep."

The light was better up here, nearer the moon. Seth produced a small medkit from the pack and sat silently as she tended the wound. The antiseptic had to hurt, but he made no reaction beyond a slight grimace.

"There." She pressed a narrow sticking plaster to the site. "It's not deep; I'd say you should be able to take the band-aid off tomorrow."

He nodded and handed her a blanket. "Thanks. Here. You might as well lie down; it'll be more comfortable. Don't worry about rolling off while you're asleep. I'll take the outside."

She was too tired to do more than glare half-heartedly at him for raising the possibility in the first place. She hadn't worried about it, but of course now that he'd mentioned rolling off into empty space, she couldn't stop thinking about it.

They settled widthwise on the branch, heads toward one edge and feet toward the other. Addy wrapped herself in her blanket and did her best to wedge herself into the gap between the trunk and Seth. Her scrunched-up hood made a poor pillow, but she was too tired to care. Seth breathed evenly beside her. The pack beneath his head rustled now and then.

Out in the darkness, something shrieked. Heart in her throat, she darted a look around, trying not to move too much in case it spotted her. On the other side of their tree, she heard a scraping noise and then a swish of movement.

Was it her imagination, or was that a pair of eyes glowing faintly a few trees over?

Addy worked saliva into her mouth. "Seth," she whispered.

No answer.

"Seth."

Silence. He must be asleep already.

The eyes had vanished. No—there they were, high up and far to the left of where they had been.

Watching her.

The swishing noise came again.

And then another shriek. She jumped.

Swish.

Rustle.

Swish.

Scraaaaaape.

CHAPTER ELEVEN

She woke to a hand on her shoulder. Seth crouched by her head; as she stared blearily up at him, he held a finger to his lips and nodded at something behind her line of sight.

She rolled over and eased to her knees before following his gaze.

Oh.

The sky above them was lighter than it had been before. It must be near dawn. Skeletons of tree branches stood out black against the grey light, dipping into thicker shadow where their leaves grew.

It was all background noise to the thing Seth had pointed out.

On a tree perhaps ten metres distant, an uneven ring of blue-white flame licked its way up the trunk. It didn't seem to scorch the bark, nor did it take hold and leave a raging fire burning in its wake. Where it passed, coarse bark vanished in a thin vapour of smoke, replaced by a smooth peel. Overgrown vines burned away, leaving new buds. One whole branch withered into nothingness, while another was taken back almost to the trunk, green as a new shoot.

It was ethereal, and breathtaking, and . . . unreal.

"What is it?" she whispered.

"Saint Juvee's Fire." Seth's eyes gleamed. "Blueburner. The Renewer's Flame." He reached for the pack and stuffed the blankets into it, hardly looking at what his hands were doing. "We need to go."

"What about breakfast?"

"Later. It's coming this way. Trust me, we don't want to be here when it reaches this branch."

The flame crawled up to the crown of the tree. She watched, fascinated, as it spread along the topmost branch, cleansing and stripping as it went. A tiny bud of a flower, white with a hint of green in its centre, sprang up on the last centimetre of slender twig. The fire came to the end and dropped onto the bough below it, a branch or two above their heads.

She had a vision of what might happen if they were still on this bough when the flame came along it. Her mouth went dry. "Right. Yes. Moving."

Climbing down was easier than climbing up had been. The improved light helped their speed, as did the glances upward to the flicker of advancing Blueburner. There was no time for talking, and no breath for it either. Addy reached the lower branches and jumped the last two metres to the ground, bending her knees to absorb the worst of the impact. It still hurt.

Seth joined her a moment later.

"This way," he said, striking off into the trees.

Every direction looked the same to Addy. She supposed he knew where he was going. She followed.

They'd walked maybe twenty metres when Seth changed course. Addy was about to ask if he'd come the wrong way when she saw a glimmer of Saint Juvee's Fire high up in a tree ahead of them. Of course. There wouldn't just be one lone flame taking care of the whole forest; they probably hunted in packs or something.

She veered left without a word.

They zig-zagged a dozen times in the next half hour, by the end of which Seth was scowling and muttering deprecations under his breath.

"Is there a problem?" Addy asked, munching on an apple as she walked.

Seth waved a hand. "Yes and no. As near as I can work out, there's a line of them working either side of us."

"I figured that, too."

"I'm trying to cut a path as straight as possible through the middle of them, but it's impossible in this jungle. We're going to be way too far north when we reach the river."

So there was a river hidden in the trees somewhere. "Does it matter?"

"There's only one bridge across the gorge, and somehow I don't think you'd fancy a thirty-metre drop off a sheer cliff into the rapids."

"Can't we get out the other side before we worry about finding the bridge? It'll be faster moving once we're out of the trees."

"Sheer cliffs," he repeated. "The forest runs right up to the cliff edge. It did on the map, at least. So there's no clear ground for us to walk along."

"But the trees should be further apart. If they're anything like the ones on the side we came in on, I mean."

Seth considered that for a moment. "It's possible. We'll keep moving, anyway. We might be able to find a break in the line to the south and get back on track."

But they didn't. In fact, the lines of Blueburner seemed determined to force them as far north as possible. Their northern zigs grew ever longer, and their southern zags grew shorter. The trees sporting blue-white flame grew more numerous.

What would happen if the lines decided to join up ahead of them? She and Seth couldn't go back; they didn't have time. Even their current northwesterly direction was better than backtracking east. If they were hemmed in by the fires, they could try to make a break for it through the line, but she didn't like their chances. The Renewer's Fire seemed to burn fast and slow with no logic to its rhythm. The line would catch them out, and she had no doubt it would be blisteringly hot to touch.

The fires, now in almost every tree on both sides of them, marked an avenue that ran unnaturally straight toward the northwest.

"Too far north," Seth muttered. "Nothing we can do about it now. Just keep moving."

They sped up again, moving at a fast jog down the lane. It was an awkward, dangerous business. They veered around trees and ducked low-hanging branches. The undergrowth lay thick and tangled, and more than once Addy almost turned her ankle when the ground dipped or rose unexpectedly beneath the shrubbery.

The lines drew closer as if they were intending to merge into one. No time for thought. Addy's mouth was dry. Her lungs protested each breath. How long had they been moving? She didn't know. Surely the sun was well up by now. The air felt warm, stifling even. And then her heart sank.

To their left, the southern line of fires curved northward to cut off their escape.

Seth saw it, too. He growled an oath and increased his pace.

The flames were now a bare five metres to either side of them. The crackling of Blueburner grew louder. The heat became unbearable. The air itself still looked clean enough; the fires made surprisingly little smoke.

Not that it mattered. They wouldn't have time to die of smoke inhalation, not once the flames caught them.

"We won't make it," Addy said, panting.

"Just keep moving."

What good would that do? They were cut off, now. The line ahead of them closed in, and they faltered to a stop.

The bubble of untouched trees grew smaller as the flames drew in, hungry for old wood. In another minute, fires would be burning in every tree around them.

"Seth . . ." She trailed off into a hacking cough. What was there to say? They would have to make a run for it—or die trying.

Bitter despair rose in her. She hadn't come this far to fail before they even reached Maunga. A dreadful thought occurred, and her stomach clenched in fear. She wouldn't die, they'd made that clear, but she didn't know about Seth. Could ghosts die? Would he die here on this doomed quest, far away from his friends, far away from any help?

Seth started and pointed. "There!"

Ahead and to their right, a single fire flickered and died. The light beside it went out a second later, and then another light behind that. They took off without another word, sprinting for the slim gap. Addy's heart leapt in her throat. Would they make it? It was a chance, if only the barest one, but it was more than they'd had a second ago.

They darted through the hole in the first line. More flames flickered and went out ahead of them, drawing back with as much precision as they'd closed in with. A narrow lane opened up, blue fire burning on either side for fifty metres.

They raced along it, heedless of the scratches and scrapes the branches were inflicting. Addy stumbled and crashed to her knees; her ankle rolled painfully under her, and then Seth lifted her to her feet and urged her on, half-shoving her forward with a hand at her back.

The flames came to an end as the trees opened up, letting more light filter down to the forest floor. Addy slowed and let Seth take the lead. She risked a glance behind her. The lane they had escaped down was filling with fire again; the wall of Blueburner flickered, still advancing northward but slower now. They would have to keep moving, but it looked like the worst of the danger was behind them.

"Addy!" Seth called over his shoulder. "Come on!" He was thirty metres ahead and gaining distance with every stride.

She jogged to catch up with him, her ankle smarting. Seth's pack bumped up and down on his back as he jumped a fallen log; she stepped over the branch and fell in beside him, glad that the trees grew less densely here and they could walk side by side for the most part.

Curiosity prodded her. "Why do you think they did that?"

He didn't answer.

"Seth?"

"What?" He shook his head and looked across at her. "Sorry. I was thinking. What did you say?"

"Why do you think they did that?"

"Opened up that escape route for us, you mean?"

She nodded.

"Blowed if I know. Maybe they don't like burning pilgrims alive."

"Or ghosts."

"Or ghosts."

They veered around a tree in their path, Addy to the left and Seth to the right, and came together again on the far side of it, past a clump of overgrown ferns.

"I've never heard that Saint Juvee's Fire is sentient," Seth said, "but they seemed to have some sort of, I don't know, agenda. Or objective."

"They did seem to be railroading us."

"Herding. Like a bunch of shepherds with a couple of recalcitrant sheep." He saw her expression and waved a hand dismissively. "I've spent a fair bit of time around farmers since I've been here. But no, I don't know why they let us go. It's possible they didn't even mean to."

He didn't sound convinced.

She glanced back and saw the faint glimmer of fire through the trees, now far behind them. "I don't think they care. They're so . . ." She groped for the right words. "They're so far beyond us, beyond anything pilgrim or ghost or human. They feel . . . otherworldly. Fey, you might say. Above caring about a couple of travellers in their realm—if they even noticed us. But I think they did. They might not be sentient, but they're not . . . *not* sentient either." She grimaced. "If that makes any sense."

"No," he said. "No sense at all. But I think I know what you mean."

They walked in silence for a few minutes, and then Seth ducked around an outthrust branch and chuckled.

"What is it?"

"Otherworldly." He grinned. "They're so otherworldly, they're even beyond ghosts. That's *very* otherworldly, love."

An answering smile tugged at her mouth. "You know what I mean." She'd grown so used to ghosts being virtual clones, she'd almost forgotten the more usual meaning of the word.

"I do. But that doesn't mean it wasn't funny."

The foliage above them thinned out. Dappled sunlight fell in dancing spots to the ground. They must be getting near the outskirts, Addy thought. Once they found the border, she doubted they'd pause for a break. She needed a rest.

"Can we stop for a bit?"

Seth slowed and looked at her. Her ankle chose that moment to send a stabbing pain up her shin. "You're hurt," he said.

"Rolled my ankle when I went down earlier. It's not broken, but I wouldn't mind some strapping tape."

They settled at the base of a nearby tree. He unslung his pack and retrieved the medkit while Addy unlaced her boot and pulled it off, trying not to jar her ankle more than she had to. She was sweating by the time she set the boot aside and tugged her sock off.

Seth lifted her ankle in his gentle hands and probed it. "Feels a bit swollen, and it looks pretty red. Not terribly bruised, though. How's it feeling?"

"Hurts," she muttered through clenched teeth. Every little movement sent sparks of fire shooting through her nerves.

"Do you want something for the pain?"

"Please."

By some miracle she managed to swallow the pills on her first attempt; grimacing at the taste, she chased them down with gulps of water. That was better. "Thanks."

"No worries," said Seth, busy massaging balm into the damaged tissue. He reached for the wrapping tape and lifted her foot again. "Can you hold it there?"

She propped her left leg on her right calf, putting the injured foot at about the level he'd requested.

"Perfect." He wrapped it around the ankle, down under the heel, over the arch, and on and around again until he came to the end of the roll, where he secured it. The splint segments activated, glowing white through the tape. "Try that."

Addy flexed her foot experimentally. It was braced well enough. The support would do wonders for helping her walk, and it remained flexible enough for comfort. "That's good."

"I can throw some heat on it if you'd like. Or some cold."

The day wasn't very hot, and warmth was tempting, but cold would be better for getting the swelling down. "Cold, please."

He tweaked the strapping around her heel, and she yelped. It felt like he'd poured a bucket of ice onto her foot. She jerked away from him, but he held fast.

"Cold!" she gasped. "Too cold!"

Another tweak, and the cold mellowed to a temperature that was still crisp but more manageable.

"Better." She caught her breath. "Thanks."

"Your knees look a bit banged up. Do you want me to . . . ?"

"I can do them. You've got your own scrapes to fix up."

Seth nodded and passed her a tub of antiseptic paste. They tended the rest of their wounds in companionable silence and took time for a drink and bite to eat before getting ready to move on.

"Where are we heading?" Addy asked, standing and shouldering the pack. "Keep on as we were, do you reckon?"

Seth looked back the way they'd come and then around at the open forest. "I'd rather head as near west as we can from here. We shouldn't have much trouble; there's no Blueburner here to flank us, and the trees aren't hemming us in anymore."

They set off due west, or as near due west as Seth could estimate. As it turned out, they didn't have far to go—fifteen minutes' walking brought them to the edge of the trees.

"Well." Addy gazed down the sheer cliff to the roaring river below. "We can't go any further west at the moment."

Seth said nothing.

"I guess we go south," she ventured after a minute. "To the bridge."

"It would take too long." His eyes rose to stare at the far side of the gorge.

"So we go north, then?"

He grunted a negative. "There's nothing there."

With a heroic effort, she refrained from rolling her eyes. "I see. So we turn back until we run into the wall of Saint Juvee's Fire, is that it?"

"Don't be daft."

"We could climb down the cliff and swim across the river," she went on, trying not to smile as her sense of the ridiculous overcame her irritation, "or fly over it from up here. Everyone knows kiwis are excellent flyers."

He grunted again.

She sidled closer to him and said in a stage whisper, "Hate to break it to you, mate, but kiwis can't fly."

That broke Seth from his reverie. "You know our Air Force logo is a kiwi, right?"

"Is it?" she said, intrigued. "Can't say I'd ever noticed."

"Black kiwi on a silver circle with black trim. Ironic, eh?"

"Using a flightless bird as the logo for our flying defence force?" Addy laughed. "That's fantastic."

He rubbed a hand across his stubbled jaw. "Now that I've shot down all your ideas . . . where do you think we should go?"

"North. Because we can't fly, swim, or go back, and going south would take too long, according to you. North seems to be the only option. And taking into account that my mind is probably still influencing the environment to some extent, who knows? We might stumble across something that isn't on the map."

Seth twitched an eyebrow. She read the thought clearly as it passed across his face: *Yeah, we might stumble across something more dangerous than that Blueburner.*

But he said nothing beyond, "Alright. North it is."

"If you don't want to . . ."

"No, it's fine." He smiled. "It's your decision. You chose north, so we'll go north. I've led us this far, but if your mind is still affecting the environment, it makes more sense for you to take the lead."

She tilted her head. "Your mind doesn't?"

"Ghost," he said, tapping his chest. "It's a privilege only given to pilgrims. I haven't had that luxury in years."

The luxury of influencing his environment? Or the luxury of being a pilgrim? Both, she reckoned.

She struck north, keeping a stone's throw from the edge of the cliff.

It would be a lonely life here, being a ghost. What had Seth said? Thirty-six of them in play at any one time but only in groups of two or three. They wouldn't get to know many people. The pilgrims would take up most of their attention, and pilgrims were like ghosts to the ghosts in the system—here for three hours and then gone forever.

It was a sobering thought.

Seth seemed to know Taieri well, though. Maybe because they both worked at the same place. She supposed there were times when they could spend all session talking while the nearest pilgrims drank themselves into a stupor. And they roamed free in the time between sessions; she'd read that in the manual. It explained how he knew Dave so well.

But the ghosts were forced to sleep for long periods if they weren't needed for a few consecutive sessions. It made sense, she had to admit. Only thirty-six ghosts per session, and there had to be . . . help . . . ten times that number alive? A hundred times? She didn't know. A virtual world this size must take a staggering amount of resources to run.

That would be horrible—going to sleep one night and waking up weeks later, knowing you were only awake because you could be of some use to the next session. She doubted Breach saw them as individuals. They wouldn't be 'Seth' and 'Taieri,' they'd be 'male club dancer number one' and 'busty barkeep number two.'

They weren't people with names and faces. They were numbers. Occupations. Utilities.

Just thinking about it made her sick.

Beside her, Seth made an involuntary noise in the back of his throat. "Look," he breathed, sounding as if he hardly believed his eyes. "It's the bridge."

The forest had been cleared of trees and undergrowth in a fifty-metre radius before them. Bright sunlight slanted down from the north, warming the air and setting Addy's skin tingling with welcome heat. Stone pavers began halfway across the grass and led to the middle point of the cliff edge where a slender stone bridge leaped the chasm in one graceful arch, heedless of the water racing through the gorge far below.

"Would you look at that," Addy said. "It's a bridge."

"Except it's not. It's not just *a* bridge. It's *the* bridge. There's only one bridge, and it should be about three hours south of us by now. But it's not; it's here."

"Maybe it just looks like that bridge? Or maybe all bridges look the same?"

He shook his head, stepped around her to get at a side pocket of the pack, and retrieved the palm-sized map projector. "No. Look."

He set the capsule on the grass and activated it. "Here's the river, running down this side. The bridge is here." He pointed to the holographic bridge spanning the river. "But," he continued, running a forefinger north up the river as far the map would move, and then back down it again as far south as possible, "there are no other bridges either north or south. At all. The map isn't out of date—it's updated live from Breach's records of the current session. It *can't* be out of date."

"That's literally the only bridge?"

"Yes. That's what I've been saying. There is only one bridge across that river, and–" he broke off, frowning perplexedly across the clearing, "—and that isn't it. It can't be."

Addy scratched her collarbone. "That can't be the bridge, but at the same time, it must be. That's a bridge, and it goes across the river, and there's only one bridge across the river."

"But it's in the wrong place."

"Unless it's not." She remembered the stairs at the mansion, endless flights and landings all looping around, leading to more flights and landings. Maybe this was more of the same. They'd come so far, they'd looped back to the start. "Maybe it's the same bridge."

"How could it be? We were meant to head due west through the forest to reach it. We're about ten kilometres to the north of where we should be."

"Maybe," she said, weighing each word before she let it fall, "we've come so far north that we're approaching the same bridge from the south. Maybe it's a loop."

"We—what?" He stared at her. "We're too far north, so we're actually south?"

"It's like the north pole." The more she thought about it, the more sense it made. "You can only go so far north, right? Eventually, you pass the pole and roll over onto the other side, so to speak. When you do that, you're facing south, because north is behind you, even though you haven't changed physical direction."

The frown cleared from his face. "Huh. I guess that works."

"It's the same bridge. We're just coming at it from the south instead of the north."

Seth nodded. "It's a better theory than none. Let's go and have a look at it, shall we?"

He retrieved the map capsule and tucked it back into the pack, and they advanced across the clearing to the paved area at the near side of the bridge.

Addy stamped on the stone pavers. They seemed solid. She touched a hand to a corner post, the dark stone rough-cut and coarse, and trailed a finger across the gritty grouting to the next block of stone. It felt real enough. There was no danger of falling over the side—waist-high walls ran along the sides of the bridge.

"Seems safe enough," said Seth from where he examined the opposite wall.

"It didn't vanish as soon as I touched it," Addy said. "So there's that." She took a cautious step up onto the arch of the bridge, poised to leap back to solid ground if she had to. Nothing happened. She relaxed. "It's fine."

They climbed to the apex together. At first muted and distant, the noise of the rapids below them swelled to a roar as they came to the middle of the bridge and then faded again as they descended the other side. In a matter of minutes, they stood on the far side. The paving formed a narrow path that dipped and curved through the trees ahead.

Seth waved for her to go in front. "You can lead."

She slipped in front without comment. If she asked, no doubt he'd just say something about *your mind influencing your environment.* It wasn't worth the words.

The path took them on a winding route westward through native bush. Half an hour's walk brought them to the edge of the trees and to a wide road that ran perpendicular to their current course. On the other side of the road, the ground rose in gentle bumps and swells to a line of green-brown hills; beyond them, nearer than she would have guessed, snow-speckled mountains stood out in jagged peaks and ridges against the skyline.

She turned right instinctively, uphill and to the north. Seth came alongside her, plucked a water bottle from an outside strap of the pack, and gulped a few mouthfuls before passing it over. It was warmer here out of the shadow of the trees. She nodded her thanks and drank.

They set a good pace. Soon the road dipped before curving to the west and rising in a set of long, switchbacking curves. Addy kept her head down and her eyes on the road as she trudged up the hill. Her feet sweltered in the leather boots; each step seemed heavier than the last. By the time she crested the brow, she was ready to shrug out of Theo's green hoodie and tie it around her waist.

Before her, the road ran level for a hundred metres before winding uphill to the right and vanishing. It appeared again on the next hill over, a narrow scar running at an angle from right to left. Another section snaked through a scattering of trees along the ridge.

Seth appeared in her peripheral vision. He carried his red jacket over one shoulder; the clean shirt Dave had lent him was damp with perspiration. She held out the water bottle.

"Further up and further in, d'you reckon?"

He nodded and held out a hand for the pack. "I can take it from here."

They started off again. Addy felt lighter and freer without the weight of the pack, and she found herself whistling. The weather grew colder as they climbed. When they made it to the ridge of the third hill and slipped in under the shadow of the trees, she untied her hoodie and shrugged it back on.

Seth called a halt twenty minutes later. He pulled his jacket on, they wolfed a handful of scroggin each, and after a short breather they went on.

The land rose steeply. The road rose with it, throwing out great loops that took them ever upward. The trees grew dense and lean, spindly roots like ageing fingers reaching out to grasp any hand-hold in the rocky soil. The silence was oppressive, but Addy had no breath left to break it. Her thighs burned. Her breath steamed in the cool air. She plodded on, trying not to think about how much further they might have to go.

The sun had long since passed its zenith. How much daylight did they have left? Two hours? Three? Seth had said they would reach their destination before dark, but it occurred to her now that he hadn't said how long before dark.

A short way past the next turn, she saw the first smatterings of snow in the shaded hollows beside the track.

"Good," said Seth when she pointed them out. He looked as tired as she felt. "We're nearly there."

"Nearly where?"

"There's a cave. Up there." He waved a hand along the track. "Not far above the snow line."

"And that's where Maunga is?"

He nodded. "It's a common destination for questers. Doesn't usually take this long to get to, though. Depends on your headspace."

Three switchbacking turns later, she could see up the path to where it vanished over a lip.

"Getting close." Seth gave her a gentle push. "Close to the cave." And then, so quietly she wasn't sure he was talking to her, "Close to the truth."

"Question is," said Addy, shivering as a gust of frozen air swept over them, "is truth the cave on the mountainside, or is truth coming out of the cave to see the world with fresh eyes? I've heard it both ways."

"Neither. The truth is the person inside the cave." They trudged for a minute or two in silence. "Funny that."

"What?"

"You, wanting me to take you to Maunga."

They crested the last bend of the track and stood panting on a snow-dusted plateau. Perhaps twenty metres away, craggy walls rose to shelter the bay. A vast arch had been hewn into the rock, leading into the mountain. Shadows danced with the sunlight at the edge of the cave, but within it lay inscrutable darkness.

"Oh?" she asked once she'd gotten her breath back. "Why's that?"

Something stirred in the shadows, and a voice said, "Because I wanted the same thing."

Maunga Richards stepped out onto the mountainside.

CHAPTER TWELVE

Addy stood frozen as Seth moved forward to greet Maunga.

What? She had asked Seth to take her to Maunga. But Seth had also volunteered—she remembered that clearly. "I should come with you," he'd said. "You don't know the way to the mountain. I do. I can get us there faster. And I'm curious . . . if Maunga knows more than she's letting on, I'd like to be there when you find out."

Of course Maunga knew more than she was letting on. And Seth had known it, too.

Bring Addy to the mountain, Maunga had said.

Take me to Maunga, Addy had said.

Seth had delivered on both promises in one clever move.

She felt sick. He had played her, and she'd played right into Maunga's hands.

Maunga and Seth met halfway across the plateau.

"Hello, love," said Seth, and kissed her.

Oh. Addy's stomach twisted. That explained a lot.

"You're alright?" Maunga asked once they'd finished. Her black hair was tied back in a dutch braid so thick it almost looked like a mohawk jutting from her head. Addy felt a pang of envy as she took in the rest of her outfit. A black leather jacket draped open over a yellow shirt. Black jeans. Yellow canvas shoes. Even in the freezing cold on a snowy mountain, Maunga looked effortlessly street-styled.

The yellow was a surprise. For some reason, she'd been expecting red. And who wore canvas shoes for climbing a mountain? They must be waterproofed. Addy stuck her hands in her pockets and huddled deeper into Theo's oversized hoodie.

Eyes soft, Seth brushed a loose strand of hair back from Maunga's face and nodded. "Fine. We've got a few bruises, and Addy twisted her ankle, but it's nothing life-threatening."

No wonder he'd looked so bleak back at the pub when Addy had told him that Maunga stole her voice. No man wanted to believe his girlfriend capable of something like that. It would be like finding out that Theo or one of her parents had done something unforgivable. The thought was both ludicrous and sickening.

Maunga looked from Seth to Addy, her expression hard to interpret. She turned back to the cave. "You'd better come inside."

Seth slid a half-guilty glance at Addy and went with Maunga.

The thought of turning and leaving crossed Addy's mind, but it was no more than a thought. Where would she go? And if she went, how would she find out what she'd come all this way to know? Better to stay. At least she knew not to trust them—either of them—now.

She followed them blindly. The arch led through a short tunnel to a vast, echoing space, lit with lanterns hidden in the tops of the many ornate pillars. Maunga muttered something to Seth about *terrible acoustics.* They crossed the space at a diagonal, slipped through a narrow doorway, and wound along a corridor and down several flights of stairs to a dry cellar. The room was small, walled with stone, and ringed with cushioned benches. Addy thought it looked like the most comfortable thing she'd seen in a long time.

Again, it wasn't what she'd been expecting. She'd rather thought they were heading for a dramatic throne room, all sharp angles and polished floors, where Maunga could lounge in villainous authority while she laid bare her plans for, say, world domination, but seeing Maunga here, Addy had to admit that the closeness and earthiness of the room suited her in a strange way.

Maunga activated the wall lamps, throwing a golden glow over the space. Seth stripped off his red jacket and sank into the curve of the cushioned bench with a long sigh. Seeing Maunga take a seat beside him, Addy crossed the floor and sat opposite the door.

"Are you hungry?" Maunga bent down to retrieve a container of what looked like cheese scones from the locker under the bench.

"Starved," said Seth. "Ta."

Maunga passed him one before crossing to stand in front of Addy. "Hungry?"

Addy stared at her. Why was Maunga offering her food? Shouldn't she be gloating over her master plan by now? A hundred questions lined up on the tip of her tongue, but the one that emerged first was, "Why am I here?"

The container lowered to a spot just in front of her nose.

"Because I need your help," Maunga said. "Now are you hungry or not?"

Addy took a scone and was surprised to find it warm. The container must've had a heating seal on it. "Thanks," she murmured, trying not to look too puzzled.

Clearly she failed because Maunga smirked and went back to her seat. They ate in silence and went back for seconds and then thirds, still in silence. It was tricky to talk when your mouth was full. A ravenous stomach was more important than discussion anyway, Addy thought. Words would wait. Food wouldn't.

She polished off her last scone and curled into the cushions, waiting for whatever came next. Seth was still eating, washing down his crumbs with a bottle of water. Maunga examined him with sharp eyes.

"What happened to your head?" Maunga asked after another minute.

Seth swallowed his mouthful. "Got tangled in some twigs climbing down a tree."

"And your cheek?"

"Overhanging branch. Ran into it in the dark." The band-aid had long since fallen off, and the scratch along his cheekbone was hardly more than a sliver of pale tissue.

"Your shirt?"

Seth looked down and raised his eyebrows at the hole near the neckline of his shirt. "Hadn't noticed that. Don't know. Must have caught it on something."

Maunga's tone sharpened. "What about your arm?" She reached for the bandaged forearm, fingers curling as if she wanted to unwrap it and see the damage for herself.

"Don't. It's stasis sealed. I'll visit Dave on my way back through the city and get him to give it a final check. He thought it would be alright. No lasting damage."

"What happened?"

"Had to convince a train that she was a ghost." He nodded at Addy. "Gouged my arm on the rim of a seat and wiped the blood on her. It did the trick."

Maunga darted Addy a glance that held equal parts amusement and mockery. "Oh, so you're a ghost now? I see."

Seth drained his water and set the empty bottle on the floor. "Anything else you'd like to know about? Or would you be satisfied with a summation, to wit, our various cuts and bruises are from running through a forest, both before and after we saw the Blueburner."

"You saw Saint Juvee's Fire?"

"We did."

A sneaking smile spread across Maunga's face, slowly, as if the muscles weren't used to the movement being genuine. Addy stared for a long minute, amazed at the change; she looked softer and younger and . . .

And, she realised as Seth pulled Maunga closer and buried his nose in her hair, very much in love.

She jerked her gaze away, feeling a flush of heat rise in her cheeks. Who would have thought? Maunga was so hard and cold. But she couldn't rid herself of the idea now, and sitting here watching them felt like an unforgivable breach of privacy.

"I suppose I'll take your word for it," Maunga said with a put-upon sigh. The smile peeped out again. "As long as you're sure you're not hurt anywhere else."

"I'm sure," Seth said.

"And you?"

It took Addy a moment to realise Maunga was talking to her. Reflex took her tongue. "I'm sorry, what?"

"Are you hurt?"

"Uh." She paused and took stock. "A bit scraped up, and my ankle's had better days, but that's about all, I think." She tried not to let her confusion show. This was possibly the oddest place she'd been in yet; mismatched stairs and gravity flips were one thing, but Maunga Richards enquiring about her health was another thing altogether.

Maunga sat forward, dark eyes intent. "I was sorry to hear about your brother."

The confusion vanished. Rage stole Addy's breath. She *dared*—! She dared to express sympathy for Addy, sympathy for *Theo?* It was her fault Addy had lost her voice in the first place! She couldn't be serious. She meant it as an insult, surely. There was no way that Maunga Richards could express sympathy for anyone and mean it, let alone sympathy for the brother of the girl whose voice she stole.

Maunga must have seen the fire in her eyes. She raised a placating hand. "No, don't get all huffy. I'm serious."

"You're serious." Addy choked on the words. "And you think you're allowed to be serious? You think you're allowed to say you're *sorry* for what happened to Theo?"

"Yes."

"You have no right—"

"I have as much right as the next human being. Although seeing as the next human being is Seth and he's a ghost, well . . ." She shrugged.

"She does mean it, Addy," Seth said.

"I am sorry about Theo," Maunga said. "And I'm serious about having as much right as anyone else to express that."

Addy gripped her knees with her hands in an effort to stop them from shaking. "You think that—"

"Yes." Maunga's voice held a bite of impatience. "I had nothing to do with him losing his voice. I barely knew him. Saw him around uni a couple of times and talked to him once in passing, but that was about it. He's a tall guy with curly hair who wears green a lot, yeah?"

Addy nodded.

"Thought so. Jirah Jenkins introduced us once at a party—at least, I think he did. It was a big party. Theo was wearing a green shirt, I remember that 'cause Ganner had spilled a beer on him and they were trying to wipe it up with a handful of paper towels. I met a lot of people that night. Hardly remember any of them."

Seth cleared his throat. "Speaking of people losing their voices. We need to have a talk about that."

"That?"

He held Maunga's gaze for a long moment before tipping his head toward Addy. "That."

"Oh," Maunga said. A muscle twitched in her jaw. She nodded. "That. Sure. In a minute?"

Seth nodded and stood. "No worries. I need to find a bathroom. Back soon."

"Down the hall to your left."

The door closed, leaving Addy alone with Maunga.

"Point is," Maunga continued as if the tangent with Seth had never happened, "I can express my sympathies for the situation the same as anyone who didn't steal his voice can. Actually—" She broke off, thought for a long minute, and then continued. "No, strike that. I can express my sympathies same as anyone can, no matter the situation. Even if I had stolen his voice—which I didn't, okay, so you can stop glaring at me like that—even if I had, I could still express genuine apology for what happened to him. Sympathy is a basic human right."

"So is freedom of expression," said Addy. Angry tears welled in her eyes; she blinked them away. "So is having a voice. And you didn't seem to care about *that* three years ago."

Maunga looked away, turning the movement almost into an eye-roll. "Can we save that discussion until Seth gets back? I'd rather not have to explain myself twice."

"What is there to explain?"

"It's not—"

"You stole my voice!" Addy spoke over the top of her—and wasn't that a heady feeling, being able to shout someone down. "You stole my voice, and now you think you can express sympathy for the same thing happening to Theo because, why, you weren't personally involved this time? Is that it?"

This time Maunga did roll her eyes. "It's not that simple."

"Really."

"Yes, really." Maunga paused as the door opened and Seth slipped back into the room, and then she continued. "It's not even half that simple, and if you think it is, you're a moron."

"Explain it to me, then. To us." She gestured to Seth, who had taken his old seat next to Maunga. "Why is you stealing my voice *not that simple?*"

Maunga rubbed a hand across her face, looking tired. "Look, I didn't want to."

"Doesn't matter," Addy said. "Whether you wanted to or not, you still did it. Intent has no bearing on the case."

"Actually—" Seth started.

Maunga held up a hand. "Let me explain it. Please."

"Alright."

"I didn't want to do it. But I had to. I was . . . approached . . . and told that if I didn't, then . . ." She trailed off, looking at Seth. Something indefinable passed between them, and then she went on. "She wanted more people infected. Said that she'd give me a month, and if I hadn't infected at least one person, she'd do it to me."

"Do what?" Addy asked.

"She'd take your voice," Seth said. The hard look in his eyes melted away; he sat as if stunned. "She said that? She blackmailed you with that, after—" He broke off, closing his eyes as if something pained him. "After everything?"

"Yeah," said Maunga. "About two weeks after *everything.*" The corner of her mouth curled in a bitter smile. "I wasn't in any sort of state to refuse, not with that hanging over my head."

Seth slid an arm around her waist. "I'm sorry."

"It's not your fault."

His gaze dropped. He didn't reply.

Maunga turned on him with fire in her eyes. "It's not. Your. Fault. We've been over this, Seth."

Addy looked between them, not understanding. Why did Seth think it was his fault? Had his original known Maunga then? Could he have stopped it? Did he know who had blackmailed her? She shifted in her seat. "Did Seth know you? His original, I mean? Back then?"

Seth barked a mirthless laugh. "They were going out."

"We," Maunga corrected.

"They. We." He rubbed his temple, wincing. "Were going out. Yes."

"Had been for a while," Maunga said. "I'd had my sixteenth birthday not long before, and we started dating a week before my fifteenth."

Addy raised her eyebrows. A thought occurred to her, and she choked back a laugh. So Maunga *had* been messaging her boyfriend that day in the tutoring session. Who'd have thought? It was such a strange idea; even when she was sitting here, seeing them interact, it was a strange idea. No wonder it had been unthinkable at the time.

"So you," she said to Seth, "or, uh, he? Your original—you think he could have stopped Maunga from being blackmailed?"

"Maybe. I don't know."

"He wasn't around by then," Maunga said, her voice hard. She shrugged. "We drifted apart. He dropped off the radar about two weeks after my sixteenth. And then I bumped into Seth the first time I came here, and we hit it off again." She frowned. "I can't decide if it's more like dating him or his identical twin."

"Both." Seth grinned. "I've said it before: I am him, but I'm also me."

Addy scratched her collarbone, trying to make sense of it all. Maunga had been involved with the original Seth for more than a year. They drifted apart and broke it off and then Maunga had somehow been blackmailed into stealing Addy's voice. Had they used Seth as leverage? Threatening Seth would be more effective than threatening Maunga if she still cared for him, wouldn't it?

"You stole my voice because if you didn't, they would have stolen yours?"

"Yeah."

But it didn't feel right. "They didn't threaten to steal Seth's?"

"No." Maunga lifted her chin. "I told you, he wasn't on the scene then. It was quite enough to threaten me with losing my voice. I'd seen what it had done to other people. Didn't want it happening to me."

Something still didn't add up. "But—"

Maunga interrupted. "You know what your problem is, kid?"

"What?"

"You're too keeking selfless, and you think everyone else is, too. Stop looking for an ulterior motive here, okay? There isn't one. I stole your voice because I didn't want them to steal mine. It's as simple and as selfish as that. I had to steal someone's voice, and you were there, and we had a few minutes spare. And once I'd done it the first time," she added, "all she had to do was remind me the threat was still there, and I'd do whatever she wanted."

The words stung. Addy blinked and sat back. "Okay," she muttered. *Whatever.* She hadn't thought she was all that selfless, but she supposed, compared to Maunga, anyone would be. The hungriest man-eating deep-sea monster, all instinct and teeth, was probably an angel compared to Maunga Richards.

Maunga was still talking, off on her own tangent. "It's so easy for her. Let's face it, I wasn't playing against type when I did it, was I?"

"What do you mean?" asked Seth.

"Who's 'she'?" asked Addy.

"I mean," Maunga said, ignoring Addy and answering Seth, "she wanted someone who looked like a bully. She wanted someone who could do what she wanted them to do and look like they enjoyed it, and she found me. Nobody asks questions; everyone just thinks 'Oh, Maunga does it because she likes being evil.' And I did it, and I enjoyed it, and once I'd done it the first time . . ." She blew out a breath. "That was all I was. Just stupid, evil Maunga who does stupid, evil things because she's a bully and she enjoys it."

She looked blindly around the room, and then her eyes landed on Addy. She frowned. "What's wrong?"

Addy started. "I'm sorry?"

"You're crying. What's the matter?"

Addy brushed a thumb under one eye. Sure enough, it came away wet. She sniffed. "I—I was just . . . thinking."

"Oh, *please*."

"What?"

"Please," Maunga drawled, "don't tell me you're crying over the mess that is my life."

Er. "I wasn't."

"Good. Don't go getting any ideas that I'm some sort of tragically misunderstood hero, because I'm not. No bones about it—if I had to sell you out again to save myself, I would."

"Good to know," Addy said, unable to keep the edge from her voice.

"So why are you crying?"

Ugh. She didn't want to tell her, but if anyone could understand—and wasn't that a strange thought—then Maunga could. It was the work of minutes to fill them in on the gallery at the top of the house and the final lines that had tipped her over the edge and sent her storming out of the mansion and into the pub.

You fear being voiceless, don't you? You fear not having a voice, not being listened to.

Yes. It's why I wrote. Because people listen when I write.

"So, what," Maunga said when she finished, "you were upset because it was private?"

"Or you were upset because it was true?" Seth asked.

"Yes," she said to Maunga and, "Yes," to Seth. And then: "No. Maybe? I don't know. It upset me because it was true, yes, but also because it's so much more than that. *I'm* so much more than that."

Seth and Maunga exchanged uncomprehending looks.

"Look, it's true that I—that I fear not having a voice. I fear not being listened to, I can admit that. And it's a large part of why I wrote. But I don't want people to look at me and see *just* my voice, or my lack of voice, or *just* my writing, or my lack of writing. My voice isn't my identity any more than my writing is. The absence of those things isn't who I am, either. They're an integral part of me, sure, but they're not the sum total of who I am."

To her surprise, Seth nodded first. "I understand. You don't want people to put you in a box."

"Yes."

"That's exactly what I was talking about." Maunga leaned forward, eyes alight. "They put you in a box. I'm just a bully, and you're a, a mute little high achiever, and Seth's—"

"A stripper," Seth said baldly. "That's me. Or rather, it's *not* me; it's only what I do."

"But you can't let them do that! Because it's not who you are. It's not who *we* are, and as soon as you start playing to that type because it's what everyone expects to see, you're not being true to yourself anymore. I might be a bully, but I can still dish out some keeking good advice about grammar usage."

Addy flushed, remembering that she'd argued in the tutoring session. What had Maunga said? Something sarcastic, no doubt. She couldn't remember the exact words.

"I don't want to be remembered," Maunga said, "as the girl who stole your voice. I don't want to be remembered as a vindictive little bully. I want to be remembered as a human being. I have faults. So what? Everybody has faults. You can't shove someone into a box and stick a label on them saying, 'This is the one aspect of your personality that anyone will see.' It doesn't work like that. I want to be remembered as someone who was loyal—"

"To a fault," Seth murmured.

"And not afraid of hard work—"

Maunga? Hard work? Yeah, right.

"And unpredictable, and—"

"You can say that again," Addy said.

Maunga stopped. "Do you know what it took to get you here?" she demanded. "Do you know how much plotting and work and patience it took? By the end of it, I was almost afraid I'd been too subtle and you were going to miss your chance."

Addy frowned. "What are you talking about?"

"Who gave you all the information packs on Breach?"

"Tuku. Kotukutuku Johnson. Her dad works at Breach."

"And her older sisters are . . . who?"

"The twins. Manatu and Tarata."

"And," Maunga said, "who was in the same class as the twins at school?"

Addy closed her eyes. "You."

"I've caught up with them once or twice over the years. Thanks to me, you got those information packs. Thanks to my little visit to your class—come on, did you really think that was a coincidence?—you knew I had a session booked with Breach and the exact time and date of it. Thanks to me—"

"Alright," Addy said, "I get it. Woop-dee-doo and congratulations. You're a criminal mastermind, not just a high school bully after all."

"Oh no, I was a high school bully. It's just that, as you said, I'm so much more than that."

"It's not what you are," Seth put in. "It's just what you do. They might be linked, but they're not one and the same."

Seth had raised a good point. Addy was curious, now.

"So what did you do?" Addy asked him. "Or who were you? Before this, I mean. Your original wasn't a, um, a s-stripper too, was he?"

The smile vanished from Seth's face.

Maunga straightened, her shoulders tense. She put a hand on his knee.

"No," Seth said. "No, he was a school kid. Skinny as anything, average height, middling intelligence. And a dancer."

Maunga relaxed a little. "He loved ballet. Had pirouettes and glissades coming out his ears."

Addy bit back a grin. It made for an amusing mental image, but the atmosphere was too serious to laugh aloud.

"I can still dance here." Seth stared at his hands. "I get to thrust my pelvis on a nightclub stage."

"Not exactly the samc," Maunga said.

"No." His smile was bitter. "But it's what they do. I may not be a stripper at heart, but I am a dancer. They take something you loved, something that was your passion, and they corrupt it. They twist it until it's the palest shadow of the thing you could have poured your life into, and then they gift it to you on a silver platter . . . and you take it gratefully because it's better than nothing."

"Is it?" Maunga's words were tired, and Addy had the feeling they'd had this conversation before.

Seth didn't answer.

Silence blanketed the small room. It wasn't the cosy silence of snuggling under a thick duvet on a frosty winter's morning; rather, it was the suffocating silence of a heavy rug thrown over a fire to smother it.

Seth frowned at the far wall. Maunga laid her head on Seth's shoulder and looked down at his bandaged forearm. Addy sat for a few minutes, fidgeting. She didn't want to break the silence, but she couldn't sit here awkwardly watching them all day. There had been something . . . oh, that's what she'd been meaning to do.

She propped her leg up on the cushioned bench, unlaced her boot, and pulled it off. The radiating cold from the strapping tape had long since worn off, or else her feet had gotten so numb tramping up the mountain that she just couldn't feel it anymore. She broke the seal, waited for the splint segments to stop glowing, and unwrapped the tape.

Hmm. Nothing felt very painful. Nothing felt at all, really. She prodded her foot. The jab felt dull, like she was touching the skin through a thick layer of cotton wool. What about if she—*ow.* Well, she could wriggle her toes; that was good news. Flexing her heel sent pins and needles flaring up her calf, but the uncomfortable prickling-tingling-itching sensation was better than nothing. The nerves had woken up now; a minute of brisk massaging brought life flooding back into her feet, and the pins and needles faded.

Addy eyed her foot, considering. She could leave the tape off, but her ankle still felt a bit weak where it had twisted under her. Better to re-wrap it.

She wrapped her foot and had just activated the splints again when Seth stirred. He drew a breath, paused, and then let it out again without saying anything.

"What is it?" Maunga asked.

"I should be going."

Already? "We just got here," said Addy. She fiddled with the temperature controls on the strapping. Cold, cold, far too cold. Warm. Warmer, that was better. And a little more heat . . . perfect.

"I know," he said. "But I told Taieri I'd be back at the pub for my sets tomorrow morning." He met Addy's eyes, smiling a little. "Of course, if your mind decides it's had enough and you vanish back into the real world, my getting back to work in time won't matter as much. But in case you have unfinished business for the next week . . . it's better that I don't rile the boss up."

She hadn't thought about that—that she was unconsciously

holding the whole session up, prolonging it far past what the ghosts were used to. "I'm sorry."

"Don't be. I like having more time with you two lovely ladies."

Maunga snorted.

"You haven't told me why you wanted me here." The question had been gnawing at Addy's mind ever since Maunga had stepped out onto the snowy plateau. The last hour had seen it pushed back by more pressing matters, but it was never far from her thoughts. She knew why *she* had wanted Seth to take her to Maunga: Maunga was her only hope of finding out more about Vox Pox. But why had Maunga asked Seth to bring Addy to the mountain?

"I did tell you," Maunga said. "I need your help."

Maunga Richards needed help—and not just any help, but Addy's help. It must be the paradox of the century. Addy bypassed the first—heavily sarcastic—answer that sprang to mind; there was no point in antagonising her. She said instead, "Help with what?"

"I know who created Vox Pox. And I know how to get to her."

For the second time in an hour, Addy's breath was stolen away. *What?* They could find the person who had invented the Silent Sickness? *Her*, Maunga had said. A woman. And Maunga knew how to get to her? "I'm in," she blurted. "Yes. Who? Where? How do we get there?"

White teeth flashed against brown skin. "Someone from Breach." Maunga's eyes gleamed with a cold light. "She has a hub in the city here; we need to get in there to see her."

"Here, as in still in the sim?"

"You remember that we're in a simulation, do you?" She waved a hand. "Obviously. Yes, here as in still in the VPR session."

"Okay. How—?"

"We can take the Tube."

Seth broke in. "I'm not invited on this jaunt, then?"

"No," Maunga said. "Sorry. But we need to get there fast."

Seth nodded, looking resigned.

"Why can't you come?" Addy asked.

"Only pilgrims can use the Tube," he said. "The mountain's a popular destination for questers, but the quest is in the journey and what you find there, not in the return. They get a free ride back to the city. Ghosts aren't questers, so of course we can't use the shortcut back. I have to go the long way—down the mountain, over the bridge, and through the forest." He let go of Maunga and stood, reaching for his jacket. "I should get started. It's a fair walk."

"Wait." He was leaving her alone with Maunga? "I still don't understand. Why do you need *me?*"

"Time," Maunga said. "We've been tracking your timer. I changed the plan as soon as I heard it had ticked over the four-hour mark."

Addy frowned. What did that have to do with anything?

"I can manipulate the session to some extent; until you got here, I put every spare bit of headspace I had into projecting a ringing certainty that my session would last for as long as it needed to. But I've never seen a timer go for as long as yours is going."

"Neither have I," said Seth.

"Anyway, I figured out how to link two timers together. They connected on line of sight as soon as I saw you outside. And now, as long as I'm with you, your timer will be influencing both of us. If I left you behind, I'd be out of the session in less than a minute."

A flood of questions poured through Addy's mind. She considered putting up a defensive front and asking what was in it for her, but that was obvious: she wanted her voice back, she wanted Theo's voice back, she wanted the cure to Vox Pox. Asking what was in it for Maunga was similarly pointless. She knew enough to work out that it had something to do with Seth, but she also knew that Maunga would never tell her the specifics.

"So there's a plan?" she asked.

Maunga and Seth traded looks, the air between them brimming with amusement.

"Of course there's a plan," Maunga said.

"Several dozen, if I know you," Seth said in an undertone.

Maunga hummed. "And a couple of backups. Just in case." She stood. "We've got a few minutes yet. We'll see you off at the door before we take the Tube."

What was the Tube? Addy imagined it as a kind of train, winding its way down the mountain and back to the city. She laced her boot as firmly as she could over her bandaged foot and joined them as Seth shouldered the pack.

"You've got enough supplies?" she asked, nodding to the pack.

"Yeah. More than enough for just me. Thanks."

Maunga led them out of the little cellar, up the stairs, along the twisting corridors, and back into the many-pillared hall near the entrance. It had started snowing outside. Addy shivered as the freezing cold hit her. She followed Maunga and Seth to the start of the path without a murmur.

They halted there at the edge of the plateau. Seth and Maunga kissed, long and deep, as if they were saying goodbye for the last time. Finally, Seth drew back and took a shuddering breath. He cradled Maunga's face in his hands and leaned forward, pressing forehead to forehead and nose to nose in a prolonged hongi that was somehow more intimate than the kiss had been.

It felt like sacrilege to watch such a display of love. But it would be just as profane to look away, Addy thought. Suffering shone in their stances and in their eyes, and she'd never been good at turning away from the pain in other people. Snow fell in whirls and eddies around them. Seth and Maunga didn't move.

"I love you," he said.

"And I love you," Maunga replied.

"I'll miss you; it's been fun. Don't come back."

Maunga made a noise somewhere between a laugh and a sob. "I couldn't even if I wanted to."

She did want to, Addy thought. Of course she did. What sane person wouldn't, when the man she loved was trapped here? No wonder they looked as if every breath was both bliss and torture;

Maunga couldn't come back here, and Seth couldn't go to her. They wouldn't see each other again.

"They've marked my file," Maunga said. "Told me on the way in. Said I'm a psychological health risk and banned me from coming back."

A belly-deep chuckle escaped from Seth. "You've got to admit they have a point."

"Three visits in twelve months isn't that many."

"Three visits in twelve months to visit your—me," said Seth, gently chiding. "Three visits in twelve months to see the virtual clone of your old boyfriend, who you've fallen in love with. What could be unhealthy about that?"

"Shut up," she murmured. "I know. But it doesn't make it any easier."

"No, it doesn't." His eyes fluttered closed. He nuzzled her nose.

There was silence for a moment, and then Maunga spoke, so quietly that Addy had to strain to hear her.

"Do you think he—?"

"Yes," Seth said.

"How do you know?"

"I'm him, remember?"

So it was Seth's original they were talking about. *Where is he now?* Had Maunga kept in touch with him? Or was it only Seth she loved and not his original? Was that even possible?

"I didn't just start loving you the first time I saw you here, you know. I have his memories. His thoughts of you. I know how he felt, how I still feel. I know I almost went crazy in here before you visited for the first time. I kept wondering where you were, if you were okay." His arms tightened around her; his eyes bore into hers. "I know he did, Maunga. I *know* he did. He loved you."

Maunga kissed him hungrily. "Thank you."

Another kiss, and then they disengaged with a sigh.

"Be safe, love." He hoisted the pack higher on his back.

Addy expected a snarky comment, but she was surprised.

"Always," Maunga said.

"And you," Seth added, turning to Addy. He bent and kissed her cheek. "You be safe too, Addy. Look after each other."

"I will," Addy said. She stepped forward and hugged him, absurdly grateful for his brief friendship, hating to leave him here alone. "We will. Thank you."

Seth turned from them and started down the track. He twitched his hood up, shoulders hunched against the cold. In clear weather they could have seen him along three or four bends of the track, each turn lower than the last, but now the snow flurries threw an ever-moving shroud of white over the landscape. It wasn't long before all they could see was a shadow and a flash of his red jacket.

A freezing wind whistled through the trees, muffled and desolate. Seth turned and lifted a hand as he reached the first bend, and then the snow covered him and he was gone.

INTERLUDE

We are the voiceless. Hear us.
Our silence is not consent, nor rejection,
nor ignorance, nor knowledge.
Our silence is the imposition of nothing
instead of something.
Our silence has been forced upon us
by you, the noisome masses.
For too long have you stolen us:
our voices, our talents, our skills—
our identities subsumed into soundlessness—
and claimed them for your own.
For too long have our choices been thus:
silent maiden or muzzled whore.
Let the reckoning commence.
We will be the voiceless no more.

CHAPTER THIRTEEN

Addy watched Maunga as Maunga watched the empty snow falling at the bend of the track.

"Right." Maunga shivered. "He'll be fine. Come on." She turned in a whirl of yellow and black and strode back to the cave.

Addy hurried after her. A few paces in front, Maunga murmured something under her breath, too low for Addy to hear. She was about to ask Maunga to repeat it when Maunga spoke again. The words were still maddeningly indistinct. The third time, the words came just loud enough that Addy could understand them.

"Requiem æternam dona ei."

Latin? Not English or Maori? *Strange.* They stepped out of the open air and back under the shelter of the arch. "Are you Catholic?"

Maunga started a little, as if she hadn't expected Addy to be right behind her. Her glance was contemptuous. "No."

Maybe she'd grown up in a religious family and distanced herself from it as she got older? "Your parents?"

"No."

The next generation up, then. "Your grandparents."

"No." Maunga rolled her eyes. "I'm not Catholic, and none of my family are. I'm also not a coward."

"I'm sorry?"

"You know how it goes. Someone spouts an obscure piece of religious whatsit, someone else questions them, and then—because the first person is a coward and doesn't want to admit to having anything to do with religion—they invent a Catholic grandmother or great-uncle or second cousin twice removed who taught them about it when they were a child."

She snorted. “That way they don’t have to say *this is what I believe;* they can present it as *this is what my grandma said* and leave it to the listener to decide if the grandmother is wise or batty. Amazing how many people sprout Catholic grandmothers when pressed for answers.”

Addy took a minute to unravel that as they crossed the pillared hall. “So you’ve been reading up on religion yourself?”

“Give the girl a prize,” Maunga muttered without any real heat. They slipped into yet another winding corridor. “Yes. Because I’m not a coward, and I don’t feel the need to ascribe my actions to other people.”

“But you’re not Catholic.”

“No.”

“So why did you—?”

They turned down a flight of broad stairs, and Addy caught the half-guilty look Maunga slid her way. She really hadn’t thought Addy could hear her. Interesting.

“Because I happen to like the words. I like the rhythm and the flow, and I agree with the sentiment.”

They reached the bottom of the stairs and stepped through another archway into a wide room. It was a dead-end. The floor sank down at the far end, forming a shallow pool filled with cloudy liquid that smelled like the ocean. Near the tiled stone wall, the pool narrowed to maybe a metre wide, and the sides curved upward to make a clear tube. A gentle current kept the flow moving out of the pool, into the enclosed tube, and through a hole in the wall.

Oh. Tube. Ha. It looked something like a waterslide. Addy had a sinking feeling about how they would be returning to the city.

“So, uh, this is the Tube, is it?”

Maunga wandered over to the pool and dipped a hand in it. “Nah,” she said. “I just felt like a bubble bath. With no bubbles. While wearing my clothes—”

"Alright," Addy muttered.

"—in a swimming pool. Filled with immersion gel. Because, hey, it's not like we're on a tight schedule or anything."

"I get it." Addy was torn between embarrassment and a perverse desire to laugh. "What's immersion gel?"

Maunga looked at her, down at the hand she was trailing through the liquid, and back up at her.

"I mean, what *is* it? What does it do?"

"You've heard about the float tanks they use for psych testing?"

The whats? "No."

"Good, so—" Maunga stopped. "You haven't?"

"No. Should I have?"

Maunga shrugged a dismissal. "I suppose not. The method of transport back to the city changes depending on the quester. I'm doing a degree in psychology, so I make sure my headspace creates the Tube. It's an extension of the float tank experiment: combines a fast ride home with a fair bit of mental stimulation."

"So, what is it?"

"Basically they're a sensory deprivation experiment. The gel matches your skin temperature so it won't feel hot or cold when you get in. The mental boundaries between your body and the liquid will blur. Your senses will dim. We've got too many layers in the way of perfect skin-to-water contact—I assume you'd rather not strip naked for the trip? Didn't think so—but it'll still be effective. Heart rate and blood pressure both drop. Your breathing slows. The aim is to float until you lose all sense of self and your mind dissolves in a puddle of goo—"

She broke off, grinning at the look on Addy's face.

"Sorry. You do float, though. You can't *not* float. It's so saturated with salt that you can't even roll over once you're lying down. I'll find us some breathing masks in a minute; float on your back or your front as you please. And really, don't worry. It's a bit like a gently moving water bed. The effect is quite pleasant, speaking from experience. Very mentally stimulating. I get a lot of thinking done whenever I'm in one."

Huh. Maybe the trip wouldn't be the cloying, suffocating nightmare she'd first envisioned.

Maunga crossed to a storage locker and pulled out what looked like a thin black scarf. "Here."

Addy took it. She'd been expecting a silky smooth texture, but instead the material was stiff and gritty with hard lines running along it at intervals.

"It's a breathing mask," Maunga said. "Wrap it around your face. Over your nose. Yeah, like that. Good."

Addy strapped the mask closed and felt for the activation switch. *There.* The hard lines along the top and bottom of the material warmed and fused to her skin, much like her shoulder piece did. The panic she'd anticipated at having a cloth covering her mouth and nose never appeared; the mask was so light she hardly felt it, and breathing came as naturally as ever.

Maunga sealed her own mask with brisk movements and waded down into the pool. "Remember to keep your weight spread out." The words came clear through her yellow mask, not muffled at all.

Addy caught a faint reverb of the words from her own mask. They had comm channels built in? That was clever.

"Trust the gel to keep you afloat and moving. And stay close—I'd hate to lose you."

"What, you're not going to rope us together?" Addy regretted the gibe as soon as the words spilled from her mouth.

A thoughtful gleam stole into Maunga's eyes.

Addy sighed.

Two minutes later they stepped down into the pool, a ten-metre length of thin rope linking their wrists. Maunga had been right about the temperature—somehow the gel felt neither hot nor cold. It was an odd sensation. Addy had to keep looking down to make sure that her bare knees were still there. Or that the liquid was still there. She couldn't decide. Maybe it was both.

She tapped her foot against the bottom. She could still feel that. Good. And her feet were more or less dry in her boots; no doubt she'd be grateful for that when they emerged at the other end.

Maunga waded closer to the narrows and eased down onto her back. "Remember, stick close. I'll know if you don't." She pulled on the rope.

Addy felt the answering strain from the loop around her wrist. "I know. I'll be right behind you. Or a maximum of ten metres behind you, anyway."

She was about to follow Maunga's example when a familiar sound caught her ear. Music. And not just any music—*her* music, coming from *her* Eareos. She lifted one side of the band to her ear, checking. Yes, that was definitely her music.

Weird.

She shrugged. Between the sea salt smell and Maunga's line about getting a lot of thinking done, perhaps it wasn't surprising. She'd always thought better around the ocean and her music.

"Are you coming?" Maunga asked, one hand outstretched, gripping the wall to keep her halted at the start of the narrows.

"Yeah." *Why not?* Might as well make the most of it. She flipped her hood up and slipped her Eareos over it until they cupped her ears. It was a snug fit but not uncomfortable. The music was still discernible through the double layer of hood and mask, loud enough without being intrusive. *Excellent.*

Ready to go. She sank to her knees and let her head and shoulders fall back. Her legs rose until she was floating, cradled by the gel. *Hmm.* It did feel rather like a water bed, but also unlike it at the same time.

"I'm letting go," Maunga said through the comm channel.

The rope tightened and yanked her wrist-first for a few metres, and then the current caught her. Once she was in the flowing narrows and she and Maunga were moving at the same speed, Addy gripped the rope and reeled in a loose metre or two. That was better.

The rope was no longer taut between them, tugging and pulling; she could rest her arms however she liked without worrying about the strain. And she didn't have to think about Maunga kicking her, either. Eight metres of rope separated them; even Maunga Richards couldn't reach that far.

The curved walls rose to enclose her in a clear tube. Addy blinked at the ceiling, such as it was, half a metre above her head. She'd expected a rush of claustrophobia, but it seemed this place lived to subvert her expectations: if anything, her mind seemed to calm even further in the confined space.

"Alright?" Maunga asked.

"Yeah. Fine."

They swept through the hole in the wall. Darkness wrapped the Tube in a gloomy embrace. Addy blinked, and blinked again, but she could see nothing beyond the dim grey light.

"You can sleep if you want," Maunga said. "It might be a while till we come out the other end."

"I might do that." Or not. She had no intention of sleeping, in all honesty. Why would she waste the mental stimulation afforded by her music and the fading ocean tang on her unconscious? Far better to stay awake and aware.

Please stop talking. This would be a terribly long trip if Maunga insisted on keeping a conversation going.

But Maunga remained silent, and after a few minutes Addy concluded that she wasn't planning to speak again.

Good. She could think in peace.

She floated at ease, cushioned by the gel, drifting with the current, barely aware of her body. But her body wasn't the important thing here; her mind was. *Deluge for the Artdom under Siege* filled her ears; Gavinoster's latest album was perfect for this journey.

The darkness came from everywhere and nowhere. She closed her eyes and let the music mingle with the sound of her breathing. She thought about Seth and wondered how far down the mountain he'd made it by now; she thought about Maunga, mere metres ahead, floating down this strange river with her; she thought about Maunga-and-Seth, about the unexpected way they fit together, about Maunga wanting to be remembered as more than just a bully and Seth's offhand comment that she was loyal to a fault.

The Tube threw her into a tight turn that went on—and on—and on, a never-ending corkscrew spiralling down into the depths of the earth. She tried counting time in her head, but the seconds seemed slow against the racing current, and she soon gave up. Her breath rose and fell as steadily as it had since entering the gel.

Trust the gel, Maunga had said. Addy did.

After what felt like the most peaceful month she'd ever experienced, the tunnel straightened out, and the steep angle eased. The current held its pace for another few minutes before slowing its headlong rush.

Addy cracked her eyes, curious to see if there had been any change in the darkness outside the Tube—and then opened them wide.

The tunnel was as black as ever; if anything, it was even blacker than it had been near the top of the mountain. High above her, shimmering and shining, a thousand white-gold stars swept in a great, patternless wave across the sky.

Her heart rose in her throat. It was stunning.

Hang on . . . Logic intruded, cutting off the swelling awe.

It couldn't be the sky, could it? They were underground, far too far underground to see the sky. And it hadn't been anywhere near night-time when they'd farewelled Seth. They must be in a cave. Not to mention that stars always had patterns. Even living in the city, she knew that. Last night Seth had guided them straight by looking at the patterns in the stars. These stars had no patterns. Some were a little larger or brighter than others, it was true, but even as she watched, they seemed to squirm and move.

Squirm? Okay, now she *knew* they weren't stars. Stars didn't squirm.

Well, whatever they were, they were beautiful.

The tunnel rushed her onward. The roof of the cave drew down, bringing the not-stars closer in all their wriggling glory. They grew bigger and brighter until she thought the roof was about to fall and crush the Tube—and then darkness swept over her, true darkness, and the star cave fell behind her and was gone. She raced on around a bend that seemed to curve forever, and then the darkness itself fell away, and daylight flooded over her.

Ow. That was *bright.* Addy squinted against the glare, blinking and blinking again to try to adjust her eyes. She caught a glimpse of blue sky far overhead; craggy cliffs rose behind and in front, and to the side, mere metres below the Tube, water raced away down the gorge in a surge of white-tipped rapids.

Almost before the sound of rushing water came to her ears through her music, she reached the far side and plunged into darkness again. At least she knew where she was, now. They were down the mountain—way, way down the mountain—and across the river. All that remained was the forest and the plain, and they'd arrive back in the city. She settled, eyes closing. *Might as well enjoy the ride.*

Anticipation built in the pit of her stomach. She didn't know what to expect at the far end. It was better not to guess; if she kept her options open, she wouldn't be as surprised.

Okay, she would be surprised. But at least she wouldn't have the surprise of dashed expectations on top of everything else.

She wondered what Maunga's plan was. Or *plans,* rather. A dozen at least, Seth had said, and from what she'd seen of Maunga—the Maunga here, multifaceted and patient and unpredictable, not the Maunga out there, brutal and bullying and positively one-dimensional—she believed it.

Addy was glad Maunga was on her side, no matter how tenuous the alliance. She had no illusions that it *was* tenuous. Maunga would drop her as soon as she'd served her purpose, whatever that purpose was. Was it the time factor? Or was it something deeper?

She didn't know. But she could start preparing. Time to think.

~

By the time she rounded the final bend of the Tube and the darkness lightened, she'd given a lot of thought to what Maunga's plans could entail. Addy wanted to reach the woman who'd created Vox Pox—so far her goals and Maunga's were in agreement. But there was more to this meeting than that, and their goals wouldn't be in common the whole time.

Addy wanted a cure: for Theo at the very least and for all four-hundred-odd victims if possible.

Somehow she doubted Maunga's end game was quite so altruistic.

Something cold and hard dropped in her gut when she realised how far she was prepared to go. Maybe she wasn't so different from Maunga. There was very little Maunga wouldn't do to achieve her end game—and now Addy knew, too, that there was very little she wouldn't do herself.

She hoped it wouldn't come to that.

"Heads up, sunshine." Maunga's voice crackled through the comm channel. "We're here."

She risked a look through her lashes, ready to slam them shut again. It was safe: no overwhelming brightness, no glaring lights. She opened her eyes and looked around.

Ambient light washed the chamber in a gentle grey-white. The top half of the Tube had vanished, leaving an indistinct roof of stone far above her. Thin ledges of polished rock, hardly wide enough for a person to edge their way along, ran down either side of the channel. Beyond them walls rose, smooth and seamless, to meet the roof.

The current slowed to a crawl. The walls drew back. Soon they were floating through the middle of a huge, subterranean chamber.

The river flowed into a larger pool, ringed with stone and perfectly circular, where it stopped.

Addy waded out of the pool to join Maunga, who stood by the side of the channel. The air felt strange—somehow hot and cold at the same time, in stark contrast to the sheer *lack* of sensation from the gel. An unsteady draught came from the open archway across the far side of the room.

Ugh. Addy's hair was wet, her clothes sopping. Her boots squelched with every step. Maunga didn't look much better. She had taken her jacket off and was wringing it out, grimacing at the water that poured from it. The leather outer might have been waterproof, but the lining clearly wasn't. Her shoes were in much the same condition.

At least Maunga had the advantage of having her hair tied back in a braid. Addy didn't even have a hair tie, let alone a comb. She scrunched her hair up into a makeshift ponytail and squeezed it out, shuddering at the trickle of gel that splashed her neck and shoulders.

Her music had stopped the moment she stepped out of the pool. She slipped her Eareos into their habitual position around her neck, threw her hood back, and unstrapped the breathing mask. It peeled away easily, leaving a faint, sticky residue on her skin and a rubbery after-smell in her nose.

"Ready to go?" Maunga asked, biting the knot at her wrist loose and letting the end of the rope drop to the floor. Sodden, her yellow shirt clung to her shoulders and stomach. She slipped her still-dripping jacket on.

"Yeah." Addy untied her own end of the rope. "It's going to be a fun walk."

The first surprise came when they stepped through the archway. A blast of hot air met them, angling straight down from the thick lintel. Addy yelped and retreated, but Maunga halted in the draught zone and laughed.

"Why are you laughing?" Addy yelled over the noise of the wind.

"Hot air," Maunga shouted. "It's a moisture regulator. We'll be dry in no time."

Oh. She stepped back into the onslaught and winced as the wind tugged at her clothes and blew the breath from her lungs. In ten seconds her hair was dry; another ten and her clothes had followed suit; ten seconds after that, her feet were toasty warm through the thick leather of her boots.

They moved forward to the hallway beyond.

Ugh. Stairs.

The flight rose steep and narrow to a landing far above them. There were no handrails and no support columns; the steps themselves were only linked together by a central spine, and the staircase seemed to float in the air. More stairs branched off from the landing, one to the right and one to the left, and—she strained to see in the uncertain light—was that a third set carrying straight on? She wasn't sure. At least it sported a different colour palette from the ghostly white-on-white of the endless stairs in the mansion.

The walls at the far edges of the great space were deep-cut stone that looked as if they had been hewn from the bones of the earth, with the stairs themselves a darker stone, gritty at the edges and worn smooth down the centre where countless feet had trodden.

"After you," she murmured and dropped back to let Maunga take the lead.

The climb proved even steeper than she'd anticipated, and longer, too. They both panted for air by the time they reached the first landing. Addy didn't dare look over the side. As soon as she'd gotten her breath back, she broached the two most important questions.

"Where are we going? And who are we going to see?"

"Caro York." Maunga turned on the spot to examine first one staircase and then another. "Caroline. At her Breach Laboratories office."

The name rang a bell, but she couldn't quite place it. *York.*

Hadn't there been a Harper York at the medico's office all those years ago? It was probably a coincidence; there were dozens of Yorks in Te Maru. "I know a Harper York, but not—"

"She's her sister. And if Harper knew what Caro was doing, she wouldn't be happy."

"Who's Caroline, then?"

Maunga looked at her sideways. "You remember meeting our session overseer? Shortish woman, black hair, slim?"

Oh. "That Caroline."

"She's the Overseer for the whole TheraRPG programme. She doesn't act as a guide for every session, I don't think, but she's overseen every session I've ever done."

It was the perfect cover, Addy thought as they began their next ascent. Of course whoever invented Vox Pox would be a scientist, and a scientist at Breach would be well respected. She shivered.

Three flights later, her legs felt like they were about to fall off. The pleasant numbness from the gel had long since worn off. All her aches and pains from the last few days returned with a vengeance. Her muscles were sore, her head throbbed, and every step on her strapped ankle sent needles jabbing into her shin.

Should've left the bandaging off. Too late now.

She was about to call for a rest stop when Maunga darted forward, over the crest of the stairs and across the landing. Addy trotted to catch her.

A square metal box waited on the far side of the landing. Its corner posts swept upward to vanish into the dim grey light above them, and the wide brass doors had been propped open, showing the empty interior. A plaque over the lintel read simply: *Breach.*

"That's what we want," said Maunga. "A lift to take us straight to the virtual hub."

"Did you know it was here?"

Maunga just grinned and moved forward into the lift. Addy followed, the doors clanged shut, and they shot upward.

The breather seemed far too short. Perhaps a minute later, the lift slowed and stopped, and the doors popped open. Maunga led the way out into a corridor that looked identical to the ones they'd seen at the non-virtual Breach facilities. She had obviously studied a map of the place—she knew her way without the barest flicker of hesitation. Addy followed her through a twisting warren of halls and stairs and admitted herself lost after the seventh turn.

They came to a door that looked just like every other door they'd passed. Maunga stopped.

"This is her office." Any lingering softness from the cave had vanished, leaving her face a hard mask. "Are you ready?"

Addy nodded and tried to ignore the nervous twitching in her stomach. "I'm ready."

Ready for what, she couldn't say. The best of fictional detectives had taught her that it was a mistake to theorise without adequate data, and she didn't intend to ignore that lesson. Trying to draw conclusions from an incomplete data set only led to erroneous results.

For the time being, best to keep her options open and her mouth shut. She still didn't know what Maunga's plan was, but she didn't doubt for a second that there was one. Addy herself was prepared. She knew the lengths she was prepared to go to. Time would tell.

They would play it by ear and trim their sails with the turning of the wind.

Maunga and Addy stepped through the door.

CHAPTER FOURTEEN

A well-lit entrance foyer greeted them. Across the room, a flock of chairs clustered around a large desk. A sensor chimed as Addy moved forward. The young man half-hidden behind a huge holo display glanced up.

"Gidday," he said, looking unsurprised at their appearance. "She's been expecting you. Half a second while I check if she's free." He strode across the room, paused, and turned back, flushing a little. "Sorry. Um. Take a seat. Watering hole—drinks station—is in the corner. Loos are through that door. Back in a tick." He vanished through the far door.

Addy turned to trade a look with Maunga, but the older girl was already across the room, heading for the bathroom door. So much for that idea.

The drinks station held not only water but coffee, tea, chocolate, and Five Spice, all of both the hot and iced varieties. Further examination revealed a six-pack of beer tucked away at the back of the cabinet, next to a corked wine bottle and several half-full bottles of liqueur. She considered the iced Five Spice but settled on water. Better to stick with the basics. She didn't want to tax her stomach after days without regular food or drink.

Addy dropped into the nearest chair, a glass of ice-cold water in hand, sighing in relief as the weight came off her aching feet. She let her head fall back against the cushioning and closed her eyes, content to sip water and wait for the receptionist to return.

A few minutes later, she heard a *thump* as someone collapsed into the chair next to her. Maunga, she guessed, cracking her eyes open long enough to confirm. Yes, that was Maunga sprawled in the next chair over with a beer in her hand. Who would've guessed?

The receptionist's name was Rawhiti Wells if the nameplate on the desk was anything to go by. He came back from the far room, leaving the door open. "She'll see you now."

"Thanks," Maunga muttered, standing up. "Very generous of her."

Rawhiti stepped aside as Maunga strode past him. Addy flashed him an apologetic look and hurried through the far door in Maunga's wake.

She was dimly aware of him shutting the door behind them, but mostly she focused on the strange sight that greeted them in Caroline's office.

A woman stood in front of a floor-to-ceiling holoboard, her back turned to them as she worked. She wore casual clothing: wedge sneakers, tights with a run down the leg, a soft black skirt. Her grey jersey had slipped down over one shoulder, showing the white singlet underneath. Addy eyed her immaculate pixie cut with no little amount of jealousy; she would never dare cut her hair that short, but she couldn't deny that it looked stunning on . . . Caroline?

Was she Caroline, though?

Across the room, another woman sat in a chair kicked back on two legs against the wall, her feet propped up on the desk. Her eyes were inscrutable as she watched the intruders; she had the same black pixie cut as the first woman, and she wore the same crisp uniform that Caroline had worn that morning: boots, tailored trousers, and a fitted grey jacket emblazoned with the Breach Laboratories logo.

Perhaps she was Caroline? Or . . .

Addy glanced from one to the other, confused. If she hadn't already met Harper, she would have thought that one of them was Caroline's sister, but as it was, neither of the women bore more than a passing resemblance to Harper York. Harper was younger and a little taller, and her hair had been much lighter, sandy blonde rather than black.

The two women here were so similar, they looked like twins.

Or . . . clones.

Oh. Right. Seth had mentioned the Overseer who kept a ghost of herself in the system.

"Hello, Caroline," said Maunga.

Addy couldn't tell which woman she had addressed the remark to. She seemed to have spoken to the space between the two figures.

"Hello, Maunga," said the woman at the desk.

Right. The one in the Breach uniform was Caroline. But was she the real one?

Caroline must have seen her confused look. She laughed.

Addy felt a surge of dislike at the sound. It should have been a harsh, grating laugh, fitting for the person who had unleashed Vox Pox on the city, but instead it was light and smooth, the sort of laugh that made one instinctively want to like the person who was laughing. Someone with a laugh that nice must be a nice person.

Or not.

"Don't look so baffled," Caroline said. "Although perhaps introductions are in order. You must be Adelaide, I think."

Addy nodded.

"And Maunga, of course, I already know." She gestured to the woman working at the holoboard. "You won't have met her—except, in a way, you will have. My VPR counterpart. We call her *B* for Beta."

"Because I'm better than you, Caro," said B without looking around.

Maunga snorted.

B turned at that, waving a hand in welcome before going back to her work.

Clever. Most virtual copies seemed to exist to help the pilgrims, but, as Seth had figured, Caroline clearly used hers to further her lab work. Two Carolines meant twice the brainpower, twice as much time, double the work. No doubt she used the time fluxes to her advantage, too. She could only have twenty-four hours in a day out in the real world; in here, the only limit would be system parameters.

Addy looked back and forth between the two Carolines, fixing them in her mind. The one in street clothes was the clone and the one in uniform was the original. Okay. She thought she had them pegged. As long as she didn't get them mixed up. That would be embarrassing.

Maunga strolled over to the holoboard and eyed the work there. Caroline—the original, not the clone—looked Addy up and down for a moment before making a thoughtful noise in the back of her throat.

"What?" Addy asked. The question emerged more aggressively than she'd intended. She hadn't meant to sound rude. She'd meant to appear polite and charming and fearless, untouchable, but her heart had started beating far too fast as soon as she laid eyes on the woman responsible for Vox Pox. Her mouth was dry. She wished she'd brought her glass of water through from the other room.

Caroline took her feet off the desk and leaned forward, eyes narrowing.

Addy's heart shivered in her chest. She licked her lips and searched for the right words, but her mind went blank.

"Nothing." Caroline relaxed back into the embrace of her leather armchair. "It's interesting, that's all."

"What's interesting?" Maunga turned and watched them both.

"The clothes."

Addy made an effort to keep her voice level. "What about them?"

"You're wearing your school uniform, which you weren't wearing when you entered the programme—I'd have noticed. It's still neat after being stuck here for ninety-odd hours with no adult supervision. Socks turned down at the knee to show the school stripes, and you've still got your tie on, even." She had very white teeth. Her smile would have been easier to look at if it had been sarcastic. "You won't get detention here for having your shirt untucked, you know."

"Habit."

"The sim left you your boots; comfortable walking must be important to you. And then there's your hoodie—or rather, *not* your hoodie. It belongs to someone else. The sleeves are too long, and it's far too big for you, not to mention the fact that you don't attend RPU."

"So what?"

"Clothes are important. Significant. There are no coincidences, not in the programme."

"If you've got a point—"

"You're a stickler for the rules, but it's more than that. Something happened at school, something you haven't moved past, or haven't been able to move past . . ."

Addy's breath froze in her lungs as Caroline went on.

"You've been here three days." Her hands moved over the desk, calling up information faster than Addy could follow. "Three days—or years? Yes. Years. Something happened three years ago at your school, something to do with Maunga, something you haven't been able to move past, and so you've come here looking for answers. Whose hoodie is it?"

The question struck home. Addy's mouth moved in automatic response. "My brother's."

"Ah." Those dark eyes lifted from the desk, piercing her. "I lose track, but of course. You were one of the early ones. Adelaide Te Ngawai. Your brother is Theo. You've had Vox Pox for three and a half years, courtesy of one Maunga Richards."

Maunga might have snarled something; it was hard to make it out through the buzzing in her ears.

"And now your brother has it, too. Naturally you'd come here."

Why had she come? Addy felt sick, drained of all energy. What had she thought would happen here? That she could grab a gun from a mount on the wall and hold Caroline hostage until she gave up the cure? There were no guns; it was an office, a working laboratory, not an armoury. There were no weapons here except the words that flew from Caroline's mouth, sharp and bright, searing as a thousand suns. There probably wasn't even a cure.

I lose track. Why had she thought she might be different? She'd never stuck out from the crowd, never been pretty, never been much more than just one smart girl in a school full of smart girls. But she'd thought Caroline would at least recognise her.

Look at me, she wanted to scream at Caroline. *Don't you know me? You ruined my life, and you don't even know me!*

But that was the point. Caroline didn't know her. She probably didn't know any of her victims, any of the countless people she'd inflicted Vox Pox on.

"I thought it might have been Seth's hoodie," Caroline said. "But of course it isn't; he's only got the one jacket, and his original isn't alive to bring him more clothes."

The words cut through the rushing in Addy's ears. She heard Maunga's sharp intake of breath.

A brief, ringing silence fell. Caroline looked from Addy to Maunga and back and then smiled again.

"Oh." There was the barest hint of delighted laughter in her voice. "She hasn't told you. Has she." It wasn't a question.

Addy shook her head. Her thoughts were unbearably slow. Seth was dead? No, not Seth—Seth's original. The boy who had been Seth, out there, in the real world. Had Maunga known?

Of course she had known. Grief lay heavy in the lines of Maunga's face. She looked weary beyond enduring. She'd known.

All this time, she'd known.

He wasn't around by then, Maunga had said. *He dropped off the radar a week or two after my sixteenth.*

It was all Addy could do to suppress a snort. *Dropped off the radar.* What a euphemism. Was it so hard to say *he's dead?*

But perhaps it was. If Maunga had been telling the truth, Seth had died soon after her sixteenth birthday. And then, two weeks after that, Caroline had approached her and told her to steal Addy's voice. As if the first present hadn't been bad enough.

She could imagine it vividly—a younger Maunga, softer around the edges, someone who didn't live in the mask of the bully so much as she slipped it on every now and again. Maunga, still reeling in the wake of her boyfriend's death. The perfect target. Her heart ached for the girl that Maunga had been. Caroline would have known just what to say, the exact words, the right balance of pity and threats and power.

Maunga would have been helpless. Addy knew all too well what that felt like.

"If she didn't tell you he was dead," Caroline said, "she wouldn't have told you how he died."

"Don't—!" Maunga broke off with a low cry of pain.

Addy turned.

B had bent Maunga's arm up behind her back at a cruel angle and was whispering in her ear. Maunga halted, teeth bared, her breathing loud and fast.

Addy's gaze swung back to Caroline. Despite the shock, despite the numb horror of the situation, she couldn't deny that she was curious. "No. She didn't tell me."

"He had Vox Pox," Caroline said.

Her words fell like stones in the silence of the room. Addy saw the ripples spreading, connecting one puddle with another and another until they were joined.

"Seth, his four sisters, his brother, his father. They all had Vox Pox." The words were matter-of-fact. "It was in the early days. I'll admit my research wasn't half so extensive as it is now. Five hundred test subjects have given me a wealth of information over the last few years. Perhaps I underestimated the ramifications of dosing an entire family all at once."

Something stirred in Addy's memory. *Not quite an entire family.* If she was right, if it was the family she was thinking of, the one she'd overheard Dad telling Mum about, Seth's mother had escaped it. What was their name? Clarence. Ettina and—and what was their dad's name? Micko. That was right. Ettina and Micko. And Seth.

Seth Clarence.

"Anyway," Caroline went on, "something went wrong with one of the boys. Perhaps he was psychologically weaker than the others. Less able to bear up under stress. I don't know." She frowned. "He visited us once for a session, long before we were open to the public, before we'd instituted the writing tests. We took a copy of him, of course. Even that early in the programme, we knew we needed backups in case of accidents. They work, but ghosts haven't proven nearly as good as the live thing. The boy committed suicide four days later."

And all the pieces fell into place.

She'd been so sure there had been something more to Maunga's blackmail. *I'd seen what it had done to others.* She'd seen it cripple her boyfriend and his family, seen it drive him to suicide because he couldn't bear the thought of never dancing again. *I didn't want it to happen to me.* Nobody in their right mind would. Not after that.

And here was Seth, or the copy of Seth, with the original Seth's memories and his own sorrow and guilt. Could he grieve for his own death, even having brought it on himself? She was sure he could—and did.

She remembered brief snatches of conversation, so much clearer in hindsight.

"She blackmailed you with that, after—after everything?"

"Yeah. About two weeks after 'everything.' I wasn't in any sort of state to refuse, not with that hanging over my head."

And: *"I'm sorry."*

"It's not your fault. . . . We've been over this."

And: *"Three visits in twelve months isn't that many."*

"Three visits in twelve months to visit your—me."

Your what? What had he been going to say? Your boyfriend who killed himself because the Vox Pox stole everything from him, everything that he was, everything that he could have been, and left him an empty wreck? The virtual clone of your old boyfriend, now stuck in endless days of emptiness and loneliness, washed in guilt for what his original had done, drowning in desperation for the girl he could never see again?

Addy thought she might throw up.

"We questioned his copy," Caroline said. "He gave us a very good picture of the original's mental state four days before his suicide. At that point we implemented the psychiatric testing for clients, both pre- and post-session."

It would have been easier to hate her if she hadn't sounded so rueful. As it was, the wordless rage spent itself crashing against Addy's breastbone without a whisper escaping her mouth.

And she knew. She knew what Maunga wanted, what Seth wanted, really, because they were one and the same. She knew what Seth longed for now that Maunga could never come back to the virtual world. She knew what Maunga had murmured on that desolate plateau when she thought Addy couldn't hear her.

Maunga would do anything to release Seth from his torment here—and anything to avenge his death, which she so clearly blamed on Caroline York.

And that, of course, was why Addy was here. So Maunga could use her as leverage.

There was only one question left to answer. How far was she prepared to go? To find the cure for Theo, for herself, for the hundreds of others?

"I see," Addy heard herself say. The words were muffled, filtering down to her from the surface, from dancing sunlight on ocean waves to the deep, dark waters below.

How far was she prepared to go? She would have to decide—fast. Once Maunga made her move, it would be too late. Maunga was neither friend nor ally. Not with what she'd brought Addy here for.

She couldn't let Maunga use her as leverage. And she couldn't walk away from Caroline, not without making an effort to find a cure. But she'd come woefully unprepared, she knew that. She couldn't threaten violence, and she had no money to barter, no firstborn child to offer, no secret to blackmail anyone with.

She had nothing to offer . . . except herself.

Addy stepped forward as if in a dream, saw Caroline's head tilt in silent enquiry, and bent down to whisper in her ear.

"Fascinating," Caroline said. Her eyes slid from Addy's face past her shoulder.

Addy turned to follow her gaze. Maunga wrestled against the clone's grip, a murderous glare on her face. Her mouth was moving, no doubt spitting curses, but Addy didn't hear her. She couldn't hear anything but the blood pounding in her ears.

She waited, poised at the edge of the chasm, heart in her mouth as Caroline's eyes came back to rest on her.

Would she accept?

"Come with me," the scientist said.

~

"Have a seat." Caroline closed the door to the inner office behind them.

The office was small and plain. It didn't smell of antiseptic like the lab behind them. It didn't smell of anything. Addy caught a faint waft of perfume from Caroline, but that was all.

A desk faced one wall, flanked by two metal chairs. Rows of shelving ran along the opposite wall, packed with jars hardly bigger than a coffee mug.

They all looked different—some were filled with bubbling

liquid that never sat still while others held a bare centimetre of waxy solid. One substance was black and clouded, another almost translucent, yet another a swaying eddy of colours. Jars in varying shades of red lined an entire shelf near floor-level. One in particular looked so much like blood that Addy found her gaze coming back to it again and again in horrified fascination.

She pulled out one of the chairs and sat, angling it so she could see both Caroline and the wall of jars.

"Does Maunga know about your offer?" Caroline sank into the second chair.

"No." Were those *bits* of something floating in that jar on the end there? "She doesn't know."

The glass of the jars turned opaque, hiding their contents. Addy looked back to Caroline to see her hand withdraw from the desk.

Caroline smiled. "I'd figured as much, from the way she was fighting B."

"Have you made a decision?"

"I'm considering it."

"You said it yourself—ghosts aren't nearly as good as the live thing. So you don't need to keep them around." Addy took a breath, her hands shaking at the realisation of what she was offering herself up for. "You won't need them anymore, not when you've got a live test subject at your beck and call. Not when you've got me."

How far was she prepared to go?

This far.

"Are you so sure that they want to be released from the simulation?" Caroline picked up a stylus from its groove and flipped it through her fingers.

"Yes," Addy said.

"And are you sure there's a cure for Vox Pox?"

She wasn't. She wasn't sure at all. But she held Caroline's gaze and let the anger steady her hands and her voice. "Is there?"

"Yes," said Caroline after a moment. "Of course there is. What sort of a scientist would I be if I created something with that much potential for harm without an antidote?" Her gaze drifted to the wall of jars. "I've stolen the voices and creative identities of five hundred people, and I can give them back at any moment—and nobody knows." Her voice was soft, her face triumphant. "I hold five hundred people in the palm of my hand, and not one of them has any idea."

The jars. Addy caught her breath. Was it that simple? "Potential for harm?" she asked, trying not to stare at the wall. *Don't let her see; don't make it obvious.* "I reckon it's gone a smidgen past *potential*."

Caroline lifted a slim shoulder. "In the short term, yes. But in the long run?" She leaned forward, eyes alight. "In the long run, what are a few years of muteness for a few hundred people compared to the progress we can make from this research, progress that will benefit *billions?* Do you have any idea the advances we've made in the last two years alone? We're doing groundbreaking science. The potential for harm is there, as in any experiment, but so is the potential for good. And the good—the good we do will far outweigh the harm."

She believes it, too. The madwoman believed it. But she wasn't mad. That was the worst of it. She was as sane as Addy herself, and she truly believed in the *rightness* of her actions.

Addy's heartbeat sounded loud in her ears, loud and slow. The breath shivered in her lungs.

"Tell that to them." A maelstrom of emotion welled up inside her; her hands shook, and her voice trembled, but she kept talking. "Tell that to the five hundred people whose lives you've ruined, and their friends and families. Theo, me, *Seth*—tell it to Seth's ghost, and his parents who were robbed of their son, and the kids who have to grow up without their brother."

"Collateral damage," said Caroline. "I regret it, I do, but it was necessary."

Addy found herself on her feet. "You killed him!"

"He killed himself."

"You drove him to it!"

Tears ran down her cheeks, but Caroline sat motionless, unbowed beneath the crushing force of her anger.

"You—you and your keeking Vox Pox! What did you think would happen? That you could dose an entire family and they'd adjust and carry on with their lives like nothing had happened? What, you thought maybe you might stop once you'd dosed ten people? Fifty, is that a big enough sample base? A hundred? But you'll always need more test subjects, won't you? You'll always want to know what could happen, what if, what if, and *people will die.* How many deaths will it take? Hundreds? Thousands? Or are they all acceptable damage? Are they all just collateral in the name of progress?"

Her words were like waves dashing themselves against the ageless cliffs until they spent their energy. Caroline sat unmoved. The cliffs would stand as firm as they always had. Despair flooded her, and then determination. She would show Caroline. She would show Caroline that not all five hundred were dead inside, not all of them were blind to her games. Because Addy had Vox Pox too, and Addy had gotten this far.

And she refused to give up now.

"Alright," she said, crossing to the wall of jars. "Alright." She ran a hand along a row, watching Caroline for any reaction. "If you won't see—" The next row followed. Halfway along, Caroline made a minute movement—a flicker of an eyelid, a stiffening in her posture. *There.* That was the reaction she'd been looking for. Addy lifted the jar out and turned to face Caroline. It felt warm in her hand, and it was heavier than she'd expected.

She wouldn't hold it for long.

"I'll just have to show you. I'm standing against it. I'll finish my session here, and I'll go to the media. The story will come out. You'll be investigated. I want to show you—" her voice shook "—that there are people who oppose you. And at least one person will be free of you."

Her trip here wouldn't be wasted. If only one person could be free of Vox Pox, it wouldn't have been a waste.

Addy let the jar fall.

Caroline's mouth curled in a slow smile. She didn't move.

The jar hit the ground in a splintering of glass. Shards flew. The insides sprayed blue liquid and white foam across the floor.

Caroline raised an eyebrow. "Are you finished?"

Addy swallowed. So much for her gesture of defiance. "Yes."

"Then sit down."

She picked her way across the glass-smattered floor and sat.

"Now," said Caroline, "let me make something clear. You accomplish nothing with your childish outbursts."

"I broke your hold on one person."

"That wasn't their creativity. That was their *cure.*"

What? Addy stared at her, her stomach sinking into her boots. *The cure?* That was a cure. It was a wall of cures. And she'd broken one.

"Can you fix it?" she blurted out.

"Of course I can fix it. But why should I? It was *your* cure."

Worse and worse. Easy enough for Caroline to react at just the right moment, of course. She'd thought it was something crucial . . . and it was. But not to Caroline.

"Um. Sorry."

Caroline snorted. "You really think you're something special, don't you? You must. One person in exchange for five hundred. Not to mention the ghosts. That's a hefty exchange rate."

Didn't everyone think they were special? It was the default setting of the human mind. *I'm unique, just like everybody else is unique.* She bit her tongue and didn't answer.

"You didn't know Seth before you came here."

"No."

"And you're not the type to risk everything on finding a cure for yourself." Flip, flip, flip went the stylus through Caroline's fingers. "You might think you're special, but you don't see yourself as important."

Who did she think she was, Dupin? Holmes? Anyone could learn to observe and induct; it was just a matter of practice and a carefully weighed gamble with words.

"But somebody is. Someone is important to you, not just special but so significant that you're willing to give up the rest of your life in exchange for their freedom." Her eyes traced Addy's frame, and the stylus paused. "The hoodie. Of course. Your brother, Theo."

There was nothing to be gained by denying it. "Yes."

"Why?"

"Because he's better than me."

"Better?" A disbelieving smile played about Caroline's mouth.

"Smarter. More intelligent. Better. More *good.*" She'd be lying if she said she didn't recognise the hero worship inherent in the words, but it didn't matter. It was true. "I can live without my voice. He can't."

"Yes, he can."

"No. He can't." Her hands shook. "He can't. It's breaking him, the—" she closed her eyes and forced the words out "—the way it broke Seth. And I can't let that happen." It raced through her in a desperate refrain: *Theo cannot be broken. He cannot be broken. Don't let him be broken. Please.*

"So you're offering yourself for him. The ghosts, the rest of the five hundred . . ."

"They're still important. But he's—he's the most important."

Caroline tipped her head to the side. "He's that significant to you." The words were musing. "You're really prepared to do this. To give yourself up. For him."

"I'd do almost anything."

"Hmm. A question for you, then."

Addy took a breath, trying to calm her jangling nerves. "Yes?"

"If you were normal and he had Vox Pox, and there was a way of transferring it—"

"Yes." She didn't need it spelled out. "I told you, I can live without my voice. He can't."

"Because you love him?"

"I—suppose so." She'd never given it much thought.

"Because he's your brother?"

"Because he's Theo. He can change the world."

He could, she knew it. What did Addy have? Words. What use were they? But Theo had his hands and his mind, and he knew his way around wood and metal and electronics. He'd built her shoulder piece and keypad when he was only eighteen; what *couldn't* he do with the experience and wisdom of years?

He needed those years. And she could give them to him.

"One live test subject," Addy said, leaning forward. "Twenty-four hours a day, seven days a week, fifty-two weeks a year. A test subject with Vox Pox who has experience with the TheraRPG programme. That would make me uniquely qualified, wouldn't it?"

"It would."

"And in return—the cure for Vox Pox, the promise that you will not create any new cases of Vox Pox, and the release of the ghosts."

"Some ghosts won't want to be released."

Addy paused. She hadn't thought of that. "So let them decide. They should at least have the choice."

"Five hundred people." Caroline gestured to the wall of jars. "That's a lot of test subjects to be letting go."

"I'm sure you've got enough data to keep your research going for years," Addy said. "And now you can study the effects of mass recovery from Vox Pox; that's worth something."

"It's worth something, yes. I'm not sure it's worth as much as you think."

Addy called her bluff. "I think it is."

Caroline held her gaze for a long moment before standing and moving to the door.

Addy followed her out into the laboratory, where B worked at the board and Maunga slouched in a chair by the desk.

"I accept your offer," Caroline said, sitting in her leather desk chair.

Maunga's eyes rose, startled.

Addy let out a breath and slumped into the spare chair. Her emotions were jumbled—relief, confusion, anxiety. Caroline had accepted. That was the main thing.

"Your first demand: cures for Vox Pox, to be released to the general population over a period of four weeks."

Caroline pulled up a datasheet and wrote as she spoke. "They're not a mass recovery aid, you realise. The method of stealing each person's creative identity was unique, and each cure is unique as well. The second demand: the promise that I will not create any new cases of Vox Pox. That's not difficult. The active testing will be shut down. As you surmised, we'll work our backlogs of data. And the third condition: the release of the ghosts."

Maunga bolted upright. "What!"

"Or rather, offering them the option of release."

"That sounds accurate," Addy said.

"And in exchange: one live test subject for twenty-four hours a day, seven days a week, fifty-two weeks a year, no end date."

Maunga stilled.

"Also accurate."

"You *sold me out?*" Maunga growled. Her eyes widened. Addy saw a flash of something that looked like fear.

"No," she said. "I sold myself out."

"Oh." Maunga looked blank, and then a flicker of confusion crossed her face. "Why?"

"Because I wasn't about to offer you up without your consent, and I was a bit short on volunteers."

"But—"

"Sign here," Caroline interrupted, spinning the datasheet around to face Addy.

Addy read it carefully—she wasn't stupid—before picking up the stylus and signing at the bottom.

"Good," said Caroline, and laughed. "You have no idea what you signed up for, did you? *Testing.* That covers a wealth of possibilities."

Her stomach clenched in sudden fear. But it was too late now.

"Don't worry. I'll honour my end of the bargain. I just wanted you to be . . . aware." Her smile vanished. "Now get out."

Addy scrambled for the door, aware of Maunga at her heels. It had hardly closed behind them when darkness fell, sudden and absolute.

It was over.

CHAPTER FIFTEEN

She came back to herself in the testing chamber, heart beating too fast, breath coming too loud, muscles cramped from three hours—three days? The thoughts clashed in her mind, beating against each other in a fury—three whatevers in the same position. Her eyes hurt, her sight blurred against the white of the room. Surely there shouldn't be so much black on the walls?

Her vision cleared. It wasn't only on the walls—it was on the floor and the ceiling as well. Every available surface was covered in black text, so minute that she couldn't read it. Her fingers screamed in agony. She must have been writing the whole time.

The actions were instinctive, even as her fingers ached—reach for the keypad at her side. Select all text. Save to shoulder piece.

Just in time. A second later, the walls wiped clean and the door sprang open.

A familiar figure stepped inside. Again her reaction was instinctive.

No.

Addy threw herself backward, scrabbling for a handhold, foothold, anything. Her back hit the wall, and then her side hit another wall. She crammed herself into the corner, knees drawn up, arms wrapped around them. Everything was too fast, too loud, too much. Not yet, please, not yet. She needed time.

Caroline moved closer and looked down at her.

"Aren't you a wreck?" Her voice was soft, barely reaching Addy's ears. "I haven't come to take you away right now—although it may have occurred to you that you failed to specify a timeframe, and as such, I would be well within my rights to do so."

Addy's hands shook. She gripped her knees, trying to hold them still, digging her nails into her skin to try to ground herself in the here and now, but it wasn't working. Breathe. In . . . two . . . three . . . out . . . two . . . three . . . and again. Come on. She could do it.

"I just came to say that I'll be in touch in the next few days. I'll come up with some pretext to explain it away to your family, don't worry. I'd hate for them to get worried and come looking for you. It will take me a few weeks to get everything organised on this end. You'll have that long, at least, before I call for you. But when I do call for you," she scuffed her boot on the ground between Addy's feet, eyes cold, "I expect you to come straightaway. Is that clear?"

Addy opened her mouth to answer, but nothing emerged. A sob caught in her throat. That was right. She couldn't talk. She couldn't *talk.* It was worse than it had been that morning, so much worse, because for three fleeting hours (days, her mind whispered, three and half days) she'd been able to speak. Amazing how quickly she'd fallen back into the old patterns. She wanted her voice back.

But now it was gone, melted away like winter's snow in the warmth of spring, and it would never come back.

"I said, is that clear?"

Addy nodded.

"Good."

Caroline turned away just as Maunga appeared in the doorway.

"Hey," Maunga snapped. "What are you doing?"

"Nothing," Caroline said lightly as she stepped into the hall. "Just filling her in on a few details. She's been in a perfect flow state for the whole session. It's amazing, really. Her body says it's been writing for three hours nonstop and her mind's telling her it's been three and a half days. She'll need a little time to resolve the difference."

Maunga watched Caroline exit the room, a dark scowl on her face, and then hurried to Addy's side. "Are you alright?"

Addy reached for Maunga's shirt. Her fingers curled deep,

anchoring her in the tight weave. She couldn't speak, and she couldn't gather her scattered thoughts enough to make her fingers talk for her. Her tongue darted out to lick dry lips; she nodded, grimaced, and nodded again.

By some miracle Maunga understood, and she sat in silence as Addy rode out the waves of panic.

She didn't know how much time passed. The panic receded enough to let her snag back some semblance of normality. She shrugged to activate her shoulder piece and typed, <THANKS.>

"No worries. What did she want?"

<JUST TELLING ME HOW MUCH FREE TIME I HAVE. OR HOW MUCH I DON'T HAVE, RATHER.>

Maunga snarled something under her breath and added aloud, "You didn't have to do that."

<YES, I DID.>

But they would never agree on that point any more than they would ever be friends, Addy thought. One shared experience couldn't bind them together as kindred spirits. Civility was perhaps all they could hope for.

Friend or not, it was a small comfort to know that someone understood.

She staggered to her feet and fought for balance as the room swayed around her. Then her legs went out from under her. She would have fallen if Maunga hadn't caught her under the arms.

"Are you sure you're okay?" Maunga asked. "Because you really don't look like it."

<I'M FINE.> She pushed the helping hand away and leaned against the wall. <GIVE ME A MINUTE.>

"Alright." Maunga retreated a couple of steps and folded her arms. That annoying smirk played about her mouth again.

Addy took a breath. She'd show Maunga. She was fine. She knew she was fine; she couldn't quite reconcile the time gap between her mind and body, but she was fine. She planted her feet and pulled her hand away from the wall. *See? Fine.* One step. Good. Another step—hello, there was the wall again.

Her second attempt went better. On her third, she made it all the way to the door before bracing herself against the frame. Maunga stayed a couple of paces away, far enough to give the illusion of independence but close enough in case anything went wrong.

Addy rested for a minute, gathering herself, and felt her old self steal back into her body with every breath she took. The pull to open her mouth to speak was fading, and the usual habit of talking with her fingers returned.

She remembered the text she'd saved to her holo. She'd have to look at it later, once she got home. Three hours of writing—or three days, if her mind was to be believed. And it hadn't been just any writing. She'd slipped into flow state once or twice in the years before she lost her voice, and she'd never forgotten it—the way the hours flew by when nothing existed but the pictures in her head, pouring out and being made real by fingers on keys, words on the page, words that she was writing.

There was nothing quite like it.

"Debriefing in two days," Caroline was saying to the gathered group when they reached the lounge. "We'll send a message out with the exact details; remember to check your mail. Please take any belongings with you. The lift is just there."

Addy joined the group and, Maunga at her side, they rose to the surface.

~

Despite Addy's protests, Maunga followed her down to the station and onto the first train that came along the Gleniti Line.

"You're still shaky as anything on your feet," she said. "I'm just making sure you get home alright. Wouldn't want anything to happen to you after the day we've had."

Maunga stretched her legs out into the aisle, humming tunelessly under her breath and scowling at the back of the seat in front. Addy curled into a window seat, Eareos over her ears, watching the advertisements go by on the tunnel walls and trying not to think.

She dozed off, head lolling back against the seat, and woke to a stiff neck and Maunga's hand on her shoulder.

"We're here," Maunga said.

It took an effort to make her legs work. Addy led her through the ticket barriers and up the flights of stairs, out onto the street, down two blocks, and around the corner to the front door. Maunga rang the bell while Addy slumped against the doorframe and yawned.

The door opened, and Mum stood before them. "Addy! Where have you been? I thought you were sick, young lady?"

Addy groped for the memory of that morning. It seemed so long ago. That was right—she'd been skipping school. *Oops. Oh well.* It didn't matter; she'd done what she'd meant to do, and besides that, she wouldn't be at school for much longer. She mustered a rueful look and shrugged at the expression on Mum's face.

"Bed." Mum stood aside to let Addy pass. "I'm sorry," she said to Maunga, "you must be one of Addy's friends, but I don't think I've met you before."

"Maunga Richards. I bumped into her at the park just now. We're not exactly friends, but she wasn't looking very well so I thought I'd bring her home. I was a few years above Adelaide at school; I'm in one of Theo's classes at uni." She paused. "He's her brother, isn't he? Theo Te Ngawai? Tall bloke with dark curly hair?"

"He is, yes." Mum's voice had warmed considerably.

Addy rolled her eyes and left Maunga to ingratiate herself with Mum. The stairs seemed endless. She reached the landing after an aeon, trudged past Theo's closed door, and into her room. There she kicked her boots off and fell full-length on her bed.

She couldn't remember ever being this worn out. It was tiredness beyond the ability of mere sleep to fix, weariness beyond thought. Exhaustion swept her into its welcome embrace, and she sank into unconsciousness.

~

Caroline released the first cures the very next day. Kaiako Georgiana walked back into the classroom after morning break and turned the wall holo on, flicking through channels until she found the one she was looking for.

"Watch this, girls," she announced with a delighted smile. "Consider it your dose of Cultural History for the day. What have I said: we're—"

"Living history," the class chorused.

"Precisely. Now hush and watch. There might be a test on this later."

Addy wriggled to get more comfortable in her chair. *A test. Yeah, right.* It was Kaiako Georgiana's favourite way of making them pay attention, but she rarely followed through on the threat.

The news showed a familiar view: the Breach reception hall, all golden wood floors and sleek metal walls. Isabel Erewhon née Mabait, still the designated Breach reporter even after Maguire Media bought out Channel 43 News last year, stood in front of the reception desk beside another familiar form: Jenkins Le Cren, Caroline's assistant. The man looked dapper in an all-black suit. Even for this formal occasion, there was no necktie in sight; his black shirt was open at the neck, and his blond hair shone under the lights.

"We're here once more in the reception foyer at Breach Laboratories," Isabel said, "where we have spent so much time over the last two years. Our team at Maguire Media has brought you many stories of the events that have gone on behind these doors."

She gestured to the door that led through from reception to the rest of the Breach building. "There have been stories of hope and joy, anger and sorrow—and, I have to say, more than a little confusion. People have come here in their thousands to find out firsthand what Breach Laboratories' Virtual Psychoreality Simulator can do. But I'm not here to talk about the TheraRPG programme. Not today."

She beamed.

The screen cut back to the studio for a moment. Rumour had it that Nigel Maguire of Maguire Media worked seven days a week, one day in each of the seven departments within the organisation he'd built from the ground up.

Rumour also said that within a week of the takeover he'd installed his secretary in the CEO's private office and claimed a desk for himself out on the open-plan floor, that he'd once worked a second job as a cleaner for his own building, that he'd been married four times, never had kids, and now lived alone with two dogs and a pet pukeko, that he was the first person in and the last person out every day, and that he fell asleep at his desk at least once a week, usually around three o'clock in the afternoon.

Today must be his rostered day to work as studio anchor. The desk hid his protruding potbelly but not the sharp gleam in his eyes or the red scratch along his jaw where he'd presumably cut himself shaving that morning. "If you're not there to spin us another yarn about the TheraRPG programme," he said while a stylus spun in hypnotic circles through his fingers, "what *are* you there for, Isabel?"

"I'm here to give some very, *very* good news." She took a breath. "Today, here and now, I am pleased to announce that after years of hard work, Breach Laboratories has finalised the cures to several individual cases of Vox Pox. One hundred cases, in fact."

"What!" Challa yelped.

"Cures!" Tuku shouted indignantly over the sudden uproar in the classroom. "We've got cures! And Dad never said a word!"

Addy could hardly hear herself think, the noise was so loud. Quite aside from Addy herself, everyone in the lower twelfth knew someone with Vox Pox or knew someone who knew someone with

Vox Pox. And everyone was hoping that, out of those one hundred cures, one of them might be for that person.

"Hannah, your sister—"

"Keek, Justin—"

Through a gap between two talking heads, Addy saw the colour drain from Aroha Waipori's face, and she mouthed a single, soundless word: *"Mum."*

Caroline had kept her promise. Addy could have cried in relief. It hadn't been in vain. She hadn't bargained herself away for nothing. She wrapped her arms around herself and took a deep breath. It hadn't been a waste. She'd done it.

"Addy." Challa turned to her. "Addy, there are cures. You'll get your voice back."

Addy jerked a nod. Maybe it shouldn't have surprised her that she was the first person Challa thought of, but to be honest, it did. Oh, they'd been the best of best friends once, but that was years ago now. They still sat next to each other; she couldn't speak for Challa, but on Addy's part, it wasn't so much out of friendship as routine. She'd rather sit next to Challa, who she could comfortably ignore, than Jessica or even Scar, where the silence would be rather more strained.

They talked a little, or Challa talked while Addy typed: cordial nothings and safe updates—*How was your weekend? Did you finish that report? Theo has a girlfriend now. Theo's broken up with his girlfriend.* Nothing deep. Nothing that might cross that fragile line.

But even so, it meant something that she was the first person Challa turned to. Challa had thought of Addy even before her cousin, who Addy knew had had Vox Pox for at least a year.

Her breath shuddered from her lungs despite her best efforts to keep it steady. Tears stung at the back of her eyes. She blinked them away and sniffed.

"Are you okay?" Challa asked.

She nodded, shrugged, and sniffed again. <YEAH,> she typed.

<YEAH, I'M OKAY. THERE'S A CURE.> Even typing the words, she could hardly believe it. Caroline had done it. She'd really done it.

Cures. They had cures for Vox Pox.

"Here with me," Isabel went on when the class settled and Kaiako Georgiana unpaused the feed, "is Jenkins Le Cren, one of the research team that has been working on developing the cures for, he tells me, the last four years. Jenkins, what can you tell us about the cures?"

Jenkins faced the camera with calm assurance. He hadn't looked much like a public relations officer when Addy had seen him down in the testing centre; he hadn't even looked much like a scientist. But he scrubbed up well.

"I can tell you that it's the end result of a —load of hard work," he said. The live censor took care of the expletive. "Sorry, that one slipped out."

No, it didn't, Addy thought. He'd done it on purpose. There was no faster way to get the public on your side than to swear on a live feed. It was a way of being human when you were stuck behind a holocam.

"We've released one hundred cures today, and I can tell you that four hundred more cures are being finalised and packaged as we speak. Every cure is highly individualised; the cures are labelled with the names of their intended recipient and will be distributed from approved medical centres so as to avoid any unfortunate mix-ups."

Isabel added, "A team of third-party scientists and experts have been on the case for months now, behind the scenes, and they're examining the cures as we speak. Just minutes ago they confirmed that each cure seems to contain a unique live component, never before seen. Verification will be ongoing, but at this point in time it looks hopeful."

Cures. Addy listened with half an ear to the continuing news feed. There were cures; live cures that could really truly cure people.

Cures that she would never get. She'd smashed hers. Oh,

Caroline could make a new one, she knew that, but Addy didn't think she would—unless, say, she decided to test the effects of giving someone the cure and then re-infecting them with Vox Pox. It was the sort of cruel thing she'd do.

Addy shuddered. The thoughts of what the *testing* might involve had preyed on her mind since she woke. Somehow she didn't think it would all be library trips and strolls through the forest.

Another news update came through after lunch, in which a grinning Isabel interviewed the first person to receive their cure. The boy couldn't have been more than ten, and he couldn't stop laughing. His parents were with him, beaming and crying and doing their best to answer Isabel's questions or to prod their son to answer. The whole thing was a happy mess, and more than one person in Addy's class surreptitiously wiped away a few tears by the end of it.

"That's one person cured," Isabel said into the holocam at the end of the interview. "Ninety-nine to go, and, with any luck, Breach will have finalised the next round before long. Back to you in the studio, Nigel. Erewhon out."

~

"You heard the news?" Maunga slipped through the swarm at the school gate and fell into step beside Addy.

<YES.>

"And?"

And what? <WHY ARE YOU HERE?> She didn't need to add the obvious—we're not friends, we're not even friendly. I don't like you. Please go away.

"To ask if you'd heard the news. They've released cures."

<I KNOW.> And this time, torn between relief and dread that her plan had, by some unfathomable stretch of the imagination, actually worked, Addy forgot herself enough to add, <YOU CAN GO NOW.>

Of course, it was Maunga Richards she was talking to. "I can," Maunga said, "but I won't."

Ugh. Addy lengthened her stride, trying to outpace the older girl. Maunga kept up effortlessly.

"Trying to get rid of me, are you?"

<YES.>

"Too bad."

Keek. She stopped in the middle of the street, ignoring the annoyed exclamation from a pedestrian behind her, and turned to face Maunga head on. <WHAT DO YOU WANT?>

They matched stares for a long minute. Maunga dropped her gaze first. "I—"

Good grief, was that *nervousness* in her voice? Addy wouldn't have believed it if she hadn't heard it for herself.

"I want to know why."

Well, that was expansive. Addy lifted an impatient eyebrow.

"Why did you do it?" Maunga asked.

Oh. That. Addy rolled her eyes and started walking again. <BECAUSE I'M TOO KEEKING SELFLESS. LIKE YOU SAID.>

"Addy—"

No. *That* was not happening. Addy pivoted on her toes and stepped into Maunga's space. <NO. YOU DO NOT GET TO CALL ME THAT. NOT AFTER WHAT YOU DID.>

This time, Maunga didn't back down. "Tell me why and I'll stop, *Addy.*"

What was it with keeking young adults and their being keeking childish? Theo was one thing, for all that he turned twenty this year, he was her brother—it was expected. Maunga, nineteen and vastly more grown up than Addy at sixteen, was another thing entirely.

<IT'S NOT CONDITIONAL. I'M NOT BARGAINING WITH YOU ON THIS.> She injected as much venom into her glare as she could. <YOU'RE NOT ONE OF CAROLINE'S MINIONS TO TELL ME WHAT TO DO. OR ARE YOU?>

It was a low blow, Addy knew, and from the way she stopped dead, Maunga knew it, too. Maybe now she'd back the keek off.

Addy walked away, flinging an obscene gesture over her shoulder at Maunga as she went.

And Maunga let her go.

CHAPTER SIXTEEN

Breach released the second round of cures at the end of the week. There was a short update on the news during their morning class, and soon the whole school was buzzing about it.

Addy received a message from Theo soon after lunch.

<THEY'VE PULLED ME OUT OF LECTURES FOR THE DAY,> the message said. <DAD'S GOT TIME OFF WORK TO COME TO THE CLINIC WITH>

He really was excited. She couldn't remember the last time he'd sent a message without finishing his sentence first.

<WITH ME.> The second message arrived a few seconds later. <IT'S MY CURE. THEY'VE GOT MY CURE.>

Thank you, Caroline. Addy bit her lip. <THAT'S GREAT! CAN'T WAIT TO GET HOME TONIGHT.>

She wasn't expecting a reply. He'd be far too busy with paperwork and everything. But to her surprise, her holo chimed halfway through her next class. Addy made sure Kaiako Georgiana was over on the far side of the room before she checked it.

Theo again. <I ASKED. THEY DIDN'T FIND YOURS IN THIS BATCH. DON'T WORRY. IT'LL BE IN THE NEXT ONE, ADS.>

She swallowed the lump in her throat. *No, it won't.* But she couldn't tell Theo that.

<THANKS,> she said instead.

~

By the end of the fourth week, seven rounds of cures had been released. Five hundred and fourteen people had miraculously recovered from Vox Pox. The media loved it: Isabel Erewhon from

Maguire Media had crested the initial wave of reports, but half a dozen other channels weren't far behind. Hardly an hour went by without another interview with a former sufferer popping up or a debate shown between leading experts in the field. All known cases of Vox Pox had been cured.

All except ten.

It came as no surprise to Addy when a list of documented Vox Pox cases was leaked by someone at Ian Tumeke's medical clinic. Harper York worked there, after all. She might not have leaked the data herself—from what Maunga had said about her, the thought wouldn't have even crossed her mind—but Caroline would have her spies there. She had them everywhere.

It was an expedient way of spilling the news that a handful of people hadn't received their cures. Oh, the media would have gotten there, even if concerned parents and caregivers hadn't spoken up, but this was faster. And Addy thought Caroline was quite concerned about speed these days.

The spreadsheet had had names removed to protect the clients' identities, but otherwise revealed the most pertinent facts about the five hundred and twenty-four cases of Vox Pox: infection dates, ongoing symptoms, and, most importantly, the date they received their cure.

All the client confidentiality in the world couldn't hide the fact that ten names were missing their cure dates.

Once the media got hold of it, the data went public, and it didn't take a genius to match birthdates and infection dates with the openly available list of patients at the medical centres across the city. Isabel Erewhon interviewed three of the unlucky victims and Channel 84 interviewed another one. Addy kept her head down. Wherever the other five were, they were laying low and staying out of the public eye.

Addy's mum and dad fielded never-ending phone calls for a week, politely but firmly declining the constant requests for interviews. The holocams managed a few shots of her in public places between home and school: two on the streets, one staring into space on the train, another one down at the Shelter watching the waves.

She'd almost thrown something when she saw that last one. The Shelter was her hiding place, her—well, her shelter. And now the media knew she went there, and the public would know it too, and—and—

"It's alright, Addy," Dad said, uncharacteristically grim. "That's enough of that carry on. I'll put a stop to it."

She never did find out quite what he'd said, but the photos stopped.

~

The letter was waiting when she got home from school. Addy eyed the entry in their home mail system.

> *To: Henry and Lana Te Ngawai.*
>
> *From: Caroline York, Overseer, TheraRPG Virtual Psychoreality Simulator Programme, Breach Laboratories.*
>
> *Subject: Adelaide's selection for the Breach Laboratories Extended Trial*

Addy was tempted to scroll down and read the first few lines of the letter, but she resisted the urge. No, she'd better not. She should wait until Mum and Dad came home, and then they could open it and give her the news.

She'd have to act like it was a surprise. Like she hadn't been sick to her stomach with dread, awaiting this development. It had taken Caroline longer than she'd expected to get organised.

Homework occupied her until Mum and Dad were both home from work. Theo was shut up in his room as usual. She waited until Mum had changed out of her business clothes before drawing her attention to the letter.

"From Breach?" Mum frowned. "Henry! Can you come here for a minute? Alright, let's see what it says . . ."

Addy read over their shoulders. It began with the usual formal greeting . . . went on to a long paragraph of obligatory preamble . . . went on again . . . and then, finally, Caroline got to the point. She was extending an apology on behalf of Breach for the lack of a cure for Addy's Vox Pox. As she was sure Henry and Lana knew, every case was individualised, and these ten cases of as-yet-uncured Vox Pox were proving resistant to any active compounds in the formulated antidotes.

Addy skimmed ahead. *Ah. There.* She was inviting Addy to participate in an extended clinical trial at Breach's new purpose-built facility out on the East Cape. The other nine people still living with Vox Pox were being sent the same letter, of course. There would be ten of them in the programme. They would be surrounded by a team of highly trained and dedicated, nay, *passionate* experts for the duration of the trial.

And as for the trial itself . . . oh, she was clever. Addy might hate the woman with every fibre of her being, but she could admit that much.

The trial would be of extended duration; it would last for as long as it took to cure the group. Caroline was frank about that. It could take months. Or years. And it would be in a controlled environment, which meant no contamination from the city. No outside influences. No visits from family or friends.

Just the ten, and the scientists, and the staff hired to keep them living in comfort. There would be a chef. There would be cleaners. There would, if the opportunity arose, be visiting speakers on a variety of topics for those who liked to keep their brains busy.

"No family visits," Mum pointed out.

"An eventual cure," Dad said.

Addy had never heard him sound so firm. His shoulders were straightening already, the strain of four years of caring for a daughter with Vox Pox lifting. "We can't refuse this, Lana."

Mum finished reading the letter before she spoke again. "It's Addy's decision."

Caroline had attached photos of the facility. It was a nondescript building in a row of similar buildings, slim and upright, with nothing more than a discreet plaque on the door to show what it was used for. The facades were old and ornate, but the inside proved itself to be modern—and more than modern.

"State-of-the-art tech room," said Dad.

"Oh, look at the wood panelling," said Mum. "They've got money."

A moment later they spoke in unison: "That's a *very* nice swimming pool."

Addy watched over their shoulders as they browsed through the photos. It didn't look too bad for a fake facility. More like a hotel than anything. The labs gleamed like they'd never been used.

"What do you think, Addy?" Mum asked. "Are you interested at all?"

<Yes . . . > Addy didn't want to agree too quickly. It was supposed to be a big decision, after all. <I'll need to think about it, but yes, I think I'd like to go. If it means a cure . . . >

"It's rather sudden." Mum looked back over the letter. "They want the trials to start in six weeks."

<We have school holidays in three weeks,> Addy pointed out. <Perfect transition time.>

A bit too perfect. But if it gave her a month and a half outside Caroline's control, she wasn't about to draw attention to it.

"It says here," Dad said, "they need a reply by the end of the month. That's the end of next week."

<I'll think on it overnight.> Addy scratched her collarbone. <And give you an answer in the morning.>

Her answer would be *yes,* of course. Caroline hadn't given her an option there.

And in the meantime . . . well, she had six weeks. She'd better make the most of it.

~

Theo found her at the park with Maunga on the first Wednesday of the holidays. Addy had crossed paths with Maunga a few times since their tiff in the middle of the street. In truth, it was too many times to be coincidence on either of their parts, but Addy had avoided the subject, and Maunga had never brought it up. Somehow the fight had cleared the air between them. Maunga seemed to have gained some respect for her, and for her own part, Addy could face the thought of seeing her with an almost disconcerting lack of animosity.

They were sitting in silence on a sun-drenched bench, watching a casual game of soccer going on among a bunch of uni students, when Theo sauntered up.

"Thought I might find you here," he said and sprawled on the grass in front of them.

Either here or the Shelter, Addy thought. She'd been spending most of her free time at one place or the other, soaking up the outdoors in these last precious weeks.

"How did you do it?" Theo's eyes stayed fixed on the field in front of them.

Addy glanced at Maunga and gestured for her to answer. Theo wouldn't see her reply; he wasn't looking at her holo.

"They're called legs," Maunga said. "I walked. Bumped into your sister and we decided to pass the time together."

Theo tipped his head back to eye them upside down. "Funny how often that seems to happen these days."

He sat upright and turned to face them, stretching out one arm and then the other. Was he missing the weight of the shoulder holo?

Addy shrugged with her free shoulder, mindful that her holo was already activated. <DID YOU HAVE A POINT?>

He sobered, looking first at Maunga and then Addy with intent eyes. "I'm not stupid. First you pull a sickie and she brings you home looking like you've both lived a week of nightmares. The next day Breach starts releasing cures, and then Mum and Dad get a letter from them offering you an extended trial, which conveniently takes you away from us for keek knows how long."

Addy swallowed.

"I looked up the place. Did a little digging." Theo scratched at his forearm under the rolled-up cuff of his green shirt. He was watching her closely. "Found the date stamps buried in the programming files. That page didn't exist before a month ago."

One point to Theo, she thought. But Caroline was still ahead by an order of magnitude.

"I know Breach said the place was purpose-built. But to pop up this soon after you two vanished for the day? You've never pulled a sickie in your entire life, Addy. Until now. And then this happens . . ." He made a moue of disbelief. "Awfully coincidental, don't you think?"

<COINCIDENCES HAPPEN.>

"Not like this." He leaned forward, but before he could speak again, Maunga broke in.

"She won't tell you. Or rather, she *can't* tell you."

"Why not?" His gaze swung back to Addy, and she closed her eyes against the expression on his face. She hadn't thought he could ever look that vulnerable. "Why can't you tell me? What happened? Why did you pull a sickie? Where did you go? What sort of deal did you have to make to pull this off?"

She flinched. Caroline's icy glare hovered in her mind, threatening her into silence.

"Theo," Maunga said in a voice hard as iron. "Leave it alone."

Addy opened her eyes to see his gaze flicker between Maunga and herself, and then he leaned back and nodded. "Alright." He didn't sound happy. "Alright. I won't push."

Addy had to know. <YOU HAVEN'T TOLD MUM AND DAD?>

"No. Haven't told anyone. I wanted to get some answers from you before I did anything else."

She hesitated. The thought of the scads of writing from the TheraRPG session was never far from her mind. She'd have to do something with it, but of course she couldn't do it herself. She'd started pulling back in preparation for whatever horrors Caroline had prepared for her; she'd never be able to summon that much energy. Even the effort she put into her schoolwork had dropped off.

<I MIGHT,> she started. Then she paused.

"You might what?"

<NO PROMISES. BUT BEFORE I LEAVE, I MIGHT BE ABLE TO MANAGE SOMETHING.>

Before she left. How long did she have now? Just over two weeks. Not long at all.

"Okay," Theo said. "Thank you."

He stretched out on the grass, soaking up the sun. Addy settled back to watch the game.

~

Addy woke sweating and shaking, tangled in twisted sheets, to the familiar silence that cloaked her room at night.

Just a dream, she told herself fiercely. It was just a dream. But the tears came nonetheless, even as she raised trembling hands to wipe them away. *Just a dream. It wasn't real. It didn't happen.*

No, it didn't happen. She threw back the heavy blankets and stood. But it could. Who knew what the testing would involve? And Seth wouldn't be there to help her this time. Neither would Maunga.

She'd be alone. Just her and Caroline.

What day was it? Sunday. Thursday night was her last at home. Five days to go. She bundled herself into a thick woollen jersey and padded to the door. Maybe Theo would still be awake.

He was.

"Couldn't sleep?" he murmured, hardly glancing up from his book as she slipped through the door into his room.

She didn't bother responding. He had eyes, didn't he? It was habit, by now, to grab the blanket off his bed and wrap it around herself before sitting next to him. They sat in silence while he finished his chapter.

Theo dog-eared the page and closed his book, dropping it on the floor beside the bed. "If your dreams are this bad before you've gone away to wherever you're going, I'd hate to see what they're like when you come back."

She wasn't coming back. She knew that. The other nine would get their cures, but her trial would be prolonged and prolonged again. It would, she thought, give a new meaning to the term *extended.*

"I wish," Theo said, frowning at the wall on the other side of the room, "that there was some way I could help you."

She huffed. Classic Theo. He hated unsolved problems. Where there was a problem, he was convinced there had to be a solution, and he'd run himself ragged looking for it. If it didn't exist yet, he'd invent it.

But he couldn't. Not this time.

<You can't. I'm sorry, I know you want a nice, tidy solution, but there isn't one. Not this time.>

"There's always a solution," he muttered. "You just have to eliminate the impossible."

Oh, well. Let him think that if it helped him cope. Who was she to begrudge him a glimmer of hope?

Addy nudged him with an elbow. <Here. I told you I'd manage something before I left.>

He startled upright. "Really?"

<Mmm-hmm. Half a tick.> She started the file transfer. <Should be coming through now.>

It was the entirety of the text from her TheraRPG session, unpolished and unedited. She'd read over it; it seemed to be a comprehensive detailing of the last three years from the day Maunga stole her voice to the session at Breach. There was nothing she could do with it, herself. She figured Theo might as well have it. Maybe he could polish it up and keep it safe until ... until he found something to do with it.

And if he never found anything to do with it, well, at least he'd know what had brought her to this point.

Theo looked over the file with wide eyes. "That's a lot of words. Who wrote it?"

<I DID.>

"*You* did? But you can't—"

<MANAGED IT SOMEHOW. DON'T ASK ME HOW, I DON'T REMEMBER.> It was true from a certain point of view. She remembered the agonising cramps afterward, just not the actual writing. <FLOW STATE, I THINK.>

"Huh."

She could have continued, but he was already absorbed in the text.

"This is good stuff, Ads," he said, breaking out of his trance for a moment. "Sorry. Did you want something else?"

<NO. THAT WAS EVERYTHING IMPORTANT, I THINK. GOING BACK TO BED.>

He murmured an absent-minded goodnight, but when she glanced back he was already poring over the file again. She left him to it.

~

A soft knock on her door heralded Theo's arrival at far-too-early o'clock two days later.

Addy cracked an eye open as he slipped inside. *Ugh.* What did he want? It was so late—or early—that even *he* was usually asleep. Whatever it was, it must be important.

She sat up and blinked at him, endeavouring to communicate that he could say whatever he'd come to say and then sod off, please, so she could go back to sleep.

"I read it," he said.

Looking at his shadowed eyes and disheveled hair, she didn't doubt it. No doubt he'd gone without such minor things as food and sleep while he did it, too. She sighed and gave in, activating her shoulder holo with a shrug. Alright. Let him talk. She wouldn't be getting back to sleep anytime soon.

She knew that look on his face, that air of repressed frenetic energy. He wanted answers.

<FIRE AWAY.> She waved for him to sit on the end of her bed.

He started pacing instead. "Just one question."

Only one? That was efficient. Maybe she would get back to sleep sometime soon, after all.

"I want to know why."

Or not.

"I know what you did. I know where you're going, more or less, and I even know who was involved." His jaw clenched.

Addy had a feeling that his next meeting with Maunga would be rather more explosive than the last.

"But *why,* Ads? Why would you do that? Why would you give up the rest of your life for us, for . . ." He ran a shaking hand across his mouth. Paused in his pacing. Looked around at her. His voice, when it came again, was little more than a whisper. "For me?"

Typical Theo. He'd never ask an easy question if there was a tricky one going begging. And she wouldn't have been able to answer this one a month ago. Maybe not even two weeks ago.

But she could answer it now.

<I HAD A FIGHT WITH MAUNGA. BACK WHEN THE FIRST ROUND OF CURES CAME OUT.>

Theo nodded, accepting the non-sequitur without pause. "I daresay she deserved it."

<SHE DID.>

"And?"

<IT MADE ME REALISE . . . >

Oh, so many things. Things she'd never thought of before, or if she had thought of them then she'd locked them away somewhere deep inside her. Caroline had been right: there were things she hadn't grown past. In some ways, in a lot of ways, there was too much thirteen-year-old in her.

The TheraRPG session might not have cured her Vox Pox, but in a way it had given her something far more valuable. Acknowledgement, they said, was the first step to healing. She'd long since acknowledged her own voicelessness—and more than acknowledged. She saw that now. She'd given it too much hold over her, let it grow until it consumed her. She'd lost herself in it.

The Vox Pox was the be-all and end-all. It had been all that mattered, all that she could see. But not anymore. That three hours in the VPR programme had forced her to acknowledge more than just the pivotal moment and the disease that came after. She'd had to face down everything that had accompanied it.

The isolation.

The depression.

The way the solid path of her future had dropped out from under her feet.

Feeling like a stranger in her own city, her own class, her own *home.*

And on and on the list went, a whole host of secondary issues that she'd barely recognised at the time or that she'd never seen as important enough to warrant a second thought.

But she'd found them there in the simulator. And faced them, even not knowing what they were at the time. And she'd overcome them.

And then, weeks later, she'd done it again.

The fight with Maunga had been the catalyst. Walking away from her, Addy hadn't experienced a blinding light, only the dull realisation that, after all these years, she hadn't needed a voice to be able to speak after all.

The creativity was a different matter. Even now she'd give anything to get it back. But talking? She could communicate just as well through her shoulder holo as she'd ever been able to through her vocal chords.

Maybe something in her had seen it long ago and had only needed the smokescreen removed. She hadn't felt nearly as surprised as she would have expected. If anything, it was more like a weight she'd never noticed before had lifted from her whole being. She felt lighter and freer, more *herself* than she could ever remember.

She'd been thirteen for far too long.

Time to grow up.

"It made you realise . . . ?" Theo prompted.

<IT MADE ME REALISE I'M ALREADY ME.>

Because that was the twisted double-nature of the thing. Vox Pox had stolen her voice, stolen her identity, and installed itself as sole occupant of her head to whisper lies: *you have nothing, you are nothing, there is only me;* and at the same time, she had felt a dead certainty that she could be herself if only she could break down the wall and free herself.

Vox Pox was everything—and she would be nothing until she was rid of it.

<I AM NOT MY VOICELESSNESS. BUT IT'S A PART OF ME. I CAN'T GO ON JUST . . . WAITING. FOREVER. WAITING FOR THE CURE, WAITING TO BE FREE OF IT, WAITING TO LIVE MY LIFE. I HAD TO DO SOMETHING.>

She didn't need a cure, not now. Not to be herself.

"So you traded your life for five hundred Vox Pox cures?" His voice was dry. "Because that's the rational thing to do in that situation."

She shrugged. <I USED MYSELF AS A BARGAINING CHIP BECAUSE THAT WAS ALL I COULD DO. THE REST CAME . . . LATER.>

Later. Later she'd woken from the deepest sleep of her life and looked, as she did every morning, at the old picture of her and Challa on the wall above her bed. And she'd laughed, very quietly, inside her head.

Truthfully, she'd been herself at thirteen when, immature and self-important, she volunteered to go with Maunga Richards to the study room to save the rest of the class from dealing with her antics.

And she'd been herself at sixteen when she volunteered to go with Caroline York. But with Caroline, at least, she'd had a little leverage, a little ability to negotiate. Kaiako Katie hadn't given her anything more than a smile and a high mark on her report; Caroline had given her five hundred and fourteen cures for Vox Pox and resolved the ghost problem.

Addy called that a win in her book.

She didn't need a cure, not now. The overwhelming black of three and a half years with Vox Pox had blown away. The despair that had come on the heels of the VPR session had lifted, too. What was left was a burning certainty, pure as any perfect mark on an assignment, that she was as much herself as she'd ever been, and that she had irrevocably done the right thing.

Which didn't make it any easier trying to explain it to Theo. But she did her best.

~

Friday morning came, and with it a sense of calm dread far beyond the shaking fright of her nightmares. It even pervaded her rock-solid surety of purpose, clinging to it like choking ash. Addy brushed it off, and the gold gleamed beneath, but it crept back again and again.

She'd packed her things the day before. She wasn't taking much—just enough to maintain the illusion that she would be at a luxury trial facility. One suitcase, packed and re-packed as if she couldn't decide what to take, and her backpack. That was all. On impulse, she'd taken the picture of her and Challa off her wall and tucked it into the front pocket. Caroline probably wouldn't let her keep it, but it was worth a try.

Maunga dropped in midmorning and took her off to the park

for an hour, where they mostly sat in silence, watching a flock of sparrows squabble on the grass of the empty cricket pitch.

"I won't follow you home," Maunga said when they parted. "Just . . ." She looked down and then away, frowning. "Look after yourself, alright?"

<I WILL. THANKS. KEEP AN EYE ON THEO, WOULD YOU?>

"Sure. Wouldn't want him doing anything rash." She paused, clasped a hand on Addy's shoulder, and walked away.

All too soon, lunch was over with. She gathered her things at the foot of the stairs.

"Are you sure you don't want us to come with you?" Mum asked for the hundredth time.

<MUM, HONESTLY,> she said, relying on her face to show fond exasperation. <I'M NEARLY SEVENTEEN, I'LL BE FINE. MIGHT NOT EVEN BE GONE THAT LONG. JUST THINK OF IT LIKE I'M GOING OFF TO UNIVERSITY, OR FINISHING SCHOOL, OR SOMETHING.> More like finishing-her-life school. But it was worth it. It would be worth it. <DON'T WORRY ABOUT ME. I LOVE YOU.>

Addy hugged them goodbye, walked to where Theo waited by the door, and stopped, unsure.

"What, no hug for me?"

She threw her arms around him and buried her head in his chest. Dimly she heard Dad mutter something about being *so glad they've learned to get along.*

"Pity it's only now that Addy's going away," Mum added.

"Hang in there," Theo murmured in her ear, too quietly for Mum and Dad to hear. *"I'll get you out, Ads. I promise."*

She gave him one last squeeze and pulled back, turning for the door so they wouldn't see her tears.

<BYE. I'LL SEE YOU AFTER. DON'T MISS ME TOO MUCH.>

And then she was out the door, bag on her back and suitcase in hand, heading for the station.

The train was on time. The journey seemed to fly by. Before she knew it, she was out on the Cape, walking down the street to the Breach East Cape trial facility.

There was the house and the discreet brass plaque on the door. It existed after all. Caroline had certainly been thorough. Addy stopped, looking up at the ancient house, the modern paint job. She took a breath and rang the bell.

How far was she prepared to go?

This far. The only way out was through.

The door opened, and she stepped inside.

CODA

We are the voiceless. Hear us.
Our silence is not consent, nor rejection,
nor ignorance, nor knowledge.
Our silence is the imposition of nothing
instead of something.
Our silence has been forced upon us
by you, the noisome masses.
For too long have you stolen us:
our voices, our talents, our skills –
our identities subsumed into soundlessness –
and claimed them for your own.
For too long have our choices been thus:
Silent maiden or muzzled whore.
Let the reckoning commence.
We will be the voiceless no more.

We are the voiceless. Hear us.
We are the voiceless. Fear us.

VOICELESS DUOLOGY BOOK 2:

EXPRESSION

E.G. WILSON

E.G. Wilson grew up on the adventures of Bilbo Baggins, those Pevensie kids, and the Swallows & Amazons. Further inspired by Sherlock, Firefly, and Tolkien's Legendarium, she turned her hand to writing stories of her own and has never looked back. Introduced to National Novel Writing Month in 2012, she has completed the challenge every November without fail. Wilson lives in South Canterbury, New Zealand. She loves mountains, hates broad beans, and never wears matching socks. In high school, Wilson was voted *Most Likely To Re-Write The Lord Of The Rings* by her classmates. She thinks *The Lord Of The Rings* is just fine the way it is.

Made in the USA
Lexington, KY
15 June 2017